THE STORY OF THE AMULET

The others stood looking after her

THE STORY
OF
THE AMULET

By

E. NESBIT

With illustrations by

H. R. MILLAR

LONDON
ERNEST BENN
LIMITED

First issued in this edition 1957
Second impression 1969
Published by Ernest Benn Limited
Bouverie House · Fleet Street · London · EC4

Printed in Great Britain

510 - 16056 - 5

TO
DR. WALLIS BUDGE
OF THE BRITISH MUSEUM
AS A SMALL TOKEN OF GRATITUDE FOR HIS
UNFAILING KINDNESS AND HELP IN
THE MAKING OF IT

CONTENTS

LIST OF ILLUSTRATIONS

CHAPTER I

THE PSAMMEAD

THERE WERE once four children who spent their summer holidays in a white house, happily situated between a sandpit and a chalkpit. One day they had the good fortune to find in the sandpit a strange creature. Its eyes were on long horns like snail's eyes, and it could move them in and out like telescopes. It had ears like a bat's ears, and its tubby body was shaped like a spider's and covered with thick soft fur—and it had hands and feet like a monkey's. It told the children—whose names were Cyril, Robert, Anthea, and Jane—that it was a Psammead or sand-fairy. (Psammead is pronounced Sammy-ad.) It was old, old, old, and its birthday was almost at the very beginning of everything. And it had been buried in the sand for thousands of years. But it still kept its fairylikeness, and part of this fairy-likeness was its power to give people whatever they wished for. You know fairies have always been able to do this. Cyril, Robert, Anthea, and Jane now found their wishes come true; but, somehow, they never could think of just the right things to wish for, and their wishes sometimes turned out very oddly indeed. In the end their unwise wishings landed them in what Robert called "a very tight place indeed," and the Psammead consented to help them out of it in return for their promise never never to ask it to grant them any more wishes, and never to tell any one about it, because it did not want to be bothered to give wishes to any one ever any more. At the moment of parting Jane said politely—

"I wish we were going to see you again some day."

And the Psammead, touched by this friendly thought, granted the wish. The book about all this is called "Five Children and It," and it ends up in a most tiresome way by saying—

"The children *did* see the Psammead again, but it was not in the sandpit; it was—but I must say no more——"

The reason that nothing more could be said was that I had not then been able to find out exactly when and where the children met the Psammead again. Of course I knew they would meet it, because it was always a beast of its word, and when it said a thing would happen, that thing happened without fail. How different from the people who tell us about what weather it is going to be on Thursday next, in London, the South Coast, and Channel!

The summer holidays during which the Psammead had been found and the wishes given had been wonderful holidays in the country, and the children had the highest hopes of just such another holiday for the next summer. The winter holidays were beguiled by the wonderful happenings of "The Pheonix and the Carpet," and the loss of these two treasures would have left the children in despair, but for the splendid hope of their next holiday in the country. The world, they felt, and indeed had some reason to feel, was full of wonderful things—and they were really the sort of people that wonderful things happen to. So they looked forward to the summer holiday; but when it came everything was different, and very, very horrid. Father had to go out to Manchuria to telegraph news about the war to the tiresome paper he wrote for—the *Daily Bellower*, or something like that, was its name. And Mother, poor dear Mother, was away in Madeira, because she had been very ill. And The Lamb—I mean the baby—was with her. And Aunt Emma, who was Mother's sister, had suddenly married Uncle Reginald, who was Father's brother, and they had gone to China, which is much too far off for you to expect to be asked to spend the holidays in, however fond your aunt and uncle may be of you. So the children were left in the care of old Nurse, who lived in Fitzroy Street, near the British Museum, and though she was always very kind to them, and indeed spoiled them far more than would be good for the most grown up of us, the four children felt perfectly wretched, and when the cab had driven off with Father and all his boxes and guns and the sheepskin, with blankets and the aluminium mess-kit inside it, the stoutest heart quailed, and the girls broke down altogether, and sobbed in each other's arms, while the boys each looked out of one of the long gloomy windows of the parlour, and tried to pretend that no boy would be such a muff as to cry.

I hope you notice that they were not cowardly enough to cry till their Father had gone; they knew he had quite enough to upset him without that. But when he was gone every one felt as if it had been trying not to cry all its life, and that it must cry now, if it died for it. So they cried.

Tea—with shrimps and watercress—cheered them a little. The watercress was arranged in a hedge round a fat glass salt-cellar, a tasteful device they had never seen before. But it was not a cheerful meal.

After tea Anthea went up to the room that had been Father's, and when she saw how dreadfully he wasn't there, and remembered how every minute was taking him further and further from her, and nearer and nearer to the guns of the Russians, she cried a little more. Then she thought of Mother, ill and alone, and perhaps at that very moment wanting a little girl to put eau-de-cologne on her head, and make her sudden cups of tea, and she cried more than ever. And then she remembered what Mother had said, the night before she went away, about Anthea being the eldest girl, and about trying to make the others happy, and things like that. So she stopped crying, and thought instead. And when she had thought as long as she could possibly bear she washed her face and combed her hair, and went down to the others, trying her best to look as though crying were an exercise she had never even heard of.

She found the parlour in deepest gloom, hardly relieved at all by the efforts of Robert, who, to make the time pass, was pulling Jane's hair—not hard, but just enough to tease.

"Look here," said Anthea. "Let's have a palaver." This word dated from the awful day when Cyril had carelessly wished that there were Red Indians in England—and there had been. The word brought back memories of last summer holidays and everyone groaned; they thought of the white house with the beautiful tangled garden—late roses, asters, marigold, sweet mignonette, and feathery asparagus—of the wilderness which some one had once meant to make into an orchard, but which was now, as Father said, "five acres of thistles haunted by the ghosts of baby cherry-trees." They thought of the view across the valley, where the lime-kilns looked like Aladdin's palaces in the sunshine, and they thought of their own sandpit, with its fringe of yellowy grasses and pale, stringy-stalked wild flowers, and the little holes in the cliff that were the little sand-martens' little front doors. And they thought of the free fresh air smelling of thyme and sweetbrier, and the scent of the wood-smoke from the cottages in the lane—and they looked round old Nurse's stuffy parlour, and Jane said—

"Oh, how different it all is!"

It was. Old Nurse had been in the habit of letting lodgings, till Father gave her the children to take care of. And her rooms were furnished "for letting". Now it is a very odd thing that no one ever seems to furnish a room "for letting" in a bit the same way as one would furnish it for living in. This room had heavy dark red stuff curtains—the colour that blood would not make a stain on—with coarse lace curtains inside. The carpet was yellow, and violet, with bits of grey and brown oilcloth in odd places. The fireplace had shavings and tinsel in it. There was a very varnished mahogany chiffonier, or side-board, with a lock that wouldn't act. There were hard chairs—far too many of them—with crochet antimacassars slipping off their seats, all of which sloped the wrong way. The table wore a cloth of a cruel green colour with a yellow chain-stitch pattern round it. Over the fireplace was a looking-glass that made you look much uglier than you really were, however plain you might be to begin with. Then there was a mantel-board with maroon plush and wool fringe that did not match the plush; a dreary clock like a black marble tomb—it was silent as the grave too, for it had long since forgotten how to tick. And there were painted glass vases that never had any flowers in, and a painted tambourine that no one ever played, and painted brackets with nothing on them.

> "And maple-framed engravings of the Queen,
> The Houses of Parliament, the Plains of Heaven,
> And of a blunt-nosed woodman's flat return."

There were two books—last December's "Bradshaw," and an odd volume of Plumridge's "Commentary on Thessalonians." There were—but I cannot dwell longer on this painful picture. It was indeed, as Jane said, very different.

"Let's have a palaver," said Anthea again.

"What about?" said Cyril, yawning.

"There's nothing to have *anything* about," said Robert kicking the leg of the table miserably.

"I don't want to play," said Jane, and her tone was grumpy.

Anthea tried very hard not to be cross. She succeeded.

"Look here," she said, "don't think I want to be preachy or a beast in any way, but I want to what Father calls define the situation. Do you agree?"

"Fire ahead," said Cyril without enthusiasm.

"Well then. We all know the reason we're staying here is because Nurse couldn't leave her house on account of the poor learned gentleman on the top-floor. And there was no one else Father could entrust to take care of us—and you know it's taken a lot of money Mother's going to Madeira to be made well."

Jane sniffed miserably.

"Yes, I know," said Anthea in a hurry, "but don't let's think about how horrid it all is. I mean we can't go to things that cost a lot, but we must do *something*. And I know there are heaps of things you can see in London without paying for them, and I thought we'd go and see them. We are all quite old now, and we haven't got The Lamb——"

Jane sniffed harder than before.

"I mean no one can say 'No' because of him, dear pet. And I thought we *must* get Nurse to see how quite old we are, and let us go out by ourselves, or else we shall never have any sort of a time at all. And I vote we see everything there is, and let's begin by asking Nurse to give us some bits of bread and we'll go to St. James's Park. There are ducks there, I know, we can feed them. Only we must make Nurse let us go by ourselves."

"Hurrah for liberty!" said Robert, "but she won't."

"Yes she will," said Jane unexpectedly. "*I* thought about that this morning, and I asked Father, and he said yes; and what's more he told old Nurse we might, only he said we must always say where we wanted to go, and if it was right she would let us."

"Three cheers for thoughtful Jane," cried Cyril, now roused at last from his yawning despair. "I say, let's go now."

So they went, old Nurse only begging them to be careful of crossings, and to ask a policeman to assist in the more difficult cases. But they were used to crossings, for they had lived in Camden Town and knew the Kentish Town Road where the trams rush up and down like mad at all hours of the day and night, and seem as though, if anything, they would rather run over you than not.

They had promised to be home by dark, but it was July, so dark would be very late indeed, and long past bedtime.

They started to walk to St. James's Park, and all their pockets were stuffed with bits of bread and the crusts of toast, to feed the ducks with. They started, I repeat, but they never got there.

Between Fitzroy Street and St. James's Park there are a great many streets, and, if you go the right way you will pass a great many shops that you cannot possibly help stopping to look at. The children stopped to look at several with gold-lace and beads and pictures and jewellery and dresses, and hats, and oysters and lobsters in their windows, and their sorrow did not seem nearly so impossible to bear as it had done in the best parlour at No. 300, Fitzroy Street.

Presently, by some wonderful chance turn of Robert's (who had been voted Captain because the girls thought it would be good for him—and indeed he thought so himself—and of course Cyril couldn't vote against him because it would have looked like a mean jealousy), they came into the little interesting criss-crossy streets that held the most interesting shops of all—the shops where live things were sold. There was one shop window entirely filled with cages, and all sorts of beautiful birds in them. The children were delighted till they remembered how they had once wished for wings themselves, and had had them—and then they felt how desperately unhappy anything with wings must be if it is shut up in a cage and not allowed to fly.

"It must be fairly beastly to be a bird in a cage," said Cyril. "Come on!"

They went on, and Cyril tried to think out a scheme for making his fortune as a gold-digger at Klondyke, and then buying all the caged birds in the world and setting them free. Then they came to a shop that sold cats, but the cats were in cages, and the children could not help wishing some one would buy all the cats and put them on hearthrugs, which are the proper places for cats. And there was the dog-shop, and that was not a happy thing to look at either, because all the dogs were chained or caged, and all the dogs, big and little, looked at the four children with sad wistful eyes and wagged beseeching tails as if they were trying to say, "Buy me! buy me! buy me! and let me go for a walk with you; oh, do buy me, and buy my poor brothers too! Do! do! do!" They almost said, "Do! do! do!" plain to the ear, as they whined; all but one big Irish terrier, and he growled when Jane patted him.

"Grrrrr," he seemed to say, as he looked at them from the back corner of his eye—"*You* won't buy me. Nobody will—ever—I shall die chained up—and I don't know that I care how soon it is, either!"

I don't know that the children would have understood all this, only once they had been in a besieged castle, so they knew how hateful it is to be kept in when you want to get out.

Of course they could not buy any of the dogs. They did, indeed, ask the price of the very, very smallest, and it was sixty-five pounds—but that was because it was a Japanese toy spaniel like the Queen once had her portrait painted with, when she was only Princess of Wales. But the children thought, if the smallest was all that money, the biggest would run into thousands—so they went on.

And they did not stop at any more cat or dog or bird shops, but passed them by, and at last they came to a shop that seemed as though it only sold creatures that did not much mind where they were—such as goldfish and white mice, and sea-anemones and other aquarium beasts, and lizards and toads, and hedgehogs and tortoises, and tame rabbits and guinea-pigs. And there they stopped for a long time, and fed the guinea-pigs with bits of bread through the cage-bars, and wondered whether it would be possible to keep a sandy-coloured double-lop in the basement of the house in Fitzroy Street.

"I don't suppose old Nurse would mind *very* much," said Jane. "Rabbits are most awfully tame sometimes. I expect it would know her voice and follow her all about."

"She'd tumble over it twenty times a day," said Cyril; "now a snake——"

"There aren't any snakes," said Robert hastily, "and besides, I never could cotton to snakes somehow—I wonder why."

"Worms are as bad," said Anthea, "and eels and slugs—I think it's because we don't like things that haven't got legs."

"Father says snakes have got legs hidden away inside of them," said Robert.

"Yes—and he says *we've* got tails hidden away inside *us*—but it doesn't either of it come to anything *really*," said Anthea. "I hate things that haven't any legs."

"It's worse when they have too many," said Jane with a shudder, "think of centipedes!"

They stood there on the pavement, a cause of some inconvenience to the passers-by, and thus beguiled the time with conversation. Cyril was leaning his elbow on the top of a hutch that had seemed empty when they had inspected the whole edifice of hutches one by one, and he was trying to reawaken the interest of a hedgehog that had curled itself into a ball earlier in the interview, when a small, soft voice just below his elbow said, quietly, plainly and quite unmistakably—not in any squeak or whine that had to be translated—but in downright common English—

"Buy me—do—please buy me!"

Cyril started as though he had been pinched, and jumped a yard away from the hutch.

"Come back—oh, come back!" said the voice, rather louder but still softly; "stoop down and pretend to be tying up your bootlace—I see it's undone, as usual."

Cyril mechanically obeyed. He knelt on one knee on the

He found himself face to face with the Psammead!

dry, hot dusty pavement, peered into the darkness of the hutch and found himself face to face with—the Psammead!

It seemed much thinner than when he had last seen it. It was dusty and dirty, and its fur was untidy and ragged. It had hunched itself up into a miserable lump, and its long snail's eyes were drawn in quite tight so that they hardly showed at all.

"Listen," said the Psammead, in a voice that sounded as though it would begin to cry in a minute, "I don't think the creature who keeps this shop will ask a very high price for me. I've bitten him more than once, and I've made myself look as common as I can. He's never had a glance from my beautiful, beautiful eyes. Tell the others I'm here—but tell them to look at some of those low, common beasts while I'm talking to you. The creature inside mustn't think you care much about me, or he'll put a price upon me far, far beyond your means. I remember in the dear old days last summer you never had much money. Oh—I never thought I should be so glad to see you—I never did." It sniffed, and shot out its long snail's eyes expressly to drop a tear well away from its fur. "Tell the others I'm here, and then I'll tell you exactly what to do about buying me."

Cyril tied his bootlace into a hard knot, stood up and addressed the others in firm tones—

"Look here," he said, "I'm not kidding—and I appeal to your honour," an appeal which in this family was never made in vain. "Don't look at that hutch—look at the white rat. Now you are not to look at that hutch whatever I say."

He stood in front of it to prevent mistakes.

"Now get yourselves ready for a great surprise. In that hutch there's an old friend of ours—*don't* look!—Yes; it's the Psammead, the good old Psammead! it wants us to buy it. It says you're not to look at it. Look at the white rat and count your money! On your honour don't look!"

The others responded nobly. They looked at the white rat till they quite stared him out of countenance, so that he went and sat up on his hind legs in a far corner and hid his eyes with his front paws, and pretended he was washing his face.

Cyril stooped again, busying himself with the other bootlace, and listened for the Psammead's further instructions.

"Go in," said the Psammead, "and ask the price of lots of other things. Then say, 'What do you want for that monkey that's lost its tail—the mangy old thing in the third hutch from the end.' Oh—don't mind *my* feelings—call me a mangy monkey—I've tried hard enough to look like one! I don't think he'll put a high price on me—I've bitten him eleven times since I came here the day before yesterday. If he names a bigger price than you can afford, say you wish you had the money."

"But you can't give us wishes. I've promised never to have another wish from you," said the bewildered Cyril.

"Don't be a silly little idiot," said the Sand-fairy in trembling but affectionate tones, "but find out how much money you've got between you, and do exactly what I tell you."

Cyril, pointing a stiff and unmeaning finger at the white rat, so as to pretend that its charms alone employed his tongue, explained matters to the others, while the Psammead hunched itself, and bunched itself, and did its very best to make itself look uninteresting.

Then the four children filed into the shop.

"How much do you want for that white rat?" asked Cyril.

"Eightpence," was the answer.

"And the guinea-pigs?"

"Eighteenpence to five bob, according to the breed."

"And the lizards?"

"Ninepence each."

"And toads?"

"Fourpence. Now look here," said the greasy owner of all this caged life with a sudden ferocity which made the whole party back hurriedly on to the wainscotting of hutches with which the shop was lined. "Lookee here. I ain't agoin' to have you a comin' in here a turnin' the whole place outer winder, 'an prizing every animile in the stock just for your larks, so don't think it! If you're a buyer, *be* a buyer—but I never had a customer yet as wanted to buy mice, and lizards, and toads, and guineas all at once. So hout you goes."

"Oh! wait a minute," said the wretched Cyril, feeling how foolishly yet well-meaningly he had carried out the Psammead's instructions. "Just tell me one thing. What do you want for the mangy old monkey in the third hutch from the end?"

The shopman only saw in this a new insult.

"Mangy young monkey yourself," said he; "get along with your blooming cheek. Hout you goes!"

"Oh! don't be so cross," said Jane, losing her head altogether, "don't you see he really *does* want to know *that*!"

"Ho! does 'e indeed?" sneered the merchant. Then he scratched his ear suspiciously, for he was a sharp business man, and he knew the ring of truth when he heard it. His hand was bandaged, and three minutes before he would have been glad to sell the "mangy old monkey" for ten shillings. Now—

"Ho! 'e does, does 'e," he said, "then two pun ten's my price. He's not got his fellow that monkey ain't, nor yet his match, not this side of the equator, which he comes from. And the only one ever seen in London. Ought to be in the Zoo. Two pun ten, down on the nail, or *hout* you goes!"

The children looked at each other—twenty-three shillings and fivepence was all they had in the world, and it would have been merely three and fivepence, but for the sovereign which Father had given to them "between them" at parting.

"We've only twenty-three shillings and fivepence," said Cyril, rattling the money in his pocket.

"Twenty-three farthings and somebody's own cheek," said the dealer, for he did not believe that Cyril had so much money.

There was a miserable pause. Then Anthea remembered, and said—

"Oh! I *wish* I had two pounds ten."

"So do I, Miss, I'm sure," said the man with bitter politeness; "I wish you 'ad, I'm sure!"

Anthea's hand was on the counter, something seemed to slide under it. She lifted it. There lay five bright half sovereigns.

"Why, I *have* got it after all," she said; "here's the money, now let's have the Sammy, . . . the monkey I mean."

The dealer looked hard at the money, but he made haste to put it in his pocket.

"I only hope you come by it honest," he said, shrugging his shoulders. He scratched his ear again.

"Well!" he said, "I suppose I must let you have it, but it's worth thribble the money, so it is——"

He slowly led the way out to the hutch—opened the door gingerly, and made a sudden fierce grab at the Psammead, which the Psammead acknowledged in one last long lingering bite.

"Here, take the brute," said the shopman, squeezing the Psammead so tight that he nearly choked it. "It's bit me to the marrow, it have."

The man's eyes opened as Anthea held out her arms. "Don't blame me if it tears your face off its bones," he said, and the Psammead made a leap from his dirty horny hands, and Anthea caught it in hers, which were not very clean, certainly, but at any rate were soft and pink, and held it kindly and closely.

"But you can't take it home like that," Cyril said, "we shall have a crowd after us," and indeed two errand-boys and a policeman had already collected.

"I can't give you nothink only a paper-bag, like what we puts the tortoises in," said the man grudgingly.

So the whole party went into the shop, and the shopman's eyes nearly came out of his head when, having given Anthea the largest paper-bag he could find, he saw her hold it open, and the Psammead carefully creep into it.

"Well!" he said, "if that there don't beat cockfighting! But p'raps you've met the brute afore."

"Yes," said Cyril affably, "he's an old friend of ours."

"If I'd a known that," the man rejoined, "you shouldn't a had him under twice the money. 'Owever," he added, as the children disappeared, "I ain't done so bad, seeing as I only give five bob for the beast. But then there's the bites to take into account!"

The children, trembling in agitation and excitement, carried home the Psammead, trembling in its paper-bag.

When they got it home, Anthea nursed it, and stroked it, and would have cried over it, if she hadn't remembered how it hated to be wet.

When it recovered enough to speak, it said—

"Get me sand; silver sand from the oil and colour shop. And get me plenty."

They got the sand, and they put it and the Psammead in the round bath together, and it rubbed itself, and rolled itself, and shook itself, and scraped itself, and scratched itself, and preened itself, till it felt clean and comfy, and then it scrabbled a hasty hole in the sand, and went to sleep in it.

The children hid the bath under the girls' bed, and had supper. Old Nurse had got them a lovely supper of bread and butter and fried onions. She was full of kind and delicate thoughts.

When Anthea woke the next morning, the Psammead was snuggling down between her shoulder and Jane's.

"You have saved my life," it said, "I know that man would have thrown cold water on me sooner or later, and then I should have died. I saw him wash out a guinea-pig's hutch yesterday morning. I'm still frightfully sleepy, I think I'll go back to sand for another nap. Wake the boys and this dormouse of a Jane, and when you've had your breakfasts we'll have a talk."

"Don't *you* want any breakfast?" asked Anthea.

"I daresay I shall pick a bit presently," it said; "but sand is all I care about—it's meat and drink to me, and coals and fire and wife and children." With these words it clambered down by the bedclothes and scrambled back into the bath, where they heard it scratching itself out of sight.

"Well!" said Anthea, "anyhow our holidays won't be dull *now*. We've found the Psammead again."

"No," said Jane, beginning to put on her stockings. "We shan't be *dull*—but it'll be only like having a pet dog now it can't give us wishes."

"Oh, don't be so discontented," said Anthea. "If it can't do anything else it can tell us about Megatheriums and things."

CHAPTER II

THE HALF AMULET

LONG AGO—that is to say last summer—the children, finding themselves embarrassed by some wish which the Psammead had granted them, and which the servants had not received in a proper spirit, had wished that the servants might not notice the gifts which the Psammead gave. And when they parted from the Psammead their last wish had been that they should meet it again. Therefore they *had* met it (and it was jolly lucky for the Psammead, as Robert pointed out). Now, of course, you see that the Psammead's being where it was, was the consequence of one of their wishes, and therefore was a Psammead-wish, and as such could not be noticed by the servants. And it was soon plain that in the Psammead's opinion old Nurse was still a servant, although she had now a house of her own, for she never noticed the Psammead at all. And that was as well, for she would never have consented to allow the girls to keep an animal and a bath of sand under their bed.

When breakfast had been cleared away—it was a very nice breakfast with hot rolls to it, a luxury quite out of the common way—Anthea went and dragged out the bath, and woke the Psammead. It stretched and shook itself.

"You must have bolted your breakfast most unwholesomely," it said, "you can't have been five minutes over it."

"We've been nearly an hour," said Anthea. "Come—you know you promised."

"Now look here," said the Psammead, sitting back on the sand and shooting out its long eyes suddenly, "we'd better begin as we mean to go on. It won't do to have any misunderstanding, so I tell you plainly that——"

"Oh, *please*," Anthea pleaded, "do wait till we get to the others. They'll think it most awfully sneakish of me to talk to you without them; do come down, there's a dear."

She knelt before the sand-bath and held out her arms. The Psammead must have remembered how glad it had been to jump into those same little arms only the day before, for it gave a little grudging grunt, and jumped once more.

Anthea wrapped it in her pinafore and carried it downstairs. It was welcomed in a thrilling silence.

At last Anthea said, "Now then!"

"What place is this?" asked the Psammead, shooting its eyes out and turning them slowly round.

"It's a sitting-room, of course," said Robert.

"Then I don't like it," said the Psammead.

"Never mind," said Anthea kindly; "we'll take you anywhere you like if you want us to. What was it you were going to say upstairs when I said the others wouldn't like it if I stayed talking to you without them?"

It looked keenly at her, and she blushed.

"Don't be silly," it said sharply. "Of course, it's quite natural that you should like your brothers and sisters to know exactly how good and unselfish you were."

"I wish you wouldn't," said Jane. "Anthea was quite right. What was it you were going to say when she stopped you?"

"I'll tell you," said the Psammead, "since you're so anxious to know. I was going to say this. You've saved my life—and I'm not ungrateful—but it doesn't change your nature or mine. You're still very ignorant, and rather silly, and I am worth a thousand of you any day of the week."

"Of course you are!" Anthea was beginning but it interrupted her.

"It's very rude to interrupt," it said; "what I mean is that I'm not going to stand any nonsense, and if you think what you've done is to give you the right to pet me or make me demean myself by playing with you, you'll find out that what you think doesn't matter a single penny. See? It's what *I* think that matters."

"I know," said Cyril, "it always was, if you remember."

"Well," said the Psammead, "then that's settled. We're to be treated as we deserve. I with respect, and all of you with—but I don't wish to be offensive. Do you want me to tell you how

I got into that horrible den you bought me out of? Oh, I'm not ungrateful! I haven't forgotten it and I shan't forget it."

"Do tell us," said Anthea. "I know you're awfully clever, but even with all your cleverness, I don't believe you can possibly know how—how respectfully we do respect you. Don't we?"

The others all said yes—and fidgeted in their chairs. Robert spoke the wishes of all when he said—"I do wish you'd go on."

So it sat up on the green-covered table and went on.

"When you'd gone away," it said, "I went to sand for a bit, and slept. I was tired out with all your silly wishes, and I felt as though I hadn't really been to sand for a year."

"To sand?" Jane repeated.

"Where I sleep. You go to bed. I go to sand."

Jane yawned; the mention of bed made her feel sleepy.

"All right," said the Psammead, in offended tones. "I'm sure I don't want to tell you a long tale. A man caught me, and I bit him. And he put me in a bag with a dead hare and a dead rabbit. And he took me to his house and put me out of the bag into a basket with holes that I could see through. And I bit him again. And then he brought me to this city, which I am told is called the Modern Babylon—though it's not a bit like the old Babylon—and he sold me to the man you bought me from, and then I bit them both. Now, what's your news?"

"There's not quite so much biting in our story," said Cyril regretfully; "in fact, there isn't any. Father's gone to Manchuria, and Mother and The Lamb have gone to Madeira because Mother was ill, and don't I just wish that they were both safe home again."

Merely from habit, the Sand-fairy began to blow itself out, but it stopped short suddenly.

"I forgot," it said; "I can't give you any more wishes."

"No—but look here," said Cyril, "couldn't we call in old Nurse and get her to say she wishes they were safe home. I'm sure she does."

"No go," said the Psammead. "It's just the same as your wishing yourself if you get some one else to wish for you. It won't act."

"But it did yesterday—with the man in the shop," said Robert.

"Ah yes," said the creature, "but you didn't *ask* him to wish, and you didn't know what would happen if he did. That can't be done again. It's played out."

"Then you can't help us at all," said Jane; "oh—I did think you could do something; I've been thinking about it ever since we saved your life yesterday. I thought you'd be certain to be able to fetch back Father, even if you couldn't manage Mother."

And Jane began to cry.

"Now *don't*," said the Psammead hastily; "you know how it always upsets me if you cry. I can't feel safe a moment. Look here; you must have some new kind of charm."

"That's easier said than done."

"Not a bit of it," said the creature; "there's one of the strongest charms in the world not a stone's throw from where you bought me yesterday. The man that I bit so—the first one, I mean—went into a shop to ask how much something cost—I think he said it was a concertina—and while he was telling the man in the shop how much too much he wanted for it, I saw the charm in a sort of tray, with a lot of other things. If you can only buy that, you will be able to have your heart's desire."

The children looked at each other and then at the Psammead. Then Cyril coughed awkwardly and took sudden courage to say what everyone was thinking.

"I do hope you won't be waxy," he said; "but it's like this: when you used to give us our wishes they almost always got us into some row or other, and we used to think you wouldn't have been pleased if they hadn't. Now, about this charm—we haven't got over and above too much tin, and if we blue it all on this charm and it turns out to be not up to much—well— you see what I'm driving at, don't you?"

"I see that *you* don't see more than the length of your nose, and *that's* not far," said the Psammead crossly. "Look here, I *had* to give you the wishes, and of course they turned out badly, in a sort of way, because you hadn't the sense to wish for what was good for you. But this charm's quite different. I haven't *got* to do this for you, it's just my own generous kindness that makes me tell you about it. So it's bound to be all right. See?"

"Don't be cross," said Anthea, "please, *please* don't. You see, it's all we've got; we shan't have any more pocket-money till Daddy comes home—unless he sends us some in a letter. But we do trust you. And I say, all of you," she went on, "don't you think it's worth spending all the money, if there's even the chanciest chance of getting Father and Mother back safe *now*? Just think of it! Oh, do let's!"

"*I* don't care what you do," said the Psammead; "I'll go back to sand again till you've made up your minds."

"No, don't!" said everybody; and Jane added, "We are quite mind made-up—don't you see we are? Let's get our hats. Will you come with us?"

"Of course," said the Psammead; "how else would you find the shop?"

So everybody got its hat. The Psammead was put into a flat bass-bag that had come from Farringdon Market with two pounds of filleted plaice in it. Now it contained about three pounds and a quarter of solid Psammead, and the children took it in turns to carry it.

"It's not half the weight of The Lamb," Robert said, and the girls sighed.

The Psammead poked a wary eye out of the top of the basket every now and then, and told the children which turnings to take.

"How on earth do you know?" asked Robert. "I can't think how you do it."

And the Psammead said sharply, "No—I don't suppose you can."

At last they came to *the* shop. It had all sorts and kinds of things in the window—concertinas, and silk handkerchiefs, china vases and tea-cups, blue Japanese jars, pipes, swords, pistols, lace collars, silver spoons tied up in half-dozens, and wedding-rings in a red lacquered basin. There were officers' epaulets and doctors' lancets. There were tea-caddies inlaid with red turtle-shell and brass curly-wurlies, plates of different kinds of money, and stacks of different kinds of plates. There was a beautiful picture of a little girl washing a dog, which Jane liked very much. And in the middle of the window there was a dirty silver tray full of mother-of-pearl card counters, old seals, paste buckles, snuff-boxes, and all sorts of little dingy odds and ends.

The Psammead put its head quite out of the fish-basket to look in the window, when Cyril said—

"There's a tray there with rubbish in it."

And then its long snail's eyes saw something that made them stretch out so much that they were as long and thin as new slate-pencils. Its fur bristled thickly, and its voice was quite hoarse with excitement as it whispered—

"That's it! That's it! There, under that blue and yellow buckle, you can see a bit sticking out. It's red. Do you see?"

"Is it that thing something like a horse-shoe?" asked Cyril. "And red, like the common sealing-wax you do up parcels with?"

"Yes, that's it," said the Psammead. "Now, you do just as you did before. Ask the price of other things. That blue buckle would do. Then the man will get the tray out of the window. I think you'd better be the one," it said to Anthea. "We'll wait out here."

So the others flattened their noses against the shop window, and presently a large, dirty, short-fingered hand with a very big diamond ring came stretching through the green half-curtains at the back of the shop window and took away the tray.

They could not see what was happening in the interview between Anthea and the Diamond Ring, and it seemed to them that she had had time—if she had had money—to buy everything in the shop before the moment came when she stood before them, her face wreathed in grins, as Cyril said later, and in her hand the charm.

It was something like this:

and it was made of a red, smooth, softly shiny stone.

"I've got it," Anthea whispered, just opening her hand to give the others a glimpse of it. "Do let's get home. We can't stand here like stuck-pigs looking at it in the street."

So home they went. The parlour in Fitzroy Street was a very flat background to magic happenings. Down in the country among the flowers and green fields anything had seemed—and indeed had been—possible. But it was hard to believe that anything really wonderful could happen so near the Tottenham Court Road. But the Psammead was there—and it in itself was wonderful. And it could talk—and it had shown them where a charm could be bought that would make the owner of it perfectly happy. So the four children hurried home, taking very long steps, with their chins stuck out, and their mouths shut very tight indeed. They went so fast that the Psammead was quite shaken about in its fish-bag, but it did not say anything—perhaps for fear of attracting public notice.

They got home at last, very hot indeed, and set the Psammead on the green tablecloth.

"Now then!" said Cyril.

But the Psammead had to have a plate of sand fetched for it, for it was quite faint. When it had refreshed itself a little it said—

"Now then! Let me see the charm," and Anthea laid it on the green table-cover. The Psammead shot out his long eyes to look at it, then it turned them reproachfully on Anthea and said—

"But there's only half of it here!"

This was indeed a blow.

"It was all there was," said Anthea, with timid firmness. She knew it was not her fault.

"There should be another piece," said the Psammead, "and a sort of pin to fasten the two together."

"Isn't half any good?"—"Won't it work without the other bit?"—"It cost seven-and-six."—"Oh, bother, bother, bother!" —"Don't be silly little idiots!" said every one and the Psammead altogether.

Then there was a wretched silence. Cyril broke it—

"What shall we do?"

"Go back to the shop and see if they haven't got the other half," said the Psammead. "I'll go to sand till you come back. Cheer up! Even the bit you've got is *some* good, but it'll be no end of a bother if you can't find the other."

So Cyril went to the shop. And the Psammead to sand. And the other three went to dinner, which was now ready. And old Nurse was very cross that Cyril was not ready too.

The three were watching at the windows when Cyril returned, and even before he was near enough for them to see his face there was something about the slouch of his shoulders and set of his knickerbockers and the way he dragged his boots along that showed but too plainly that his errand had been in vain.

"Well?" they all said, hoping against hope on the front-door step.

"No go," Cyril answered; "the man said the thing was per-

"But there's only half of it here!"

fect. He said it was a Roman lady's locket, and people shouldn't
buy curios if they didn't know anything about arky—something
or other, and that he never went back on a bargain, because
it wasn't business, and he expected his customers to act the
same. He was simply nasty—that's what he was, and I want my
dinner."

It was plain that Cyril was not pleased.

The unlikeliness of anything really interesting happening in
that parlour lay like a weight of lead on every one's spirits.
Cyril had his dinner, and just as he was swallowing the last
mouthful of apple-pudding there was a scratch at the door.
Anthea opened it and in walked the Psammead.

"Well," it said, when it had heard the news, "things might
be worse. Only you won't be surprised if you have a few
adventures before you get the other half. You want to get it,
of course."

"Rather," was the general reply. "And we don't mind
adventures."

"No," said the Psammead, "I seem to remember that about
you. Well, sit down and listen with all your ears. Eight, are
there? Right—I am glad you know arithmetic. Now pay
attention, because I don't intend to tell you everything twice
over."

As the children settled themselves on the floor—it was far
more comfortable than the chairs, as well as more polite to the
Psammead, who was stroking its whiskers on the hearth-rug—
a sudden cold pain caught at Anthea's heart. Father—Mother
—the darling Lamb—all far away. Then a warm, comfortable
feeling flowed through her. The Psammead was here, and at
least half a charm, and there were to be adventures. (If you
don't know what a cold pain is, I am glad for your sakes, and
I hope you never may.)

"Now," said the Psammead cheerily, "you are not particularly nice, nor particularly clever, and you're not at all good-
looking. Still, you've saved my life—oh, when I think of that
man and his pail of water!—so I'll tell you all I know. At least,
of course I can't do that, because I know far too much. But
I'll tell you all I know about this red thing."

"Do! Do! Do! Do!" said every one.

"Well, then," said the Psammead. "This thing is half of an Amulet that can do all sorts of things; it can make the corn grow, and the waters flow, and the trees bear fruit, and the little new beautiful babies come. (Not that babies *are* beautiful, of course," it broke off to say, "but their mothers think they are—and as long as you think a thing's true it *is* true as far as you're concerned.")

Robert yawned.

The Psammead went on.

"The complete Amulet can keep off all the things that make people unhappy—jealousy, bad temper, pride, disagreeableness, greediness, selfishness, laziness. Evil spirits, people called them when the Amulet was made. Don't you think it would be nice to have it?"

"Very," said the children, quite without enthusiasm.

"And it can give you strength and courage."

"That's better," said Cyril.

"And virtue."

"I suppose it's nice to have that," said Jane, but not with much interest.

"And it can give you your heart's desire."

"Now you're talking," said Robert.

"Of course I am," retorted the Psammead tartly, "so there's no need for you to."

"Heart's desire is good enough for me," said Cyril.

"Yes, but," Anthea ventured, "all that's what the *whole* charm can do. There's something that the half we've got can win off its own bat—isn't there?" She appealed to the Psammead. It nodded.

"Yes," it said; "the half has the power to take you anywhere you like to look for the other half."

This seemed a brilliant prospect till Robert asked—

"Does it know where to look?"

The Psammead shook its head and answered.

"I don't think it's likely."

"Do you?"

"No."

"Then," said Robert, "we might as well look for a needle in a bottle of hay. Yes—it *is* bottle, and not bundle, Father said so."

"Not at all," said the Psammead briskly; "you think you know everything, but you are quite mistaken. The first thing is to get the thing to talk."

"Can it?" Jane questioned. Jane's question did not mean that she thought it couldn't, for in spite of the parlour furniture the feeling of magic was growing deeper and thicker, and seemed to fill the room like a dream of a scented fog.

"Of course it can. I suppose you can read."

"Oh yes!" Every one was rather hurt at the question.

"Well, then—all you've got to do is to read the name that's written on the part of the charm that you've got. And as soon as you say the name out loud the thing will have power to do —well, several things."

There was a silence. The red charm was passed from hand to hand.

"There's no name on it," said Cyril at last.

"Nonsense," said the Psammead; "what's that?"

"Oh, *that*!" said Cyril, "it's not reading. It looks like pictures of chickens and snakes and things."

This was what was on the charm:

"I've no patience with you," said the Psammead; "if you can't read you must find some one who can. A priest now?"

"We don't know any priests," said Anthea; "we know a clergyman—he's called a priest in the prayer-book, you know —but he only knows Greek and Latin and Hebrew, and this isn't either of those—I know."

The Psammead stamped a furry foot angrily.

"I wish I'd never seen you," it said; "you aren't any more good than so many stone images. Not so much, if I'm to tell the truth. Is there no wise man in your Babylon who can pronounce the names of the Great Ones."

"There's a poor learned gentleman upstairs," said Anthea, "we might try him. He has a lot of stone images in his room, and iron-looking ones too—we peeped in once when he was out. Old Nurse says he doesn't eat enough to keep a canary alive. He spends it all on stones and things."

"Try him," said the Psammead, "only be careful. If he knows a greater name than this and uses it against you, your charm will be of no use. Bind him first with the chains of honour and upright dealing. And then ask his aid—oh, yes, you'd better all go; you can put me to sand as you go upstairs. I must have a few minutes' peace and quietness."

So the four children hastily washed their hands and brushed their hair—this was Anthea's idea—and went up to knock at the door of the "poor learned gentleman," and to "bind him with the chains of honour and upright dealing."

CHAPTER III

THE PAST

THE LEARNED gentleman had let his dinner get quite cold. It was mutton chop, and as it lay on the plate it looked like a brown island in the middle of a frozen pond, because the grease of the gravy had become cold, and consequently white. It looked very nasty, and it was the first thing the children saw when, after knocking three times and receiving no reply, one of them ventured to turn the handle and softly to open the door. The chop was on the end of a long table that ran down one side of the room. The table had images on it and queer-shaped stones, and books. And there were glass cases fixed against the wall behind, with little strange things in them. The cases were rather like the one you see in jewellers' shops.

The "poor learned gentleman" was sitting at a table in the window, looking at something very small which he held in a pair of fine pincers. He had a round spy-glass sort of thing in one eye—which reminded the children of watchmakers, and also of the long snail's eyes of the Psammead.

The gentleman was very long and thin, and his long, thin boots stuck out under the other side of his table. He did not hear the door open, and the children stood hesitating. At last Robert gave the door a push, and they all startled back, for in the middle of the wall that the door had hidden was a mummy-case—very, very, very big—painted in red and yellow and green and black, and the face of it seemed to look at them quite angrily.

You know what a mummy-case is like, of course? If you don't you had better go to the British Museum at once and find out. Any way, it is not at all the sort of thing that you expect to meet in a top-floor front in Bloomsbury, looking as though it would like to know what business you had there.

36

In the middle of the wall was a mummy-case

So every one said, "Oh!" rather loud, and their boots clattered as they stumbled back.

The learned gentleman took the glass out of his eye and said—

"I beg your pardon," in a very soft, quiet pleasant voice—the voice of a gentleman who has been to Oxford.

"It's us that beg yours," said Cyril politely. "We are sorry to disturb you."

"Come in," said the gentleman, rising—with the most distinguished courtesy, Anthea told herself. "I am delighted to see you. Won't you sit down? No, not there; allow me to move that papyrus."

He cleared a chair, and stood smiling and looking kindly through his large, round spectacles.

"He treats us like grown-ups," whispered Robert, "and he doesn't seem to know how many of us there are."

"Hush," said Anthea, "it isn't manners to whisper. You say, Cyril—go ahead."

"We're very sorry to disturb you," said Cyril politely, "but we did knock three times, and you didn't say 'Come in,' or 'Run away now,' or that you couldn't be bothered just now, or to come when you weren't so busy, or any of the things people do say when you knock at doors, so we opened it. We knew you were in because we heard you sneeze while we were waiting."

"Not at all," said the gentleman; "do sit down."

"He has found out there are four of us," said Robert, as the gentleman cleared three more chairs. He put the things off them carefully on the floor. The first chair had things like bricks that tiny, tiny birds' feet have walked over when the bricks were soft, only the marks were in regular lines. The second chair had round things on it like very large, fat, long, pale beads. And the last chair had a pile of dusty papers on it.

The children sat down.

"We know you are very, very learned," said Cyril, "and we have got a charm, and we want you to read the name on it, because it isn't in Latin or Greek, or Hebrew, or any of the languages *we* know——"

"A thorough knowledge of even those languages is a very fair foundation on which to build an education," said the gentleman politely.

"Oh!" said Cyril blushing, "but we only know them to look at, except Latin—and I'm only in Cæsar with that."

The gentleman took off his spectacles and laughed. His laugh sounded rusty, Cyril thought, as though it wasn't often used.

"Of course!" he said. "I'm sure I beg your pardon. I think I must have been in a dream. You are the children who live downstairs, are you not? Yes. I have seen you as I have passed in and out. And you have found something that you think to be an antiquity, and you've brought it to show me? That was very kind. I should like to inspect it."

"I'm afraid we didn't think about your liking to inspect it," said the truthful Anthea. "It was just for *us*—because we wanted to know the name on it——"

"Oh, yes—and, I say," Robert interjected, "you won't think it rude of us if we ask you first, before we show it, to be bound in the what-do-you-call-it of——"

"In the bonds of honour and upright dealing," said Anthea.

"I'm afraid I don't quite follow you," said the gentleman, with gentle nervousness.

"Well, it's this way," said Cyril. "We've got part of a charm. And the Sammy—I mean, something told us it would work, though it's only half a one; but it won't work unless we can say the name that's on it. But, of course, if you've got another name that can lick ours, our charm will be no go; so we want you to give us your word of honour as a gentleman —though I'm sure, now I've seen you, that it's not necessary; but still I've promised to ask you, so we must. Will you please give us your honourable word not to say any name stronger than the name on our charm?"

The gentleman had put on his spectacles again and was looking at Cyril through them. He now said: "Bless me!" more than once, adding, "Who told you all this?"

"I can't tell you," said Cyril. "I'm very sorry, but I can't."

Some faint memory of a far-off childhood must have come to the learned gentleman just then, for he smiled.

"I see," he said. "It is some sort of game that you are engaged in? Of course! Yes! Well, I will certainly promise. Yet I wonder how you heard of the names of power?"

"We can't tell you that either," said Cyril; and Anthea said, "Here is our charm," and held it out.

With politeness, but without interest, the gentleman took it. But after the first glance all his body suddenly stiffened, as a pointer's does when he sees a partridge.

"Excuse me," he said in quite a changed voice, and carried the charm to the window.

He looked at it; he turned it over. He fixed his spy-glass in his eye and looked again. No one said anything. Only Robert made a shuffling noise with his feet till Anthea nudged him to shut up.

At last the learned gentleman drew a long breath.

"Where did you find this?" he asked.

"We didn't find it. We bought it at a shop. Jacob Absalom the name is—not far from Charing Cross," said Cyril.

"We gave seven-and-sixpence for it," added Jane.

"It is not for sale, I suppose? You do not wish to part with it? I ought to tell you that it is extremely valuable—extraordinarly valuable, I may say."

"Yes," said Cyril, "we know that, so of course we want to keep it."

"Keep it carefully, then," said the gentleman impressively; "and if ever you should wish to part with it, may I ask you to give me the refusal of it?"

"The refusal?"

"I mean, do not sell it to any one else until you have given me the opportunity of buying it."

"All right," said Cyril, "we won't. But we don't want to sell it. We want to make it do things."

"I suppose you can play at that as well as at anything else," said the gentleman; "but I'm afraid the days of magic are over."

"They aren't *really*," said Anthea earnestly. "You'd see they aren't if I could tell you about our last summer holidays. Only I mustn't. Thank you very much. And can you read the name?"

He fixed his spy-glass in his eye and looked again

"Yes, I can read it."

"Will you tell it us?"

"The name," said the gentleman, "is Ur Hekau Setcheh."

"Ur Hekau Setcheh," repeated Cyril. "Thanks awfully. I do hope we haven't taken up too much of your time."

"Not at all," said the gentleman. "And do let me entreat you to be very, very careful of that most valuable specimen."

They said "Thank you" in all the different polite ways they could think of, and filed out of the door and down the stairs. Anthea was last. Half-way down to the first landing she turned and ran up again.

The door was still open, and the learned gentleman and the mummy-case were standing opposite to each other, and both looked as though they had stood like that for years.

The gentleman started when Anthea put her hand on his arm.

"I hope you won't be cross and say it's not my business," she said, "but do look at your chop! Don't you think you ought to eat it? Father forgets his dinner sometimes when he's writing, and Mother always says I ought to remind him if she's not at home to do it herself, because it's so bad to miss your regular meals. So I thought perhaps you wouldn't mind my reminding you, because you don't seem to have any one else to do it."

She glanced at the mummy-case; *it* certainly did not look as though it would ever think of reminding people of their meals.

The learned gentleman looked at her for a moment before he said—

"Thank you, my dear. It was a kindly thought. No, I haven't any one to remind me about things like that."

He sighed, and looked at the chop.

"It looks very nasty," said Anthea.

"Yes," he said, "it does. I'll eat it immediately, before I forget."

As he ate it he sighed more than once. Perhaps because the chop was nasty, perhaps because he longed for the charm which the children did not want to sell, perhaps because it was so long since any one had cared whether he ate his chops or forgot them.

Anthea caught the others at the stair-foot. They woke the Psammead, and it taught them exactly how to use the word of power, and to make the charm speak. I am not going to tell you how this is done, because you might try to do it. And for you any such trying would be almost sure to end in disappointment. Because in the first place it is a thousand million to one against your ever getting hold of the right sort of charm, and if you did, there would be hardly any chance at all of your finding a learned gentleman clever enough and kind enough to read the word for you.

The children and the Psammead crouched in a circle on the floor—in the girls' bedroom, because in the parlour they might have been interrupted by old Nurse's coming in to lay the cloth for tea—and the charm was put in the middle of the circle.

The sun shone splendidly outside, and the room was very light. Through the open window came the hum and rattle of London, and in the street below they could hear the voice of the milkman.

When all was ready, the Psammead signed to Anthea to say the word. And she said it.

Instantly the whole light of all the world seemed to go out. The room was dark. The world outside was dark—darker than the darkest night that ever was. And all the sounds went out too, so that there was a silence deeper than any silence you have ever even dreamed of imagining. It was like being suddenly deaf and blind, only darker and quieter even than that.

But before the children had got over the sudden shock of it enough to be frightened, a faint, beautiful light began to show in the middle of the circle, and at the same moment a faint, beautiful voice began to speak. The light was too small for one to see anything by, and the voice was too small for you to hear what it said. You could just see the light and just hear the voice.

But the light grew stronger. It was greeny, like glow-worms' lamps, and it grew and grew till it was as though thousands and thousands of glow-worms were signalling to their winged sweethearts from the middle of the circle. And the voice grew, not so much in loudness as in sweetness (though it grew louder, too), till it was so sweet that you wanted to cry with pleasure just at the sound of it. It was like nightingales, and the sea, and the fiddle, and the voice of your mother when you have been a long time away, and she meets you at the door when you get home.

And the voice said—

"Speak. What is it that you would hear?"

I cannot tell you what language the voice used. I only know that every one present understood it perfectly. If you come to think of it, there must be some language that every one could understand, if we only knew what it was. Nor can I tell you how the charm spoke, nor whether it was the charm that spoke, or some presence in the charm. The children could not have told you either. Indeed, they could not look at the charm while it was speaking, because the light was too bright. They looked instead at the green radiance on the faded Kidderminster carpet at the edge of the circle. They all felt very quiet, and not inclined to ask questions or fidget with their feet. For this was not like the things that had happened in the country when the Psammead had given them their wishes. That had been funny somehow, and this was not. It was something like Arabian Nights magic, and something like being in church. No one cared to speak.

It was Cyril who said at last—

"Please we want to know where the other half of the charm is."

"The part of the Amulet which is lost," said the beautiful voice, "was broken and ground into the dust of the shrine that held it. It and the pin that joined the two halves are themselves dust, and the dust is scattered over many lands and sunk in many seas."

"Oh, I say!" murmured Robert, and a blank silence fell.

"Then it's all up?" said Cyril at last; "it's no use our looking for a thing that's smashed into dust, and the dust scattered all over the place."

"If you would find it," said the voice, "you must seek it where it still is, perfect as ever."

"I don't understand," said Cyril.

"In the Past you may find it," said the voice.

"I wish we *may* find it," said Cyril.

The Psammead whispered crossly, "Don't you understand? The thing existed in the Past. If you were in the Past, too, you could find it. It's very difficult to make you understand things. Time and space are only forms of thought."

"I see," said Cyril.

"No, you don't," said the Psammead, "and it doesn't matter if you don't, either. What I mean is that if you were only made the right way, you could see everything happening in the same place at the same time. Now do you see?"

"I'm afraid *I* don't," said Anthea; "I'm sorry I'm so stupid."

"Well, at any rate you see this. That lost half of the Amulet is in the Past. Therefore it's in the Past we must look for it. I mustn't speak to the charm myself. Ask it things! Find out!"

"Where can we find the other part of you?" asked Cyril obediently.

"In the Past," said the voice.

"What part of the Past?"

"I may not tell you. If you will choose a time, I will take you to the place that then held it. You yourselves must find it."

"When did you see it last?" asked Anthea—"I mean, when was it taken away from you?"

The beautiful voice answered—

"That was thousands of years ago. The Amulet was perfect then, and lay in a shrine, the last of many shrines, and I worked wonders. Then came strange men with strange weapons and destroyed my shrine, and the Amulet they bore away with many captives. But of these, one, my priest, knew the word of power, and spoke it for me, so that the Amulet became invisible, and thus returned to my shrine, but the shrine was broken down, and ere any magic could rebuild it, one spoke a word before which my power bowed down and was still. And the Amulet lay there, still perfect, but enslaved. Then one coming with stones to rebuild the shrine, dropped a hewn stone on the

Amulet as it lay, and one half was sundered from the other. I had no power to seek for that which was lost. And there being none to speak the word of power, I could not rejoin it. So the Amulet lay in the dust of the desert many thousand years, and at last came a small man, a conqueror with an army, and after him a crowd of men who sought to seem wise, and one of these found half the Amulet and brought it to this land. But none could read the name. So I lay still. And this man dying and his son after him, the Amulet was sold by those who came after to a merchant, and from him you bought it, and it is here, and now, the name of power having been spoken, I also am here."

This is what the voice said. I think it must have meant Napoleon by the small man, the conqueror. Because I know I have been told that he took an army to Egypt, and that afterwards a lot of wise people went grubbing in the sand, and fished up all sorts of wonderful things, older than you would think possible. And of these I believe this charm to have been one, and the most wonderful one of all.

Every one listened: and every one tried to think. It is not easy to do this clearly when you have been listening to the kind of talk I have told you about.

At last Robert said—

"Can you take us into the Past—to the shrine where you and the other thing were together. If you could take us there, we might find the other part still there after all these thousands of years."

"Still there? silly!" said Cyril. "Don't you see, if we get back into the Past it won't be thousands of years ago. It will be *now* for us—won't it?" He appealed to the Psammead, who said—

"You're not so far off the idea as you usually are!"

"Well," said Anthea, "will you take us back to when there was a shrine and you were safe in it—all of you?"

"Yes," said the voice. "You must hold me up, and speak the word of power, and one by one, beginning with the first-born, you shall pass through me into the Past. But let the last that passes be the one that holds me, and let him not loose his hold, lest you lose me, and so remain in the Past for ever."

"That's a nasty idea," said Robert.

"When you desire to return," the beautiful voice went on, "hold me up towards the East, and speak the word. Then, passing through me, you shall return to this time and it shall be the present to you."

"But how——"

A bell rang loudly.

"Oh crikey!" exclaimed Robert, "that's tea! Will you please make it proper daylight again so that we can go down. And thank you so much for all your kindness."

"We've enjoyed ourselves very much indeed, thank you!" added Anthea politely.

The beautiful light faded slowly. The great darkness and silence came and these suddenly changed to the dazzlement of day and the great soft, rustling sound of London, that is like some vast beast turning over in its sleep.

The children rubbed their eyes, the Psammead ran quickly to its sandy bath, and the others went down to tea. And until the cups were actually filled tea seemed less real than the beautiful voice and the greeny light.

After tea Anthea persuaded the others to allow her to hang the charm round her neck with a piece of string.

"It would be so awful if it got lost," she said; "it might get lost anywhere, you know, and it would be rather beastly for us to have to stay in the Past for ever and ever, wouldn't it?"

CHAPTER IV

EIGHT THOUSAND YEARS AGO

Next morning Anthea got old Nurse to allow her to take up the "poor learned gentleman's" breakfast. He did not recognise her at first, but when he did he was vaguely pleased to see her.

"You see I'm wearing the charm round my neck," she said; "I'm taking care of it—like you told us to."

"That's right," said he; "did you have a good game last night?"

"You will eat your breakfast before it's cold, won't you?" said Anthea. "Yes, we had a splendid time. The charm made it all dark, and then greeny light, and then it spoke. Oh! I wish you could have heard it—it was such a darling voice—and it told us the other half of it was lost in the Past, so of course we shall have to look for it there!"

The learned gentleman rubbed his hair with both hands and looked anxiously at Anthea.

"I suppose it's natural—youthful imagination and so forth," he said. "Yet some one must have. . . . Who told you that some part of the charm was missing?"

"I can't tell you," she said. "I know it seems most awfully rude, especially after you being so kind about telling us the name of power, and all that, but really, I'm not allowed to tell anybody anything about the—the—the person who told me. You won't forget your breakfast, will you?"

The learned gentleman smiled feebly and then frowned—not a cross-frown, but a puzzle-frown.

"Thank you," he said, "I shall always be pleased if you'll look in—any time you're passing you know—at least. . . ."

"I will," she said; "goodbye. I'll always tell you anything I *may* tell."

He had not had many adventures with children in them,

and he wondered whether all children were like these. He spent quite five minutes in wondering before he settled down to the fifty-second chapter of his great book on "The Secret Rites of the Priests of Amen Rā."

It is no use to pretend that the children did not feel a good deal of agitation at the thought of going through the charm into the Past. That idea, that perhaps they might stay in the Past and never get back again, was anything but pleasing. Yet no one would have dared to suggest that the charm should not be used; and though each was in its heart very frightened indeed, they would all have joined in jeering at the cowardice of any one of them who should have uttered the timid but natural suggestion, "Don't let's!"

It seemed necessary to make arrangements for being out all day, for there was no reason to suppose that the sound of the dinner-bell would be able to reach back into the Past, and it seemed unwise to excite old Nurse's curiosity when nothing they could say—not even the truth—could in any way satisfy it. They were all very proud to think how well they had understood what the charm and the Psammead had said about Time and Space and things like that, and they were perfectly certain that it would be quite impossible to make old Nurse understand a single word of it. So they merely asked her to let them take their dinner out into Regent's Park—and this, with the implied cold mutton and tomatoes, was readily granted.

"You can get yourselves some buns or sponge-cakes, or whatever you fancy-like," said old Nurse, giving Cyril a shilling. "Don't go getting jam-tarts, now—so messy at the best of times, and without forks and plates ruination to your clothes, besides your not being able to wash your hands and faces afterwards."

So Cyril took the shilling, and they all started off. They went round by the Tottenham Court Road to buy a piece of waterproof sheeting to put over the Psammead in case it should be raining in the Past when they got there. For it is almost certain death to a Psammead to get wet.

The sun was shining very brightly, and even London looked

pretty. Women were selling roses from big baskets-full, and Anthea bought four roses, one each, for herself and the others. They were red roses and smelt of summer—the kind of roses you always want so desperately at about Christmas-time when you can only get mistletoe, which is pale right through to its very scent, and holly which pricks your nose if you try to smell it. So now every one had a rose in its buttonhole, and soon every one was sitting on the grass in Regent's Park under trees whose leaves would have been clean, clear green in the country, but here were dusty and yellowish, and brown at the edges.

"We've got to go on with it," said Anthea, "and as the eldest has to go first, you'll have to be last, Jane. You quite understand about holding on to the charm as you go through, don't you, Pussy?"

"I wish I hadn't got to be last," said Jane.

"You shall carry the Psammead if you like," said Anthea. "That is," she added, remembering the beast's queer temper, "if it'll let you."

The Psammead, however, was unexpectedly amiable.

"*I* don't mind," it said, "who carries me, so long as it doesn't drop me. I can't bear being dropped."

Jane with trembling hands took the Psammead and its fish-basket under one arm. The charm's long string was hung round her neck. Then they all stood up. Jane held out the charm at arm's length, and Cyril solemnly pronounced the word of power.

As he spoke it the charm grew tall and broad, and he saw that Jane was just holding on to the edge of a great red arch of very curious shape. The opening of the arch was small, but Cyril saw that he could go through it. All round and beyond the arch were the faded trees and trampled grass of Regent's Park, where the little ragged children were playing Ring o' Roses. But through the opening of it shone a blaze of blue and yellow and red. Cyril drew a long breath and stiffened his legs so that the others should not see that his knees were trembling and almost knocking together. "Here goes!" he said, and, stepping up through the arch, disappeared. Then followed

*The opening of the arch was small, but Cyril saw that
he could get through it*

Anthea. Robert, coming next, held fast, at Anthea's suggestion, to the sleeve of Jane, who was thus dragged safely through the arch. And as soon as they were on the other side of the arch there was no more arch at all and no more Regent's Park either, only the charm in Jane's hand, and it was its proper size again. They were now in a light so bright that they winked and blinked and rubbed their eyes. During this dazzling interval Anthea felt for the charm and pushed it inside Jane's frock, so that it might be quite safe. When their eyes got used to the new wonderful light the children looked around them. The sky was very, very blue, and it sparkled and glittered and dazzled like the sea at home when the sun shines on it.

They were standing on a little clearing in a thick, low forest; there were trees and shrubs and a close, thorny, tangly undergrowth. In front of them stretched a bank of strange black mud, then came the browny-yellowy shining ribbon of a river. Then more dry, caked mud and more greeny-browny jungle. The only things that told that human people had been there were the clearing, a path that led to it, and an odd arrangement of cut reeds in the river.

They looked at each other.

"Well!" said Robert, "this *is* a change of air!"

It was. The air was hotter than they could have imagined, even in London in August.

"I wish I knew where we were," said Cyril.

"Here's a river, now—I wonder whether it's the Amazon or the Tiber, or what."

"It's the Nile," said the Psammead, looking out of the fish-bag.

"Then this is Egypt," said Robert, who had once taken a geography prize.

"I don't see any crocodiles," Cyril objected. His prize had been for natural history.

The Psammead reached out a hairy arm from its basket and pointed to a heap of mud at the edge of the water.

"What do you call that?" it said; and as it spoke the heap of mud slid into the river just as a slab of badly mixed mortar will slip from a bricklayer's trowel.

"Oh!" said everybody.

There was a crashing among the reeds on the other side of the water.

"And there's a river-horse!" said the Psammead, as a great beast like an enormous slaty-blue slug showed itself against the black bank on the far side of the stream.

"It's a hippopotamus," said Cyril; "it seems much more real somehow than the one at the Zoo, doesn't it?"

"I'm glad it's being real on the other side of the river," said Jane.

And now there was a crackling of reeds and twigs behind them. This was horrible. Of course it might be another hippopotamus, or a crocodile, or a lion—or, in fact, almost anything.

"Keep your hand on the charm, Jane," said Robert hastily. "We ought to have a means of escape handy. I'm dead certain this is the sort of place where simply anything *might* happen to us."

"I believe a hippopotamus is going to happen to us," said Jane—"a very, very big one."

They had all turned to face the danger.

"Don't be silly little duffers," said the Psammead in its friendly, informal way; "it's not a river-horse. It's a human."

It was. It was a girl—of about Anthea's age. Her hair was short and fair, and though her skin was tanned by the sun, you could see that it would have been fair too if it had had a chance. She had every chance of being tanned, for she had no clothes to speak of, and the four English children, carefully dressed in frocks, hats, shoes, stockings, coats, collars, and all the rest of it, envied her more than any words of theirs or of mine could possibly say. There was no doubt that here was the right costume for that climate.

She carried a pot on her head, of red and black earthenware. She did not see the children, who shrank back against the edge of the jungle, and she went forward to the brink of the river to fill her pitcher. As she went she made a strange sort of droning, humming, melancholy noise all on two notes. Anthea could not help thinking that perhaps the girl thought this noise was singing.

The girl filled the pitcher and set it down by the river bank. Then she waded into the water and stooped over the circle of cut reeds. She pulled half a dozen fine fish out of the water within the reeds, killing each as she took it out, and threading it on a long osier that she carried. Then she knotted the osier, hung it on her arm, picked up the pitcher and turned to come back. And as she turned she saw the four children. The white dresses of Jane and Anthea stood out like snow against the dark forest background. She screamed and the pitcher fell, and the water was spilled out over the hard mud surface and over the fish, which had fallen too. Then the water slowly trickled away into the deep cracks.

"Don't be frightened," Anthea cried, "we won't hurt you."

"Who are you?" said the girl.

Now, once for all, I am not going to be bothered to tell you how it was that the girl could understand Anthea and Anthea could understand the girl. *You*, at any rate, would not understand *me*, if I tried to explain it, any more than you can understand about time and space being only forms of thought. You may think what you like. Perhaps the children had found out the universal language which everyone can understand, and which wise men so far have not found. You will have noticed long ago that they were singularly lucky children, and they may have had this piece of luck as well as others. Or it may have been that . . . but why pursue the question farther? The fact remains that in all their adventures the muddle-headed inventions which we call foreign languages never bothered them in the least. They could always understand and be understood. If you can explain this, please do. I daresay I could understand your explanation, though you could never understand mine.

So when the girl said, "Who are you?" every one understood at once, and Anthea replied—

"We are children—just like you. Don't be frightened. Won't you show us where you live?"

Jane put her face right into the Psammead's basket, and burrowed her mouth into its fur to whisper—

"Is it safe? Won't they eat us? Are they cannibals?"

The Psammead shrugged its fur.

"Don't make your voice buzz like that, it tickles my ears," it said rather crossly. "You can always get back to Regent's Park in time if you keep fast hold of the charm," it said.

The strange girl was trembling with fright.

Anthea had a bangle on her arm. It was a sevenpenny-half-penny trumpery brass thing that pretended to be silver; it had a glass heart of turquoise blue hanging from it, and it was the gift of the maid-of-all-work at the Fitzroy Street house.

"Here," said Anthea, "this is for you. That is to show we will not hurt you. And if you take it I shall know that you won't hurt us."

The girl held out her hand. Anthea slid the bangle over it, and the girl's face lighted up with the joy of possession.

"Come," she said, looking lovingly at the bangle; "it is peace between your house and mine."

She picked up her fish and pitcher and led the way up the narrow path by which she had come and the others followed.

"This is something like!" said Cyril, trying to be brave.

"Yes!" said Robert, also assuming a boldness he was far from feeling, "this really and truly *is* an adventure! Its being in the Past makes it quite different from the Phœnix and Carpet happenings."

The belt of thick-growing acacia trees and shrubs—mostly prickly and unpleasant-looking—seemed about half a mile across. The path was narrow and the wood dark. At last, ahead, daylight shone through the boughs and leaves.

The whole party suddenly came out of the wood's shadow into the glare of the sunlight that shone on a great stretch of yellow sand, dotted with heaps of grey rocks where spiky cactus plants showed gaudy crimson and pink flowers among their shabby, sand-peppered leaves. Away to the right was something that looked like a grey-brown hedge, and from beyond it blue smoke went up to the bluer sky. And over all the sun shone till you could hardly bear your clothes.

"That is where I live," said the girl pointing.

"I won't go," whispered Jane into the basket, "unless you say it's all right."

The Psammead ought to have been touched by this proof of

The girl held out her hand. Anthea slid the bangle on it

confidence. Perhaps, however, it looked upon it as a proof of doubt, for it merely snarled—

"If you don't go now I'll never help you again."

"*Oh*," whispered Anthea, "dear Jane, don't! Think of Father and Mother and all of us getting our heart's desire. And we can go back any minute. Come on!"

"Besides," said Cyril, in a low voice, "the Psammead must know there's no danger or it wouldn't go. It's not so over and above brave itself. Come on!"

This Jane at last consented to do.

As they got nearer to the browny fence they saw that it was a great hedge about eight feet high, made of piled-up thorn bushes.

"What's that for?" asked Cyril.

"To keep out foes and wild beasts," said the girl.

"I should think it ought to, too," said he. "Why, some of the thorns are as long as my foot."

There was an opening in the hedge, and they followed the girl through it. A little way further on was another hedge, not so high, also of dry thorn bushes, very prickly and spiteful-looking, and within this was a sort of village of huts.

There were no gardens and no roads. Just huts built of wood and twigs and clay, and roofed with great palm-leaves, dumped down anywhere. The doors of these houses were very low, like the doors of dog-kennels. The ground between them was not paths or streets, but just yellow sand trampled very hard and smooth.

In the middle of the village there was a hedge that enclosed what seemed to be a piece of ground about as big as their own garden in Camden Town.

No sooner were the children well within the inner thorn hedge than dozens of men and women and children came crowding round from behind and inside the huts.

The girl stood protectingly in front of the four children, and said—

"They are wonder-children from beyond the desert. They bring marvellous gifts, and I have said that it is peace between us and them."

She held out her arm with the Lowther Arcade bangle on it.

The children from London, where nothing now surprises any one, had never before seen so many people look so astonished.

They crowded round the children, touching their clothes, their shoes, the buttons on the boys' jackets, and the coral of the girls' necklaces.

"Do say something," whispered Anthea.

"We come," said Cyril, with some dim remembrance of a dreadful day when he had had to wait in an outer office while his father interviewed a solicitor, and there had been nothing to read but the *Daily Telegraph*—"we come from the world where the sun never sets. And peace with honour is what we want. We are the great Anglo-Saxon or conquering race. Not that we want to conquer *you*," he added hastily. "We only want to look at your houses and your—well, at all you've got here, and then we shall return to our own place, and tell of all that we have seen so that your name may be famed."

Cyril's speech didn't keep the crowd from pressing round and looking as eagerly as ever at the clothing of the children. Anthea had an idea that these people had never seen woven stuff before, and she saw how wonderful and strange it must seem to people who had never had any clothes but the skins of beasts. The sewing, too, of modern clothes seemed to astonish them very much. They must have been able to sew themselves, by the way, for men who seemed to be the chiefs wore knickerbockers of goat-skin or deer-skin, fastened round the waist with twisted strips of hide. And the women wore long skimpy skirts of animals' skins. The people were not very tall, their hair was fair, and men and women both had it short. Their eyes were blue, and that seemed odd in Egypt. Most of them were tattooed like sailors, only more roughly.

"What is this? What is this?" they kept asking touching the children's clothes curiously.

Anthea hastily took off Jane's frilly lace collar and handed it to the woman who seemed most friendly.

"Take this," she said, "and look at it. And leave us alone. We want to talk among ourselves."

She spoke in the tone of authority which she had always found successful when she had not time to coax her baby brother to do as he was told. The tone was just as successful now. The children were left together and the crowd retreated. It paused a dozen yards away to look at the lace collar and to go on talking as hard as it could.

The children will never know what those people said, though they know well enough that they, the four strangers, were the subject of the talk. They tried to comfort themselves by remembering the girl's promise of friendliness, but of course the thought of the charm was more comfortable than anything else. They sat down on the sand in the shadow of the hedged-round place in the middle of the village, and now for the first time they were able to look about them and to see something more than a crowd of eager, curious faces.

They here noticed that the women wore necklaces made of beads of different coloured stone, and from these hung pendants of odd, strange shapes, and some of them had bracelets of ivory and flint.

"I say," said Robert, "what a lot we could teach them if we stayed here!"

"I expect they could teach us something too," said Cyril. "Did you notice that flint bracelet the woman had that Anthea gave the collar to? That must have taken some making. Look here, they'll get suspicious if we talk among ourselves, and I do want to know about how they do things. Let's get the girl to show us round, and we can be thinking about how to get the Amulet at the same time. Only mind, we must keep together."

Anthea beckoned to the girl, who was standing a little way off looking wistfully at them, and she came gladly.

"Tell us how you make the bracelets, the stones ones," said Cyril.

"With other stones," said the girl; "the men make them; we have men of special skill in such work."

"Haven't you any iron tools?"

"Iron," said the girl, "I don't know what you mean." It was the first word she had not understood.

"Are all your tools of flint?" asked Cyril.

*The crowd paused a dozen yards away to look at
the lace collar*

"Of course," said the girl, opening her eyes wide.

I wish I had time to tell you of that talk. The English children wanted to hear all about this new place, but they also wanted to tell of their own country. It was like when you come back from your holidays and you want to hear and to tell everything at the same time. As the talk went on there were more and more words that the girl could not understand, and the children soon gave up the attempt to explain to her what their own country was like, when they began to see how very few of the things they had always thought they could not do without were really not at all necessary to life.

The girl showed them how the huts were made—indeed, as one was being made that very day she took them to look at it. The way of building was very different to ours. The men stuck long pieces of wood into a piece of ground the size of the hut they wanted to make. These were about eight inches apart; then they put in another row about eight inches away from the first, and then a third row still further out. Then all the space between was filled up with small branches and twigs, and then daubed over with black mud worked with the feet till it was soft and sticky like putty.

The girl told them how the men went hunting with flint spears and arrows, and how they made boats with reeds and clay. Then she explained the reed thing in the river that she had taken the fish out of. It was a fish-trap—just a ring of reeds set up in the water with only one little opening in it, and in this opening, just below the water, were stuck reeds slanting the way of the river's flow, so that the fish, when they had swum sillily in, sillily couldn't get out again. She showed them the clay pots and jars and platters, some of them ornamented with black and red patterns, and the most wonderful things made of flint and different sorts of stone, beads, and ornaments, and tools and weapons of all sorts and kinds.

"It is really wonderful," said Cyril patronisingly, "when you consider that it's all eight thousand years ago——"

"I don't understand you," said the girl.

"It *isn't* eight thousand years ago," whispered Jane. "It's *now*—and that's just what I don't like about it. I say, *do* let's get home again before anything more happens. You can see for yourselves the charm isn't here."

"What's in that place in the middle?" asked Anthea, struck by a sudden thought, and pointing to the fence.

"That's the secret sacred place," said the girl in a whisper. "No one knows what is there. There are many walls, and inside the insidest one *It* is, but no one knows what *It* is except the headmen."

"I believe *you* know," said Cyril, looking at her very hard.

"I'll give you this if you'll tell me," said Anthea taking off a bead-ring which had already been much admired.

"Yes," said the girl, catching eagerly at the ring. "My father is one of the heads, and I know a water charm to make him talk in his sleep. And he has spoken. I will tell you. But if they know I have told you they will kill me. In the insidest inside there is a stone box, and in it there is the Amulet. None knows whence it came. It came from very far away."

"Have you seen it?" asked Anthea.

The girl nodded.

"Is it anything like this?" asked Jane, rashly producing the charm.

The girl's face turned a sickly greenish-white.

"Hide it, hide it," she whispered. "You must put it back. If they see it they will kill us all. You for taking it, and me for knowing that there was such a thing. Oh, woe—woe! why did you ever come here?"

"Don't be frightened," said Cyril. "They shan't know. Jane, don't you be such a little jack-ape again—that's all. You see what will happen if you do. Now, tell me——" He turned to the girl, but before he had time to speak the question there was a loud shout, and a man bounded in through the opening in the thorn-hedge.

"Many foes are upon us!" he cried. "Make ready the defences!"

His breath only served for that, and he lay panting on the ground.

"Oh, *do* let's go home!" said Jane. "Look here—I don't care —I *will*!"

A man bounded in through the opening in the thorn-hedge

She held up the charm. Fortunately all the strange, fair people were too busy to notice *her*. She held up the charm. And nothing happened.

"You haven't said the word of power," said Anthea.

Jane hastily said it—and still nothing happened.

"Hold it up towards the East, you silly!" said Robert

"Which is the East?" said Jane, dancing about in her agony of terror.

Nobody knew. So they opened the fish-bag to ask the Psammead.

And the bag had only a waterproof sheet in it.

The Psammead was gone.

"Hide the sacred thing! Hide it! Hide it!" whispered the girl.

Cyril shrugged his shoulders, and tried to look as brave as he knew he ought to feel.

"Hide it up, Pussy," he said. "We are in for it now. We've just got to stay and see it out."

CHAPTER V

THE FIGHT IN THE VILLAGE

HERE WAS a horrible position! Four English children, whose proper date was A.D 1905, and whose proper address was London, set down in Egypt in the year 6000 B.C. with no means whatever of getting back into their own time and place. They could not find the East, and the sun was of no use at the moment, because some officious person had once explained to Cyril that the sun did not really set in the West at all—nor rise in the East either, for the matter of that.

The Psammead had crept out of the bass-bag when they were not looking and had basely deserted them.

An enemy was approaching. There would be a fight. People get killed in fights, and the idea of taking part in a fight was one that did not appeal to the children.

The man who had brought the news of the enemy still lay panting on the sand. His tongue was hanging out, long and red, like a dog's. The people of the village were hurriedly filling the gaps in the fence with thorn-bushes from the heap that seemed to have been piled there ready for just such a need. They lifted the clustering thorns with long poles—much as men at home, nowadays, lift hay with a fork.

Jane bit her lip and tried to decide not to cry.

Robert felt in his pocket for a toy pistol and loaded it with a pink paper cap. It was his only weapon.

Cyril tightened his belt two holes.

And Anthea absently took the drooping red roses from the buttonholes of the others, bit the ends of the stalks, and set them in a pot of water that stood in the shadow by a hut door. She was always rather silly about flowers.

"Look here!" she said. "I think perhaps the Psammead is really arranging something for us. I don't believe it would go away and leave us all alone in the Past. I'm certain it wouldn't."

Jane succeeded in deciding not to cry—at any rate yet.

"But what can we do?" Robert asked.

"Nothing," Cyril answered promptly, "except keep our eyes and ears open. Look! That runner chap's getting his wind. Let's go and hear what he's got to say."

The runner had risen to his knees and was sitting back on his heels. Now he stood up and spoke. He began by some respectful remarks addressed to the heads of the village. His speech got more interesting when he said—

"I went out in my raft to snare ibises, and I had gone up the stream an hour's journey. Then I set my snares and waited. And I heard the sound of many wings, and looking up, saw many herons circling in the air. And I saw that they were afraid; so I took thought. A beast may scare one heron, coming upon it suddenly, but no beast will scare a whole flock of herons. And still they flew and circled, and would not alight. So then I knew that what had scared the herons must be men, and men who know not our ways of going softly so as to take the birds and beasts unawares. By this I knew they were not of our race or of our place. So, leaving my raft, I crept along the riverbank, and at last came upon the strangers. They are many as the sands of the desert, and their spear-heads shine red like the sun. They are a terrible people, and their march is towards us. Having seen this, I ran, and did not stay till I was before you."

"These are *your* folk," said the headman, turning suddenly and angrily on Cyril, "you came as spies for them."

"We did *not*," said Cyril indignantly. "We wouldn't be spies for anything. I'm certain these people aren't a bit like us. Are they now?" he asked the runner.

"No," was the answer. "These men's faces were darkened, and their hair black as night. Yet these strange children, maybe, are their gods, who have come before to make ready the way for them."

A murmur ran through the crowd.

"No, *no*," said Cyril again. "We are on your side. We will help you to guard your sacred things."

The headman seemed impressed by the fact that Cyril knew that there *were* sacred things to be guarded. He stood a moment gazing at the children. Then he said—

*"These are your folk," said the headman, turning suddenly
and angrily on Cyril*

"It is well. And now let all make offering, that we may be strong in battle."

The crowd dispersed, and nine men, wearing antelope-skins, grouped themselves in front of the opening in the hedge in the middle of the village. And presently, one by one, the men brought all sort of things—hippopotamus flesh, ostrich-feathers, the fruit of the date palms, red chalk, green chalk, fish from the river, and ibex from the mountains; and the headman received these gifts. There was another hedge inside the first, about a yard from it, so that there was a lane inside between the hedges. And every now and then one of the headmen would disappear along this lane with full hands and come back with hands empty.

"They're making offerings to their Amulet," said Anthea. "We'd better give something too."

The pockets of the party, hastily explored, yielded a piece of pink tape, a bit of sealing-wax, and part of the Waterbury watch that Robert had not been able to help taking to pieces at Christmas and had never had time to rearrange. Most boys have a watch in this condition.

They presented their offerings, and Anthea added the red roses.

The headman who took the things looked at them with awe, especially at the red roses and the Waterbury-watch fragment.

"This is a day of very wondrous happenings," he said. "I have no more room in me to be astonished. Our maiden said there was peace between you and us. But for this coming of a foe we should have made sure."

The children shuddered.

"Now speak. Are you upon our side?"

"*Yes.* Don't I keep telling you we are?" Robert said. "Look here. I will give you a sign. You see this." He held out the toy pistol. "I shall speak to it, and if it answers me you will know that I and the others are come to guard your sacred thing—that we've just made the offerings to."

"Will that god whose image you hold in your hand speak to you alone, or shall I also hear it?" asked the man cautiously.

"You'll be surprised when you *do* hear it," said Robert. "Now, then." He looked at the pistol and said—

"If we are to guard the sacred treasure within"—he pointed to the hedged-in space—"speak with thy loud voice, and we shall obey."

He pulled the trigger, and the cap went off. The noise was loud, for it was a two-shilling pistol, and the caps were excellent.

Every man, woman, and child in the village fell on its face on the sand.

The headman who had accepted the test rose first.

"The voice has spoken," he said. "Lead them into the anteroom of the sacred thing."

So now the four children were led in through the opening of the hedge and round the lane till they came to an opening in the inner hedge, and they went through an opening in that, and so passed into another lane.

The thing was built something like this, and all the hedges were of brushwood and thorns:

"It's like the maze at Hampton Court," whispered Anthea.

The lanes were all open to the sky, but the little hut in the middle of the maze was round-roofed, and a curtain of skins hung over the doorway.

"Here you may wait," said their guide; "but do not dare to pass the curtain." He himself passed it and disappeared.

"But look here," whispered Cyril, "some of us ought to be outside, in case the Psammead turns up."

"Don't let's get separated from each other, whatever we do,"

*Every man, woman and child in the village fell on its
face on the sand*

said Anthea. "It's quite bad enough to be separated from the Psammead. We can't do anything while that man is in there. Let's all go out into the village again. We can come back later now we know the way in. That man'll have to fight like the rest, most likely, if it comes to fighting. If we find the Psammead we'll go straight home. It must be getting late, and I don't much like this mazy place."

They went out and told the headman that they would protect the treasure when the fighting began. And now they looked about them and were able to see exactly how a first-class worker in flint flakes and notches an arrow-head or the edge of an axe—an advantage which no other person now alive has ever enjoyed. The boys found the weapons most interesting. The arrow-heads were not on arrows such as you shoot from a bow, but on javelins, for throwing from the hand. The chief weapon was a stone fastened to a rather short stick something like the things gentlemen used to carry about and call life-preservers in the days of the garrotters. Then there were long things like spears or lances, with flint knives— horribly sharp—and flint battle-axes.

Every one in the village was so busy that the place was like an ant-heap when you have walked into it by accident. The women were busy and even the children.

Quite suddenly all the air seemed to glow and grow red— it was like the sudden opening of a furnace door, such as you may see at Woolwich Arsenal if you ever have the luck to be taken there—and then almost as suddenly it was as though the furnace doors had been shut. For the sun had set, and it was night.

The sun had that abrupt way of setting in Egypt eight thousand years ago, and I believe it has never been able to break itself of the habit, and sets in exactly the same manner to the present day. The girl brought the skins of wild deer and led the children to a heap of dry sedge.

"My father says they will not attack yet. Sleep!" she said, and it really seemed a good idea. You may think that in the midst of all these dangers the children would not have been able to sleep—but somehow, though they were rather frightened now and then, the feeling was growing in them—deep down and almost hidden away, but still growing—that the Psammead was to be trusted, and that they were really and truly safe. This did not prevent their being quite as much frightened as they could bear to be without being perfectly miserable.

"I suppose we'd better go to sleep," said Robert. "I don't know what on earth poor old Nurse will do with us out all night; set the police on our tracks, I expect. I only wish they could find us! A dozen policemen would be rather welcome just now. But it's no use getting into a stew over it," he added soothingly. "Good-night."

And they all fell asleep.

They were awakened by long, loud, terrible sounds that seemed to come from everywhere at once—horrible threatening shouts and shrieks and howls that sounded, as Cyril said later, like the voices of men thirsting for their enemies' blood.

"It is the voice of the strange men," said the girl, coming to them trembling through the dark. "They have attacked the walls, and the thorns have driven them back. My father says they will not try again till daylight. But they are shouting to frighten us. As though we were savages! Dwellers in the swamps!" she said indignantly.

All night the terrible noise went on, but when the sun rose, as abruptly as he had set, the sound suddenly ceased.

The children had hardly time to be glad of this before a shower of javelins came hurtling over the great thorn-hedge, and every one sheltered behind the huts. But next moment another shower of weapons came from the opposite side, and the crowd rushed to other shelter. Cyril pulled out a javelin that had stuck in the roof of the hut beside him. Its head was of brightly burnished copper.

Then the sound of shouting arose again and the crackle of dried thorns. The enemy was breaking down the hedge. All the villagers swarmed to the point whence the crackling and the shouting came; they hurled stones over the hedges, and short arrows with flint heads. The children had never before seen men with the fighting light in their eyes. It was very strange and terrible, and gave you a queer thick feeling in your throat; it was quite different from the pictures of fights in the illustrated papers at home.

It seemed that the shower of stones had driven back the besiegers. The besieged drew breath, but at that moment the shouting and the crackling arose on the opposite side of the village and the crowd hastened to defend that point, and so the fight swayed to and fro across the village, for the besieged had not the sense to divide their forces as their enemies had done.

Cyril noticed that every now and then certain of the fighting-men would enter the maze, and come out with brighter faces, a braver aspect, and a more upright carriage.

"I believe they go and touch the Amulet," he said. "You know the Psammead said it could make people brave."

They crept through the maze, and watching they saw that Cyril was right. A headman was standing in front of the skin curtain, and as the warriors came before him he murmured a word they could not hear, and touched their foreheads with something that they could not see. And this something he held in his hands. And through his fingers they saw the gleam of a red stone that they knew.

The fight raged across the thorn-hedge outside. Suddenly there was a loud and bitter cry.

"They're in! They're in! The hedge is down!"

The headman disappeared behind the deer-skin curtain.

"He's gone to hide it," said Anthea. "Oh, Psammead dear, how could you leave us!"

Suddenly there was a shriek from inside the hut, and the headman staggered out white with fear and fled out through the maze. The children were as white as he.

"Oh! What is it? What is it?" moaned Anthea. "Oh, Psammead, how could you! How could you!"

And the sound of the fight sank breathlessly and swelled fiercely all around. It was like the rising and falling of the waves of the sea.

Anthea shuddered and said again, "Oh, Psammead, Psammead!"

"Well?" said a brisk voice, and the curtain of skins was lifted at one corner by a furry hand, and out peeped the bat's ears and snail's eyes of the Psammead.

Anthea caught it in her arms and a sigh of desperate relief was breathed by each of the four.

"Oh! which is the East!" Anthea said, and she spoke hurriedly, for the noise of wild fighting drew nearer and nearer.

"Don't choke me," said the Psammead, "come inside."

The inside of the hut was pitch dark.

"I've got a match;" said Cyril, and struck it. The floor of the hut was of soft, loose sand.

"I've been asleep here," said the Psammead; "most comfortable it's been, the best sand I've had for a month. It's all right. Everything's all right. I knew your only chance would be while the fight was going on. That man won't come back. I bit him, and he thinks I'm an Evil Spirit. Now you've only got to take the thing and go.

The hut was hung with skins. Heaped in the middle were the offerings that had been given the night before, Anthea's roses fading on the top of the heap. At one side of the hut stood a large square stone block, and on it an oblong box of earthenware with strange figures of men and beasts on it.

"Is the thing in there?" asked Cyril, as the Psammead pointed a skinny finger at it.

"You must judge of that," said the Psammead. "The man was just going to bury the box in the sand when I jumped out at him and bit him."

"Light another match, Robert," said Anthea. "Now, then quick! which is the East?"

"Why, where the sun rises, of course!"

"But some one told us——"

"Oh, they'll tell you anything!" said the Psammead impatiently, getting into its bass-bag and wrapping itself in its waterproof sheet.

"But we can't see the sun in here, and it isn't rising anyhow," said Jane.

"How you do waste time!" the Psammead said. "Why, the East's where the shrine is, of course. *There!*"

Out peeped the bat's ears and snail's eyes of the Psammead

It pointed to the great stone.

And still the shouting and the clash of stone on metal sounded nearer and nearer. The children could hear that the headmen had surrounded the hut to protect their treasure as long as might be from the enemy. But none dare to come in after the Psammead's sudden fierce biting of the headman.

"Now, Jane," said Cyril, very quickly. "I'll take the Amulet, you stand ready to hold up the charm, and be sure you don't let it go as you come through."

He made a step forward, but at that instant a great crackling overhead ended in a blaze of sunlight. The roof had been broken in at one side, and great slabs of it were being lifted off by two spears. As the children trembled and winked in the new light, large dark hands tore down the wall, and a dark face, with a blobby fat nose, looked over the gap. Even at that awful moment Anthea had time to think that it was very like the face of Mr. Jacob Absalom, who had sold them the charm in the shop near Charing Cross.

"Here is their Amulet," cried a harsh, strange voice; "it is this that makes them strong to fight and brave to die. And what else have we here—gods or demons?"

He glared fiercely at the children, and the whites of his eyes were very white indeed. He had a wet, red copper knife in his teeth. There was not a moment to lose.

"Jane, *Jane*, QUICK!" cried every one passionately.

Jane with trembling hands held up the charm towards the East, and Cyril spoke the word of power. The Amulet grew to a great arch. Out beyond it was the glaring Egyptian sky, the broken wall, the cruel, dark, big-nosed face with the red, wet knife in its gleaming teeth. Within the arch was the dull, faint, greeny-brown of London grass and trees.

"Hold tight, Jane!" Cyril cried, and he dashed through the arch, dragging Anthea and the Psammead after him. Robert followed, clutching Jane. And in the ears of each, as they passed through the arch of the charm, the sound and fury of battle died out suddenly and utterly, and they heard only the low, dull, discontented hum of vast London, and the peeking and patting of the sparrows on the gravel and the voices of the

*Out beyond it was the glaring Egyptian sky, the broken
wall, the cruel, dark, big-nosed face*

ragged baby children playing Ring-o'-Roses on the yellow trampled grass. And the charm was a little charm again in Jane's hand, and there was the basket with their dinner and the bath-buns lying just where they had left it.

"My hat!" said Cyril, drawing a long breath; "that was something like an adventure."

"It was rather like one, certainly," said the Psammead.

They all lay still, breathing in the safe, quiet air of Regent's Park.

"We'd better go home at once," said Anthea presently. "Old Nurse will be most frightfully anxious. The sun looks about the same as it did when we started yesterday. We've been away twenty-four hours."

"The buns are quite soft still," said Cyril, feeling one; "I suppose the dew kept them fresh."

They were not hungry, curiously enough.

They picked up the dinner-basket and the Psammead-basket, and went straight home.

Old Nurse met them with amazement.

"Well, if ever I did!" she said. "What's gone wrong? You've soon tired of your picnic."

The children took this to be bitter irony, which means saying the exact opposite of what you mean in order to make yourself disagreeable; as when you happen to have a dirty face, and some one says, "How nice and clean you look!"

"We're very sorry," began Anthea, but old Nurse said—

"Oh, bless me, child, I don't care! Please yourselves and you'll please me. Come in and get your dinners comf'table. I've got a potato on a-boiling."

When she had gone to attend to the potatoes the children looked at each other. Could it be that old Nurse had so changed that she no longer cared that they should have been away from home for twenty-four hours—all night in fact—without any explanation whatever?

But the Psammead put its head out of its basket and said—

"What's the matter? Don't you understand? You come back through the charm-arch at the same time as you go through it. This isn't to-morrow!"

"Is it still yesterday?" asked Jane.

"No, it's to-day. The same as it's always been. It wouldn't do to go mixing up the present and the Past, and cutting bits out of one to fit into the other."

"Then all that adventure took no time at all?"

"You can call it that if you like," said the Psammead. "It took none of the modern time, anyhow."

That evening Anthea carried up a steak for the learned gentleman's dinner. She persuaded Beatrice, the maid-of-all-work, who had given her the bangle with the blue stone, to let her do it. And she stayed and talked to him, by special invitation, while he ate the dinner.

She told him the whole adventure, beginning with—

"This afternoon we found ourselves on the bank of the River Nile," and ending up with, "And then we remembered how to get back, and there we were in Regent's Park, and it hadn't taken any time at all."

She did not tell anything about the charm or the Psammead, because that was forbidden, but the story was quite wonderful enough even as it was to entrance the learned gentleman.

"You are a most unusual little girl," he said. "Who tells you all these things?"

"No one," said Anthea, "they just happen."

"Make-believe," he said slowly, as one who recalls and pronounces a long-forgotten word.

He sat long after she had left him. At last he roused himself with a start.

"I really must take a holiday," he said; "my nerves must be all out of order. I actually have a perfectly distinct impression that the little girl from the rooms below came in and gave me a coherent and graphic picture of life as I conceive it to have been in pre-dynastic Egypt. Strange what tricks the mind will play! I shall have to be more careful."

He finished his bread conscientiously, and actually went for a mile walk before he went back to his work.

CHAPTER VI

THE WAY TO BABYLON

"How many miles to Babylon?
Three score and ten!
Can I get there by candle light?
Yes, and back again!"

JANE WAS singing to her doll, rocking it to and fro in the house which she had made for herself and it. The roof of the house was the dining-table, and the walls were table-cloths and antimacassars hanging all round, and kept in their places by books laid on their top ends at the table edge.

The others were tasting the fearful joys of domestic tobogganing. You know how it is done—with the largest and best tea-tray and the surface of the stair carpet. It is best to do it on the days when the stair rods are being cleaned, and the carpet is only held by the nails at the top. Of course, it is one of the five or six thoroughly tip-top games that grown-up people are so unjust to—and old Nurse, though a brick in many respects, was quite enough of a standard grown-up to put her foot down on the tobogganing long before any of the performers had had half enough of it. The tea-tray was taken away, and the baffled party entered the sitting-room, in exactly the mood not to be pleased if they could help it.

So Cyril said, "What a beastly mess!"

And Robert added, "Do shut up, Jane!"

Even Anthea, who was almost always kind, advised Jane to try another song. "I'm sick to death of that," said she.

It was a wet day, so none of the plans for seeing all the sights of London that can be seen for nothing, could be carried out. Every one had been thinking all the morning about the wonderful adventures of the day before, when Jane had held up the charm and it had turned into an arch, through which they had walked straight out of the present time and the Regent's Park into the land of Egypt eight thousand years ago. The memory of yesterday's happenings was still extremely fresh and frightening, so that every one hoped that no one would suggest another excursion into the past, for it seemed to all that yesterday's adventures were quite enough to last for at least a week. Yet each felt a little anxious that the others should not think it was afraid, and presently Cyril, who really was not a coward, began to see that it would not be at all nice if he should have to think himself one. So he said—

"I say—about that charm—Jane—come out. We ought to talk about it, anyhow."

"Oh, if that's all," said Robert.

Jane obediently wriggled to the front of her house and sat there. She felt for the charm, to make sure that it was still round her neck.

"It *isn't* all," said Cyril, saying much more than he meant because he thought Robert's tone had been rude—as indeed it had. "We ought to go and look for that Amulet. What's the good of having a first-class charm and keeping it idle, just eating its head off in the stable."

"*I'm* game for anything, of course," said Robert; but he added, with a fine air of chivalry, "only I don't think the girls are keen to-day somehow."

"Oh, yes; I am," said Anthea hurriedly. "If you think I'm afraid, I'm not."

"I am though," said Jane heavily; "I didn't like it, and I won't go there again—not for anything I won't."

"We shouldn't go *there* again, silly," said Cyril; "it would be some other place."

"I daresay; a place with lions and tigers in it as likely as not."

Seeing Jane so frightened, made the others feel quite brave. They said they were certain they ought to go.

"It's so ungrateful to the Psammead not to," Anthea added, a little primly.

Jane stood up. She was desperate.

"I won't!" she cried; "I won't, I won't, I won't! If you make me I'll scream and I'll scream, and I'll tell old Nurse, and I'll get her to burn the charm in the kitchen fire. So now, then!"

You can imagine how furious every one was with Jane for feeling what each of them had felt all the morning. In each breast the same thought arose, "No one can say it's *our* fault." And they at once began to show Jane how angry they all felt that all the fault was hers. This made them feel quite brave.

"Tell-tale tit, its tongue shall be split,
  And all the dogs in our town shall have a little bit,"
sang Robert.

"It's always the way if you have girls in anything." Cyril spoke in a cold displeasure that was worse than Robert's cruel quotation, and even Anthea said, "Well, *I'm* not afraid if I *am* a girl," which of course, was the most cutting thing of all.

Jane picked up her doll and faced the others with what is sometimes called the courage of despair.

"I don't care," she said; "I *won't*, so there! It's just silly going to places when you don't want to, and when you don't know what they're going to be like! You can laugh at me as much as you like. You're beasts—and I hate you all!"

With these awful words she went out and banged the door.

Then the others would not look at each other, and they did not feel so brave as they had done.

Cyril took up a book, but it was not interesting to read. Robert kicked a chair-leg absently. His feet were always eloquent in moments of emotion. Anthea stood pleating the end of the table-cloth into folds—she seemed earnestly anxious to get all the pleats the same size. The sound of Jane's sobs had died away.

Suddenly Anthea said, "Oh! let it be 'pax'—poor little Pussy —you know she's the youngest."

"She called us beasts," said Robert, kicking the chair suddenly.

"Well," said Cyril, who was subject to passing fits of justice, "we began, you know. At least you did." Cyril's justice was always uncompromising.

"I'm not going to say I'm sorry if you mean that," said

Robert, and the chair-leg cracked to the kick he gave as he said it.

"Oh, do let's," said Anthea, "we're three to one, and Mother does so hate it if we row. Come on. I'll say I'm sorry first, though I didn't say anything, hardly."

"All right, let's get it over," said Cyril opening the door. "Hi—you—Pussy!"

Far away up the stairs a voice could be heard singing brokenly, but still defiantly—

> "How many miles (sniff) to Babylon?
> Three score and ten! (sniff)
> Can I get there by candle light?
> Yes (sniff), and back again!"

It was trying, for this was plainly meant to annoy. But Anthea would not give herself time to think this. She led the way up the stairs, taking three at a time, and bounded to the level of Jane, who sat on the top step of all, thumping her doll to the tune of the song she was trying to sing.

"I say, Pussy, let it be pax! We're sorry if you are——"

It was enough. The kiss of peace was given by all. Jane being the youngest was entitled to this ceremonial.

Anthea added a special apology of her own.

"I'm sorry if I was a pig, Pussy dear," she said—"especially because in my really and truly inside mind I've been feeling a little as if I'd rather not go into the Past again either. But then, do think. If we don't go we shan't get the Amulet, and oh, Pussy, think if we could only get Father and Mother and The Lamb safe back! We *must* go, but we'll wait a day or two if you like and then perhaps you'll feel braver."

"Raw meat makes you brave, however cowardly you are," said Robert, to show that there was now no ill-feeling, "and cranberries—that's what Tartars eat, and they're so brave it's simply awful. I suppose cranberries are only for Christmas time, but I'll ask old Nurse to let you have your chop very raw if you like."

"I think I could be brave without that," said Jane hastily; she hated underdone meat. "I'll try."

At this moment the door of the learned gentleman's room opened, and he looked out.

"Excuse me," he said, in that gentle, polite weary voice of his, "but was I mistaken in thinking that I caught a familiar word just now? Were you not singing some old ballad of Babylon?"

"No," said Robert, "at least Jane was singing 'How many miles', but I shouldn't have thought you could have heard the words for——"

He would have said, "for the sniffing," but Anthea pinched him just in time.

"I did not hear *all* the words," said the learned gentleman. "I wonder would you recite them to me?"

So they all said together—

> "How many miles to Babylon?
>   Three score and ten!
>   Can I get there by candle light?
>   Yes, and back again!"

"I wish one could," the learned gentleman said with a sigh.

"Can't you?" asked Jane.

"Babylon has fallen," he answered with a sigh. "You know it was once a great and beautiful city, and the centre of learning and Art, and now it is only ruins, and so covered up with earth that people are not even agreed as to where it once stood."

He was leaning on the banisters, and his eyes had a far-away look in them, as though he could see through the stair-case window the splendour and glory of ancient Babylon.

"I say," Cyril remarked abruptly. "You know that charm we showed you, and you told us how to say the name that's on it?"

"Yes!"

"Well, do you think that charm was ever in Babylon?"

"It's quite possible," the learned gentleman replied. "Such charms have been found in very early Egyptian tombs, yet their origin has not been accurately determined as Egyptian. They may have been brought from Asia. Or, supposing the charm to have been fashioned in Egypt, it might very well have been carried to Babylon by some friendly embassy, or brought back by the Babylonish army from some Egyptian campaign as part of the spoils of war. The inscription may be much later than the charm. Oh, yes! it is a pleasant fancy, that that splendid specimen of yours was once used amid Babylonish surroundings."

The others looked at each other, but it was Jane who spoke.

"Were the Babylon people savages, were they always fighting and throwing things about?" For she had read the thoughts of the others by the unerring light of her own fears.

"The Babylonians were certainly more gentle than the Assyrians," said the learned gentleman. "And they were not savages by any means. A very high level of culture," he looked doubtfully at his audience and went on, "I mean that they made beautiful statues and jewellery, and built splendid palaces. And they were very learned; they had glorious libraries and high towers for the purpose of astrological and astronomical observation."

"Er?" said Robert.

"I mean for—star-gazing and fortune-telling," said the learned gentleman, "and there were temples and beautiful hanging gardens——"

"I'll go to Babylon if you like," said Jane abruptly, and the others hastened to say "Done!" before she should have time to change her mind.

"Ah," said the learned gentleman, smiling rather sadly, "one can go so far in dreams, when one is young." He sighed again, and then adding with a laboured briskness, "I hope you'll have a—a—jolly game," he went into his room and shut the door.

"He said 'jolly' as if it was a foreign language," said Cyril. "Come on, let's get the Psammead and go now. I think Babylon seems a most frightfully jolly place to go to."

So they woke the Psammead and put it in its bass-bag with the waterproof sheet, in case of inclement weather in Babylon. It was very cross, but it said it would as soon go to Babylon as anywhere else. "The sand is good thereabouts," it added.

Then Jane held up the charm, and Cyril said—

"We want to go to Babylon to look for the part of you that was lost. Will you please let us go there through you?"

"Please put us down just outside," said Jane hastily; "and then if we don't like it we needn't go inside."

"Don't be all day," said the Psammead.

So Anthea hastily uttered the word of power, without which the charm could do nothing.

"Ur—Hekau—Setcheh!" she said softly, and as she spoke the charm grew into an arch so tall that the top of it was close against the bedroom ceiling. Outside the arch was the bedroom painted chest-of-drawers and the Kidderminster carpet, and the washhand-stand with the riveted willow-pattern jug, and the faded curtains, and the dull light of indoors on a wet day. Through the arch showed the gleam of soft green leaves and white blossoms. They stepped forward quite happily. Even Jane felt that this did not look like lions, and her hand hardly trembled at all as she held the charm for the others to go through, and last, slipped through herself, and hung the charm, now grown small again, once more round her neck.

The children found themselves under a white-blossomed, green-leafed fruit-tree, in what seemed to be an orchard of such trees, all white-flowered and green-foliaged. Among the long green grass under their feet grew crocuses and lilies, and strange blue flowers. In the branches overhead thrushes and blackbirds were singing, and the coo of a pigeon came softly to them in the green quietness of the orchard.

"Oh, how perfectly lovely!" cried Anthea.

"Why, it's like home exactly—I mean England—only everything's bluer, and whiter, and greener, and the flowers are bigger."

The boys owned that it certainly was fairly decent, and even Jane admitted that it was all very pretty.

"I'm certain there's nothing to be frightened of here," said Anthea.

"I don't know," said Jane. "I suppose the fruit-trees go on just the same even when people are killing each other. I didn't half like what the learned gentleman said about the hanging

In front of them they could see a great mass of buildings

gardens. I suppose they have gardens on purpose to hang people in. I do hope this isn't one."

"Of course it isn't," said Cyril. "The hanging gardens are just gardens hung up—I think on chains between houses, don't you know, like trays. Come on; let's get somewhere."

They began to walk through the cool grass. As far as they could see was nothing but trees, and trees, and more trees. At the end of their orchard was another one, only separated from theirs by a little still stream of clear water. They jumped this, and went on. Cyril, who was fond of gardening—which meant that he liked to watch the gardener at work—was able to command the respect of the others by telling them the names of a good many trees. There were nut-trees and almond-trees, and apricots, and fig-trees with their big five-fingered leaves. And every now and then the children had to cross another brook.

"It's like between the squares in 'Through the Looking-glass,'" said Anthea.

At last they came to an orchard which was quite different from the other orchards. It had a low building in one corner.

"These are vines," said Cyril superiorly, "and I know this is a vineyard. I shouldn't wonder if there was a wine-press inside that place over there."

At last they got out of the orchards and on to a sort of road, very rough, and not at all like the roads you are used to. It had cypress-trees and acacia-trees along it, and a sort of hedge of tamarisks, like those you see on the road between Nice and Cannes, or near Littlehampton, if you've only been as far as that.

And now in front of them they could see a great mass of buildings. There were scattered houses of wood and stone here and there among green orchards, and beyond these a great wall that shone red in the early morning sun. The wall was enormously high—more than half the height of St. Paul's—and in the wall were set enormous gates that shone like gold as the rising sun beat on them. Each gate had a solid square tower on each side of it that stood out from the wall and rose above it. Beyond the wall were more towers and houses, gleaming with gold and bright colours. Away to the left ran the steel-blue swirl of a great river. And the children could see, through a gap in the trees, that the river flowed out from the town under a great arch in the wall.

"Those feathery things along by the water are palms," said Cyril instructively.

"Oh, yes; you know everything," Robert replied. "What's all that grey-green stuff you see away over there, where it's all flat and sandy?"

"All right," said Cyril loftily, "*I* don't want to tell you anything. I only thought you'd like to know a palm-tree when you saw it again."

"Look!" cried Anthea; "they're opening the gates."

And indeed the great gates swung back with a brazen clang, and instantly a little crowd of a dozen or more people came out and along the road towards them.

The children, with one accord, crouched behind the tamarisk hedge.

"I don't like the sound of those gates," said Jane. "Fancy being inside when they shut. You'd never get out."

"You've got an arch of your own to go out by," the Psammead put its head out of the basket to remind her. "Don't behave so like a girl. If I were you I should just march right into the town and ask to see the king."

There was something at once simple and grand about this idea, and it pleased every one.

So when the work-people had passed (they *were* work-people, the children felt sure, because they were dressed so plainly—just one long blue shirt thing—of blue or yellow) the four children marched boldly up to the brazen gate between the towers. The arch above the gate was quite a tunnel, the walls were so thick.

"Courage," said Cyril. "Step out. It's no use trying to sneak past. Be bold!"

Robert answered this appeal by unexpectedly bursting into "The British Grenadiers," and to its quick-step they approached the gates of Babylon.

They approached the gates of Babylon

"Some talk of Alexander,
      And some of Hercules,
Of Hector and Lysander,
      And such great names as these.
But of all the gallant heroes . . . ."

This brought them to the threshold of the gate, and two men in bright armour suddenly barred their way with crossed spears.

"Who goes there?" they said.

(I think I must have explained to you before how it was that the children were always able to understand the language of any place they might happen to be in, and to be themselves understood. If not, I have no time to explain it now.)

"We come from very far," said Cyril mechanically. "From the Empire where the sun never sets, and we want to see your King."

"If it's quite convenient," amended Anthea.

"The King (may he live for ever!)," said the gatekeeper, "is gone to fetch home his fourteenth wife. Where on earth have you come from not to know that?"

"The Queen then," said Anthea hurriedly, and not taking any notice of the question as to where they had come from.

"The Queen," said the gatekeeper, "(may she live for ever!) gives audience to-day three hours after sun-rising."

"But what are we to do till the end of the three hours?" asked Cyril.

The gatekeeper seemed neither to know nor to care. He appeared less interested in them than they could have thought possible. But the man who had crossed spears with him to bar the children's way was more human.

"Let them go in and look about them," he said. "I'll wager my best sword they've never seen anything to come near our little—village."

He said it in the tone people use for when they call the Atlantic Ocean the "herring pond".

The gatekeeper hesitated.

"They're only children, after all," said the other, who had children of his own. "Let me off for a few minutes, Captain, and I'll take them to my place and see if my good woman can't fit them up in something a little less outlandish than their present rig. Then they can have a look round without being mobbed. May I go?"

"Oh yes, if you like," said the Captain, "but don't be all day."

The man led them through the dark arch into the town. And it was very different to London. For one thing, everything in London seems to be patched up out of odds and ends, but these houses seemed all to have been built by people who liked the same sort of things. Not that they were all alike, for though all were squarish, they were of different sizes, and decorated in all sorts of different ways, some with paintings in bright colours, some with black and silver designs. There were terraces, and gardens, and balconies, and open spaces with trees. Their guide took them to a little house in a back street, where a kind-faced woman sat spinning at the door of a very dark room.

"Here," he said, "just lend these children a mantle each, so that they can go about and see the place till the Queen's audience begins. You leave that wool for a bit, and show them round if you like. I must be off now."

The woman did as she was told, and the four children, wrapped in fringed mantles, went with her all about the town, and oh! how I wish I had time to tell you all that they saw. It was all so wonderfully different from anything you have ever seen. For one thing, all the houses were dazzlingly bright, and many of them covered with pictures. Some had great creatures carved in stone at each side of the door. Then the people—there were no black frock-coats and tall hats; no dingy coats and skirts of good, useful, ugly stuffs warranted to wear. Everyone's clothes were bright and beautiful with blue and scarlet and green and gold.

The market was brighter than you would think anything could be. There were stalls for everything you could possibly want—and for a great many things that if you wanted here and now, want would be your master. There were pineapples and peaches in heaps—and stalls of crockery and glass things,

beautiful shapes and glorious colours—there were stalls for
necklaces, and clasps, and bracelets, and brooches, for woven
stuffs, and furs, and embroidered linen. The children had never
seen half so many beautiful things, together, even at Liberty's.

It seemed no time at all before the woman said—

"It's nearly time now. We ought to be getting on towards
the palace. It's as well to be early."

So they went to the palace, and when they got there it was
more splendid than anything they had seen yet.

For it was glowing with colours, and with gold and silver
and black and white—like some magnificent embroidery.
Flight after flight of broad marble steps led up to it, and at the
edges of the stairs stood great images, twenty times as big as a
man—images of men with wings like chain armour, and hawks'
heads, and winged men with the heads of dogs. And there
were the statues of great kings.

Between the flights of steps were terraces where fountains
played, and the Queen's Guard in white and scarlet, and
armour that shone like gold, stood by twos lining the way up
the stairs; and a great body of them was massed by the vast
door of the palace itself, where it stood glittering like an im-
possibly radiant peacock in the noon-day sun.

All sorts of people were passing up the steps to seek audience
of the Queen. Ladies in richly-embroidered dresses with fringy
flounces, poor folks in plain and simple clothes, dandies with
beards oiled and curled.

And Cyril, Robert, Anthea and Jane, went with the crowd.

At the gate of the palace the Psammead put one eye
cautiously out of the basket and whispered—

"I can't be bothered with queens. I'll go home with this good
lady. I'm sure she'll get me some sand if you ask her to."

"Oh! don't leave us," said Jane.

The woman was giving some last instructions in Court eti-
quette to Anthea, and did not hear Jane.

"Don't be a little muff," said the Psammead quite fiercely.
"It's not a bit of good your having a charm. You never use it.
If you want me you've only got to say the name of power and
ask the charm to bring me to you."

"I'd rather go with you," said Jane. And it was the most surprising thing she had ever said in her life.

Everyone opened its mouth without thinking of manners, and Anthea, who was peeping into the Psammead's basket, saw that its mouth opened wider than anybody's.

"You needn't gawp like that," Jane went on. "I'm not going to be bothered with queens any more than *it* is. And I know, wherever it is, it'll take jolly good care that it's safe."

"She's right there," said everyone, for they had observed that the Psammead had a way of knowing which side its bread was buttered.

She turned to the woman and said, "You'll take me home with you, won't you? And let me play with your little girls till the others have done with the Queen."

"Surely I will, little heart!" said the woman.

And then Anthea hurriedly stroked the Psammead and embraced Jane, who took the woman's hand, and trotted contentedly away with the Psammead's bag under the other arm.

The others stood looking after her till she, the woman, and the basket were lost in the many-coloured crowd. Then Anthea turned once more to the palace's magnificent doorway and said—

"Let's ask the porter to take care of our Babylonian overcoats."

So they took off the garments that the woman had lent them and stood amid the jostling petitioners of the Queen in their own English frocks and coats and hats and boots.

"We want to see the Queen," said Cyril; "we come from the far Empire where the sun never sets!"

A murmur of surprise and a thrill of excitement ran through the crowd. The door-porter spoke to a black man, he spoke to some one else. There was a whispering, waiting pause. Then a big man, with a cleanly-shaven face, beckoned them from the top of a flight of red marble steps.

They went up; the boots of Robert clattering more than usual because he was so nervous. A door swung open, a curtain was drawn back. A double line of bowing forms in gorgeous raiment formed a lane that led to the steps of the throne, and

as the children advanced hurriedly there came from the throne
a voice very sweet and very kind.

"Three children from the land where the sun never sets!
Let them draw hither without fear."

In another minute they were kneeling at the throne's foot,
saying, "Oh, Queen, live for ever!" exactly as the woman had
taught them. And a splendid dream-lady, all gold and silver
and jewels and snowy drift of veils, was raising Anthea, and
saying—

"Don't be frightened, I really am *so* glad you came! The
land where the sun never sets! I am delighted to see you! I was
getting quite too dreadfully bored for anything!"

And behind Anthea the kneeling Cyril whispered in the ear
of the respectful Robert—

"Bobs, don't say anything to Panther. It's no use upsetting
her, but we didn't ask for Jane's address, and the Psammead's
with her."

"Well," whispered Robert, "the charm can bring them to us
at any moment. *It* said so."

"Oh, yes," whispered Cyril, in miserable derision, "*we're* all
right of course. So we are! Oh, yes! If we'd only *got* the
charm."

Then Robert saw, and he murmured, "Crikey!" at the foot
of the throne of Babylon; while Cyril hoarsely whispered the
plain English fact—

"Jane's got the charm round her neck, you silly cuckoo."

"Crikey!" Robert repeated in heart-broken undertones.

"Three children from the land where the sun never sets!"

CHAPTER VII

"THE DEEPEST DUNGEON BELOW
THE CASTLE MOAT"

THE QUEEN threw three of the red and gold embroidered cushions off the throne down on to the marble steps that led up to it.

"Just make yourselves comfortable there," she said. "I'm simply dying to talk to you, and to hear all about your wonderful country and how you got here, and everything, but I have to do justice every morning. Such a bore, isn't it? Do you do justice in your own country?"

"No," said Cyril; "at least of course we try to, but not in this public sort of way, only in private."

"Ah, yes," said the Queen, "I should much prefer a private audience myself—much easier to manage. But public opinion has to be considered. Doing justice is very hard work, even when you're brought up to it."

"We don't do justice, but we have to do scales, Jane and me," said Anthea, "twenty minutes a day. It's simply horrid."

"What are scales?" asked the Queen, "and what is Jane?"

"Jane is my little sister. One of the guards-at-the-gate's wife is taking care of her. And scales are music."

"I never heard of the instrument," said the Queen. "Do you sing?"

"Oh, yes. We can sing in parts," said Anthea.

"That *is* magic," said the Queen. "How many parts are you each cut into before you do it?"

"We aren't cut at all," said Robert hastily. "We couldn't sing if we were. We'll show you afterwards."

"So you shall, and now sit quiet like dear children and hear me do justice. The way I do it has always been admired. I oughtn't to say that, ought I? Sounds so conceited. But I don't mind with you, dears. Somehow I feel as though I'd known you quite a long time already."

The Queen settled herself on her throne and made a signal to her attendants. The children, whispering together among the cushions on the steps of the throne, decided that she was very beautiful and very kind, but perhaps just the least bit flighty.

The first person who came to ask for justice was a woman whose brother had taken the money the father had left for her. The brother said it was the uncle who had the money. There was a good deal of talk and the children were growing rather bored, when the Queen suddenly clapped her hands, and said—

"Put both the men in prison till one of them owns up that the other is innocent."

"But suppose they both did it?" Cyril could not help interrupting.

"Then prison's the best place for them," said the Queen.

"But suppose neither did it."

"That's impossible," said the Queen; "a thing's not done unless some one does it. And you mustn't interrupt."

Then came a woman, in tears, with a torn veil and real ashes on her head—at least Anthea thought so, but it may have been only road-dust. She complained that her husband was in prison.

"What for?" said the Queen.

"They *said* it was for speaking evil of your Majesty," said the woman, "but it wasn't. Some one had a spite against him. That was what it was."

"How do you know he hadn't spoken evil of me?" said the Queen.

"No one could," said the woman simply, "when they'd once seen your beautiful face."

"Let the man out," said the Queen, smiling. "Next case."

The next case was that of a boy who had stolen a fox. "Like the Spartan boy," whispered Robert. But the Queen ruled that nobody could have any possible reason for owning a fox, and still less for stealing one. And she did not believe that there were any foxes in Babylon; she, at any rate, had never seen one. So the boy was released.

The people came to the Queen about all sorts of family quarrels and neighbourly mis-understandings—from a fight between brothers over the division of an inheritance, to the dishonest and unfriendly conduct of a woman who had borrowed a cooking-pot at the last New Year's festival, and not returned it yet.

And the Queen decided everything, very, very decidedly indeed. At last she clapped her hands quite suddenly and with extreme loudness, and said—

"The audience is over for to-day."

Everyone said, "May the Queen live for ever!" and went out.

And the children were left alone in the justice-hall with the Queen of Babylon and her ladies.

"There!" said the Queen, with a long sigh of relief. "*That's* over! I couldn't have done another stitch of justice if you'd offered me the crown of Egypt! Now come into the garden, and we'll have a nice, long, cosy talk."

She led them through long, narrow corridors whose walls, they somehow felt, were very, very thick, into a sort of garden courtyard. There were thick shrubs closely planted, and roses were trained over trellises, and made a pleasant shade—needed, indeed, for already the sun was as hot as it is in England in August at the seaside.

Slaves spread cushions on a low, marble terrace, and a big man with a smooth face served cool drink in cups of gold studded with beryls. He drank a little from the Queen's cup before handing it to her.

"That's rather a nasty trick," whispered Robert, who had been carefully taught never to drink out of one of the nice, shiny, metal cups that are chained to the London drinking fountains without first rinsing it out thoroughly.

The Queen overheard him.

"Not at all," said she. "Ritti-Marduk is a very clean man. And one has to have *someone* as taster, you know, because of poison."

The word made the children feel rather creepy; but Ritti-Marduk had tasted all the cups, so they felt pretty safe. The drink was delicious—very cold, and tasting partly like lemonade and partly like penny ices.

"Leave us," said the Queen. And all the Court ladies, in their beautiful, many-folded, many-coloured, fringed dresses, filed out slowly, and the children were left alone with the Queen.

"Now," she said, "tell me all about yourselves."

They looked at each other.

"You, Bobs," said Cyril.

"No—Anthea," said Robert.

"No—you—Cyril," said Anthea. "Don't you remember how pleased the Queen of India was when you told her all about us?"

Cyril muttered that it was all very well, and so it was. For when he had told the tale of the Phœnix and the Carpet to the Ranee, it had been only the truth—and all the truth that he had to tell. But now it was not easy to tell a convincing story without mentioning the Amulet—which, of course, it wouldn't have done to mention—and without owning that they were really living in London, about two thousand five hundred years later than the time they were talking in.

Cyril took refuge in the tale of the Psammead and its wonderful power of making wishes come true. The children had never been able to tell any one before, and Cyril was surprised to find that the spell which kept them silent in London did not work here. "Something to do with our being in the Past, I suppose," he said to himself.

"This is *most* interesting," said the Queen. "We must have this Psammead for the banquet to-night. Its performance will be one of the most popular turns in the whole programme. Where is it?"

Anthea explained that they did not know; also why it was that they did not know.

"Oh, *that's* quite simple," said the Queen, and every one breathed a deep breath of relief as she said it. "Ritti-Marduk shall run down to the gates and find out which guard your sister went home with."

"Might he"—Anthea's voice was tremulous—"might he— would it interfere with his meal-times, or anything like that, if he went *now*?"

"Of course he shall go now. He may think himself lucky if

he gets his meals at any time," said the Queen heartily, and clapped her hands.

"May I send a letter?" asked Cyril, pulling out a red-backed, penny account-book, and feeling in his pockets for a stump of pencil that he *knew* was in one of them.

"By all means. I'll call my scribe."

"Oh, I can scribe right enough, thanks," said Cyril, finding the pencil and licking its point. He even had to bite the wood a little, for it was very blunt.

"Oh, you clever, clever boy!" said the Queen. "Do let me watch you do it!"

Cyril wrote on a leaf of the book—it was of rough, woolly paper, with hairs that stuck out and would have got in his pen if he had been using one, and ruled for accounts.

"Hide IT most carefully before you come here," he wrote, "and don't mention it—and destroy this letter. Everything is going A1. The Queen is a fair treat. There's nothing to be afraid of."

"What curious characters, and what a strange flat surface!" said the Queen. "What have you inscribed?"

"I've 'scribed," replied Cyril cautiously, "that you are fair, and a—and like a—like a festival; and that she need not be afraid, and that she is to come at once."

Ritti-Marduk, who had come in and had stood waiting while Cyril wrote, his Babylonish eyes nearly starting out of his Babylonish head, now took the letter, with some reluctance.

"Oh, Queen, live for ever! Is it a charm?" he timidly asked. "A strong charm, most great lady?"

"*Yes*," said Robert, unexpectedly, "it *is* a charm, but it won't hurt any one until you've given it to Jane. And then she'll destroy it, so that it *can't* hurt any one. It's most awful strong! —as strong as—Peppermint!" he ended abruptly.

"I know not the god," said Ritti-Marduk, bending timorously.

"She'll tear it up directly she gets it," said Robert, "That'll end the charm. You needn't be afraid if you go now."

Ritti-Marduk went, seeming only partly satisfied; and then the Queen began to admire the penny account-book and the bit of pencil in so marked and significant a way that Cyril felt he could not do less than press them upon her as a gift. She ruffled the leaves delightedly.

"What a wonderful substance!" she said. "And with this style you make charms? Make a charm for me! Do you know," her voice sank to a whisper, "the names of the great ones of your own far country?"

"Rather!" said Cyril, and hastily wrote the names of Alfred the Great, Shakespeare, Nelson, Gordon, Lord Beaconsfield, Mr. Rudyard Kipling, and Mr. Sherlock Holmes, while the Queen watched him with "unbaited breath," as Anthea said afterwards.

She took the book and hid it reverently among the bright folds of her gown.

"You shall teach me later to say the great names," she said. "And the names of their Ministers—perhaps the great Nisroch is one of them?"

"I don't think so," said Cyril. "Mr. Campbell Bannerman's Prime Minister and Mr. Burns a Minister, and so is the Archbishop of Canterbury, I think, but I'm not sure—and Dr. Parker was one, I know, and—

"No more," said the Queen, putting her hands to her ears. "My head's going round with all those great names. You shall teach them to me later—because of course you'll make us a nice long visit now you have come, won't you? Now tell me—but no, I am quite tired out with your being so clever. Besides, I'm sure you'd like *me* to tell *you* something, wouldn't you?"

"Yes," said Anthea. "I want to know how it is that the King has gone——"

"Excuse me, but you should say 'the King may-he-live-for-ever,'" said the Queen gently.

"I beg your pardon," Anthea hastened to say—"the King may-he-live-for-ever has gone to fetch home his fourteenth wife? I don't think even Bluebeard had as many as that. And, besides, he hasn't killed *you* at any rate."

The Queen looked bewildered.

"She means," explained Robert, "that English kings only

have one wife—at least, Henry the Eighth had seven or eight, but not all at once."

"In our country," said the Queen scornfully, "a king would not reign a day who had only one wife. No one would respect him, and quite right too."

"Then are all the other thirteen alive?" asked Anthea.

"Of course they are—poor mean-spirited things! I don't associate with them, of course, I am the Queen: they're only the wives."

"I see," said Anthea, gasping.

"But oh, my dears," the Queen went on, "such a to-do as there's been about this last wife! You never did! It really was *too* funny. We wanted an Egyptian princess. The King may-he-live-for-ever has got a wife from most of the important nations, and he had set his heart on an Egyptian one to complete his collection. Well, of course, to begin with, we sent a handsome present of gold. The Egyptian king sent back some horses—quite a few; he's fearfully stingy!—and he said he liked the gold very much, but what they were really short of was lapis lazuli, so of course we sent him some. But by that time he'd begun to use the gold to cover the beams of the roof of the Temple of the Sun-God, and he hadn't nearly enough to finish the job, so we sent more. And so it went on, oh, for years. You see each journey takes at least six months. And at last we asked the hand of his daughter in marriage."

"Yes, and then?" said Anthea, who wanted to get to the princess part of the story.

"Well, then," said the Queen, "when he'd got everything out of us that he could, and only given the meanest presents in return, he sent to say he would esteem the honour of an alliance very highly, only unfortunately he hadn't any daughter, but he hoped one would be born soon, and if so, she should certainly be reserved for the King of Babylon!"

"What a trick!" said Cyril.

"Yes, wasn't it? So then we said his sister would do, and then there were more gifts and more journeys; and now at last the tiresome, black-haired thing is coming, and the King may-he-live-for-ever has gone seven days' journey to meet her at

Carchemish. And he's gone in his best chariot, the one inlaid with lapis lazuli and gold, with the gold-plated wheels and onyx-studded hubs—much too great an honour in my opinion. She'll be here to-night; there'll be a grand banquet to celebrate her arrival. *She* won't be present, of course. She'll be having her baths and her anointings, and all that sort of thing. We always clean our foreign brides very carefully. It takes two or three weeks. Now it's dinner-time, and you shall eat with me, for I can see that you are of high rank."

She led them into a dark, cook hall, with many cushions on the floor. On these they sat, and low tables were brought— beautiful tables of smooth, blue stone mounted in gold. On these, golden trays were placed; but there were no knives, or forks, or spoons. The children expected the Queen to call for them; but no. She just ate with her fingers, and as the first dish was a great tray of boiled corn, and meat and raisins all mixed up together, and melted fat poured all over the tray, it was found difficult to follow her example with anything like what we are used to think of as good table manners. There were stewed quinces afterwards, and dates in syrup, and thick yellowy cream. It was the kind of dinner you hardly ever get in Fitzroy Street.

After dinner everybody went to sleep, even the children.

The Queen awoke with a start.

"Good gracious!" she cried, "what a time we've slept! I must rush off and dress for the banquet. I shan't have much more than time."

"Hasn't Ritti-Marduk got back with our sister and the Psammead yet?" Anthea asked.

"I *quite* forgot to ask. I'm sorry," said the Queen. "And of course they wouldn't announce her unless I told them to, except during justice hours. I expect she's waiting outside. I'll see."

Ritti-Marduk came in a moment later.

"I regret," he said, "that I have been unable to find your sister. The beast she bears with her in a basket has bitten the child of the guard, and your sister and the beast set out to come to you. The police say they have a clue. No doubt we shall

Different people came and did amusing things

have news of her in a few weeks." He bowed and withdrew.

The horror of this threefold loss—Jane, the Psammead, and the Amulet—gave the children something to talk about while the Queen was dressing. I shall not report their conversation; it was very gloomy. Everyone repeated himself several times, and the discussion ended in each of them blaming the other two for having let Jane go. You know the sort of talk it was, don't you? At last Cyril said—

"After all, she's with the Psammead, so *she's* all right. The Psammead is jolly careful of itself too. And it isn't as if we were in any danger. Let's try to buck up and enjoy the banquet."

They did enjoy the banquet. They had a beautiful bath, which was delicious, where heavily oiled all over, including their hair, and that was most unpleasant. Then they dressed again and were presented to the King, who was most affable. The banquet was long; there were all sorts of nice things to eat, and everybody seemed to eat and drink a good deal. Every one lay on cushions and couches, ladies on one side and gentlemen on the other; and after the eating was done each lady went and sat by some one gentleman, who seemed to be her sweetheart or her husband, for they were very affectionate to each other. The Court dresses had gold threads woven in them, very bright and beautiful.

The middle of the room was left clear, and different people came and did amusing things. There were conjurers and jugglers and snake-charmers, which last Anthea did not like at all.

When it got dark torches were lighted. Cedar splinters dipped in oil blazed in copper dishes set high on poles.

Then there was a dancer, who hardly danced at all, only just struck attitudes. She had hardly any clothes, and was not at all pretty. The children were rather bored by her, but every one else was delighted, including the King.

"By the beard of Nimrod!" he cried, "ask what you like, girl, and you shall have it!"

"I want nothing," said the dancer; "the honour of having pleased the King may-he-live-for-ever is reward enough for me."

And the King was so pleased with this modest and sensible reply that he gave her the gold collar off his own neck.

"I say!" said Cyril, awed by the magnificence of the gift.

"It's all right," whispered the Queen, "it's not his best collar by any means. We always keep a stock of cheap jewellery for these occasions. And now—you promised to sing us something. Would you like my minstrels to accompany you?"

"No, thank you," said Anthea quickly. The minstrels had been playing off and on all the time, and their music reminded Anthea of the band she and the others had once had on the fifth of November—with penny horns, a tin whistle, a tea tray, the tongs, a policeman's rattle, and a toy drum. They had enjoyed this band very much at the time. But it was quite different when some one else was making the same kind of music. Anthea understood now that Father had not been really heartless and unreasonable when he had told them to stop that infuriating din.

"What shall we sing?" Cyril was asking.

"Sweet and low?" suggested Anthea.

"Too soft—I vote for 'Who will o'er the downs.' Now then —one, two, three."

> "Oh, who will o'er the downs so free,
>   Oh, who will with me ride,
> Oh, who will up and follow me,
>   To win a blooming bride?
>
> Her father he has locked the door,
>   Her mother keeps the key;
> But neither bolt nor bar shall keep
>   My own true love from me."

Jane, the alto, was missing, and Robert, unlike the mother of the lady in the song, never could "keep the key," but the song, even so, was sufficiently unlike anything any of them had ever heard to rouse the Babylonian Court to the wildest enthusiasm.

"More, more," cried the King; "by my beard, this savage music is a new thing. Sing again!"

So they sang:

> "I saw her bower at twilight gray,
>   'Twas guarded safe and sure.
> I saw her bower at break of day,
>   'Twas guarded then no more.
>
> The varlets they were all asleep,
>   And there was none to see
> The greeting fair that passèd there
>   Between my love and me."

Shouts of applause greeted the ending of the verse, and the King would not be satisfied till they had sung all their part-songs (they only knew three) twice over, and ended up with "Men of Harlech" in unison. Then the King stood up in his royal robes with his high, narrow crown on his head and shouted—

"By the beak of Nisroch, ask what you will, strangers from the land where the sun never sets!"

"We ought to say it's enough honour, like the dancer, did," whispered Anthea.

"No, let's ask for *It*," said Robert.

"No, no, I'm sure the other's manners," said Anthea. But Robert, who was excited by the music, and the flaring torches, and the applause and the opportunity, spoke up before the others could stop him.

"Give us the half of the Amulet that has on it the name UR HEKAU SETCHEH," he said, adding as an afterthought, "O King, live-for-ever."

As he spoke the great name those in the pillared hall fell on their faces, and lay still. All but the Queen, who crouched amid her cushions with her head in her hands, and the King, who stood upright, perfectly still, like the statue of a king in stone. It was only for a moment though. Then his great voice thundered out—

"Guard, sieze them!"

Instantly, from nowhere as it seemed, sprang eight soldiers in bright armour inlaid with gold, and tunics of red and white. Very splendid they were, and very alarming.

"Impious and sacrilegious wretches!" shouted the King, "To the dungeons with them! We will find a way, to-morrow, to make them speak. For without doubt they can tell us where to find the lost half of *It*."

A wall of scarlet and white and steel and gold closed up round the children and hurried them away among the many pillars of the great hall. As they went they heard the voices of the courtiers loud in horror.

"You've done it this time," said Cyril with extreme bitterness.

"Oh, it will come right. It *must*. It always does," said Anthea desperately.

The king stood upright, perfectly still

They could not see where they were going, because the guard surrounded them so closely, but the ground under their feet, smooth marble at first, grew rougher like stone, then it was loose earth and sand, and they felt the night air. Then there was more stone, and steps down.

"It's my belief we really *are* going to the deepest dungeon below the castle moat this time," said Cyril.

And they were. At least it was not below a moat, but below

the river Euphrates, which was just as bad if not worse. In a most unpleasant place it was. Dark, very, very damp, and with an odd, musty smell rather like the shells of oysters. There was a torch—that is to say, a copper basket on a high stick with oiled wood burning in it. By its light the children saw that the walls were green, and that trickles of water ran down them and dripped from the roof. There were things on the floor that looked like newts, and in the darker corners creepy, shiny things moved sluggishly, uneasily, horribly.

Robert's heart sank right into those really reliable boots of his. Anthea and Cyril each had a private struggle with that inside disagreeableness which is part of all of us, and which is sometimes called the Old Adam—and both were victors. Neither of them said to Robert (and both tried hard not even to think it), "This is *your* doing." Anthea had the additional temptation to add, "I told you so." And she resisted it successfully.

"Sacrilege, and impious cheek," said the captain of the guard to the gaoler. "To be kept during the King's pleasure. I expect he means to get some pleasure out of them to-morrow! He'll tickle them up!"

"Poor little kids," said the gaoler.

"Oh, yes," said the captain. "I've got kids of my own too. But it doesn't do to let domestic sentiment interfere with one's public duties. Good-night."

The soldiers tramped heavily off in their white and red and steel and gold. The gaoler, with a bunch of big keys in his hand, stook looking pityingly at the children. He shook his head twice and went out.

"Courage!" said Anthea. "I know it will be all right. It's only a dream *really*, you know. It *must* be! I don't believe about time being only a something or other of thought. It *is* a dream, and we're bound to wake up all right and safe."

"Humph," said Cyril bitterly. And Robert suddenly said—

"It's all my doing. If it really is all up do please not keep a down on me about it, and tell Father——Oh, I forgot."

What he had forgotten was that his Father was three

thousand miles and five thousand or more years away from him.

"All right, Bobs, old man," said Cyril; and Anthea got hold of Robert's hand and squeezed it.

Then the gaoler came back with a platter of hard, flat cakes made of coarse grain, very different from the cream-and-juicy-date feasts of the palace; also a pitcher of water.

"There," he said.

"Oh, thank you so very much. You *are* kind," said Anthea feverishly.

"Go to sleep," said the goaler, pointing to a heap of straw in a corner; "to-morrow comes soon enough."

"Oh, dear Mr. Gaoler," said Anthea, "whatever will they do to us to-morrow?"

"They'll try to make you tell things," said the gaoler grimly, "and my advice is if you've nothing to tell, make up something. Then perhaps they'll sell you to the Northern nations. Regular savages *they* are. Good-night."

"Good-night," said three trembling voices, which their owners strove in vain to render firm. Then he went out, and the three were left alone in the damp, dim vault.

"I know the light won't last long," said Cyril, looking at the flickering brazier.

"Is it any good, do you think, calling on the name when we haven't got the charm?" suggested Anthea.

"I shouldn't think so. But we might try."

So they tried. But the blank silence of the damp dungeon remained unchanged.

"What was the name the Queen said?" asked Cyril suddenly. "Nisbeth—Nesbit—something? You know, the slave of the great names?"

"Wait a sec," said Robert, "though I don't know why you want it. Nusroch—Nisrock—Nisroch—That's it."

Then Anthea pulled herself together. All her muscles tightened, and the muscles of her mind and soul, if you can call them that, tightened too.

"Ur Hekau Setcheh," she cried in a fervent voice. "Oh, Nisroch, servant of the Great Ones, come and help us!"

There was a waiting silence. Then a cold, blue light awoke in the corner where the straw was—and in the light they saw coming towards them a strange and terrible figure. I won't try to describe it, because the drawing shows it, exactly as it was, and exactly as the old Babylonians carved it on their stones, so that you can see it in our own British Museum at this day. I will just say that it had eagle's wings and an eagle's head and the body of a man.

It came towards them, strong and unspeakably horrible.

"Oh, go away," cried Anthea; but Cyril cried, "No; stay!"

The creature hesitated, then bowed low before them on the damp floor of the dungeon.

"Speak," it said, in a harsh, grating voice like large rusty keys being turned in locks. "The servant of the Great Ones is *your* servant. What is your need that you call on the name of Nisroch?"

"We want to go home," said Robert.

"No, no," cried Anthea; "we want to be where Jane is."

Nisroch raised his great arm and pointed at the wall of the dungeon. And, as he pointed, the wall disappeared, and instead of the damp, green, rocky surface, there shone and glowed a room with rich hangings of red silk embroidered with golden water-lilies, with cushioned couches and great mirrors of polished steel; and in it was the Queen, and before her, on a red pillow, sat the Psammead, its fur hunched up in an irritated, discontented way. On a blue-covered couch lay Jane fast asleep.

"Walk forward without fear," said Nisroch. "Is there aught else that the Servant of the great Name can do for those who speak that name?"

"No—oh, *no*," said Cyril. "It's all right now. Thanks ever so."

"You are a dear," cried Anthea, not in the least knowing what she was saying. "Oh, thank you—thank you. But *do* go *now*!"

She caught the hand of the creature, and it was cold and hard in hers, like a hand of stone.

"Go forward," said Nisroch. And they went.

Nisroch raised his great arm and pointed at the wall of the dungeon

"Oh, my good gracious," said the Queen as they stood before her. "How did you get here? I *knew* you were magic. I meant to let you out the first thing in the morning, if I could slip away—but thanks be to Dagon, you've managed it for yourselves. You must get away. I'll wake my chief lady and she shall call Ritti-Marduk, and he'll let you out the back way, and——"

"Don't rouse anybody for goodness' sake," said Anthea, "except Jane, and I'll rouse her."

She shook Jane with energy, and Jane slowly awoke.

"Ritti-Marduk brought them in hours ago, really," said the Queen, "but I wanted to have the Psammead all to myself for a bit. You'll excuse the little natural deception?—it's part of the Babylonish character, don't you know? But I don't want anything to happen to you. Do let me rouse someone."

"No, no, no, no," said Anthea with desperate earnestness. She thought she knew enough of what the Babylonians were like when they were roused. "We can go by our own magic. And you will tell the King it wasn't the gaoler's fault. It was Nisroch."

"Nisroch!" echoed the Queen. "You are indeed magicians."

Jane sat up, blinking stupidly.

"Hold *It* up, and say the word," cried Cyril, catching up the Psammead, which mechanically bit him, but only very slightly.

"Which is the East?" asked Jane.

"Behind me," said the Queen. "Why?"

"Ur Hekau Setcheh," said Jane sleepily, and held up the charm.

And there they all were in the dining-room at 300 Fitzroy Street.

"Jane," said Cyril with great presence of mind, "go and get the plate of sand down for the Psammead."

Jane went.

"Look here!" he said quickly, as the sound of her boots grew less loud on the stairs, "don't let's tell her about the dungeon and all that. It'll only frighten her so that she'll never want to go anywhere else."

"Hold it up, and say the word," cried Cyril

"Righto!" said Cyril; but Anthea felt that she could not have said a word to save her life.

"Why did you want to come back in such a hurry?" asked Jane, returning with the plate of sand. "It was awfully jolly in Babylon, I think! I liked it no end."

"Oh, yes," said Cyril carelessly. "It was jolly enough, of course, but I thought we'd been there long enough. Mother always says you oughtn't to wear out your welcome!"

CHAPTER VIII

THE QUEEN IN LONDON

"Now TELL us what happened to you," said Cyril to Jane, when he and the others had told her all about the Queen's talk and the banquet, and the variety entertainment, carefully stopping short before the beginning of the dungeon part of the story.

"It wasn't much good going," said Jane, "if you didn't even try to get the Amulet."

"We found out it was no go," said Cyril; "it's not to be got in Babylon. It was lost before that. We'll go to some other jolly friendly place, where every one is kind and pleasant, and look for it there. Now tell about your part."

"Oh," said Jane, "the Queen's man with the smooth face—what was his name?"

"Ritti-Marduk," said Cyril.

"Yes," said Jane, "Ritti-Marduk, he came for me just after the Psammead had bitten the guard-of-the-gate's wife's little boy, and he took me to the Palace. And we had supper with the new little Queen from Egypt. She is a dear—not much older than you. She told me heaps about Egypt. And we played ball after supper. And then the Babylon Queen sent for me. I like her too. And she talked to the Psammead and I went to sleep. And then you woke me up. That's all."

The Psammead, roused from its sound sleep, told the same story.

"But," it added, "what possessed you to tell that Queen that I could give wishes? I sometimes think you were born without even the most rudimentary imitation of brains."

The children did not know the meaning of rudimentary, but it sounded a rude, insulting word.

"I don't see that we did any harm," said Cyril sulkily.

"Oh, no," said the Psammead with withering irony, "not at

all! Of course not! Quite the contrary! Exactly so! Only she happened to wish that she might soon find herself in your country. And soon may mean any moment."

"Then it's your fault," said Robert, "because you might just as well have made 'soon' mean some moment next year or next century."

"That's where you, as so often happens, make the mistake," rejoined the Sand-fairy. "*I* couldn't mean anything but what *she* meant by 'soon'. It wasn't my wish. And what she meant was the next time the King happens to go out lion hunting. So she'll have a whole day, and perhaps two, to do as she wishes with. She doesn't know about time only being a mode of thought."

"Well," said Cyril, with a sigh of resignation, "we must do what we can to give her a good time. She was jolly decent to us. I say, suppose we were to go to St. James's Park after dinner and feed those ducks that we never did feed. After all that Babylon and all those years ago, I feel as if I should like to see something *real*, and *now*. You'll come, Psammead?"

"Where's my priceless woven basket of sacred rushes?" asked the Psammead morosely. "I can't go out with nothing on. And I won't, what's more."

And then everybody remembered with pain that the bass bag had, in the hurry of departure from Babylon, not been remembered.

"But it's not so extra precious," said Robert hastily. "You get them given to you for nothing if you buy fish in Farringdon Market."

"Oh," said the Psammead very crossly indeed, "so you presume on my sublime indifference to the things of this disgusting modern world, to fob me off with a travelling equipage that costs you nothing. Very well, I shall go to sand. Please don't wake me."

And it went then and there to sand, which, as you know, meant to bed. The boys went to St. James's Park to feed the ducks, but they went alone.

Anthea and Jane sat sewing all the afternoon. They cut off half a yard from each of their best green Liberty sashes.

A towel cut in two formed a lining; and they sat and sewed and
sewed and sewed. What they were making was a bag for the
Psammead. Each worked at a half of the bag. Jane's half had
four-leaved shamrocks embroidered on it. They were the only
things she could do (because she had been taught how at school,
and, fortunately, some of the silk she had been taught with was
left over). And even so, Anthea had to draw the pattern for
her. Anthea's side of bag had letters on it—worked hastily but
affectionately in chain stitch. They were something like this:—

She would have put "travelling carriage," but she made the
letters too big, so there was no room. The bag was made *into*
a bag with old Nurse's sewing machine, and the strings of it
were Anthea's and Jane's best red hair ribbons.

At tea-time, when the boys had come home with a most un-
favourable report of the St. James's Park ducks, Anthea ventured to awaken the Psammead, and to show it its new travelling
bag.

"Humph," it said, sniffing a little contemptuously, yet at the
same time affectionately, "it's not so dusty."

The Psammead seemed to pick up very easily the kind of
things that people said nowadays. For a creature that had in its
time associated with Megatheriums and Pterodactyls, its quickness was really wonderful.

"It's more worthy of me," it said, "than the kind of bag
that's given away with a pound of plaice. When do you pro-
pose to take me out in it?"

"I should like a rest from taking you or us anywhere," said Cyril. But Jane said—

"I want to go to Egypt. I did like that Egyptian Princess that came to marry the King in Babylon. She told me about the larks they have in Egypt. And the cats. Do let's go there. And I told her what the bird things on the Amulet were like. And she said it was Egyptian writing."

The others exchanged looks of silent rejoicing at the thought of their cleverness in having concealed from Jane the terrors they had suffered in the dungeon below the Euphrates.

"Egypt's so nice too," Jane went on, "because of Doctor Brewer's Scripture History. I would like to go there when Joseph was dreaming those curious dreams, or when Moses was doing wonderful things with snakes and sticks."

"I don't care about snakes," said Anthea shuddering.

"Well, we needn't be in at that part, but Babylon was lovely! We had cream and sweet, sticky stuff. And I expect Egypt's the same."

There was a good deal of discussion, but it all ended in everybody's agreeing to Jane's idea. And next morning directly after breakfast (which was kippers, and very nice) the Psammead was invited to get into his travelling carriage.

The moment after it had done so, with stiff, furry reluctance, like that of a cat when you want to nurse it, and its ideas are not the same as yours, old Nurse came in.

"Well, chickies," she said, "are you feeling very dull?"

"Oh, no, Nurse dear," said Anthea; "we're having a lovely time. We're just going off to see some old ancient relics."

"Ah," said old Nurse, "the Royal Academy, I suppose? Don't go wasting your money too reckless, that's all."

She cleared away the kipper bones and the tea-things, and when she had swept up the crumbs and removed the cloth, the Amulet was held up and the order given—just as Duchesses (and other people) give it to their coachmen.

"To Egypt, please!" said Anthea, when Cyril had uttered the wonderful Name of Power.

"When Moses was there," added Jane.

And there, in the dingy Fitzroy Street dining-room, the

Amulet grew big, and it was an arch, and through it they saw a blue, blue sky and a running river.

"No, stop!" said Cyril, and pulled down Jane's hand with the Amulet in it.

"What silly cuckoos we all are," he said. "Of course we can't go. We daren't leave home for a single minute now, for fear that minute should be *the* minute."

"What minute be *what* minute?" asked Jane impatiently, trying to get her hand away from Cyril.

"The minute when the Queen of Babylon comes," said Cyril. And then everyone saw it.

For some days life flowed in a very slow, dusty, uneventful stream. The children could never go out all at once, because they never knew when the King of Babylon would go out lion hunting and leave his Queen free to pay them that surprise visit to which she was, without doubt, eagerly looking forward.

So they took it in turns, two and two, to go out and to stay in.

The stay-at-homes would have been much duller than they were but for the new interest taken in them by the learned gentleman.

He called Anthea in one day to show her a beautiful necklace of purple and gold beads.

"I saw one like that," she said, "in——"

"In the British Museum, perhaps?"

"I like to call the place where I saw it Babylon," said Anthea cautiously.

"A pretty fancy," said the learned gentleman, "and quite correct too, because, as a matter of fact, these beads did come from Babylon."

The other three were all out that day. The boys had been going to the Zoo, and Jane had said so plaintively, "I'm sure I am fonder of rhinoceroses than either of you are," that Anthea had told her to run along then. And she had run, catching the boys before that part of the road where Fitzroy Street suddenly becomes Fitzroy Square.

"I think Babylon is most frightfully interesting," said

Anthea. "I do have such interesting dreams about it—at least, not dreams exactly, but quite as wonderful."

"Do sit down and tell me," said he. So she sat down and told. And he asked her a lot of questions, and she answered them as well as she could.

"Wonderful—wonderful!" he said at last. "One's heard of thought-transference, but I never thought *I* had any power of that sort. Yet it must be that, and very bad for *you*, I should think. Doesn't your head ache very much?"

He suddenly put a cold, thin hand on her forehead.

"No thank you, not at all," said she.

"I assure you it is not done intentionally," he went on. "Of course I know a good deal about Babylon, and I unconsciously communicate it to you; you've heard of thought-reading, but some of the things you say, I don't understand; they never enter my head, and yet they're so astoundingly probable."

"It's all right," said Anthea reassuringly. "*I* understand. And don't worry. It's all quite simple really."

It was not quite so simple when Anthea, having heard the others come in, went down, and before she had had time to ask how they had liked the Zoo, heard a noise outside, compared to which the wild beasts' noises were gentle as singing birds.

"Good gracious!" cried Anthea, "what's that?"

The loud hum of many voices came through the open window. Words could be distinguished.

" 'Ere's a guy!"

"This ain't November. That ain't no guy. It's a ballet lady, that's what it is."

"Not it—it's a bloomin' looney, I tell you."

Then came a clear voice that they knew.

"Retire, slaves!" it said.

"What's she a saying of?" cried a dozen voices.

"Some blamed foreign lingo," one voice replied.

The children rushed to the door. A crowd was on the road and pavement.

In the middle of the crowd, plainly to be seen from the top

of the steps, were the beautiful face and bright veil of the Babylonian Queen.

"Jimminy!" cried Robert, and ran down the steps, "here she is!"

"Here!" he cried, "look out—let the lady pass. She's a friend of ours, coming to see us."

"Nice friend for a respectable house," snorted a fat woman with marrows on a hand-cart.

All the same the crowd made way a little. The Queen met Robert on the pavement, and Cyril joined them, the Psammead bag still on his arm.

"Here," he whispered; "here's the Psammead; you can get wishes."

"*I* wish you'd come in a different dress, if you *had* to come," said Robert; "but it's no use my wishing anything."

"No," said the Queen. "I wish I was dressed—no, I don't— I wish *they* were dressed properly, then they wouldn't be so silly."

The Psammead blew itself out till the bag was a very tight fit for it; and suddenly every man, woman, and child in that crowd felt that it had not enough clothes on. For, of course, the Queen's idea of proper dress was the dress that had been proper for the working-classes three thousand years ago in Babylon— and there was not much of it.

"Lawky me!" said the marrow-selling woman, "whatever could a-took me to come out this figure?" and she wheeled her cart away very quickly indeed.

"Some one's made a pretty guy of you—talk of guys," said a man who sold bootlaces.

"Well, don't you talk," said the man next him. "Look at your own silly legs; and where's your boots?"

"I never come out like this, I'll take my sacred," said the bootlace-seller. "I wasn't quite myself last night, I'll own, but not to dress up like a circus."

The crowd was all talking at once, and getting rather angry. But no one seemed to think of blaming the Queen.

Anthea bounded down the steps and pulled her up; the others followed, and the door was shut.

"I never come out like this," said the bootlace-seller

"Blowed if I can make it out!" they heard. "I'm off home, I am."

And the crowd, coming slowly to the same mind, dispersed, followed by another crowd of persons who were not dressed in what the Queen thought was the proper way.

"We shall have the police here directly," said Anthea in the tones of despair. "Oh, why did you come dressed like that?"

The Queen leaned against the arm of the horse-hair sofa.

"How else can a queen dress I should like to know?" she questioned.

"Our Queen wears things like other people," said Cyril.

"Well, I don't. And I must say," she remarked in an injured tone, "that you don't seem very glad to see me now I *have* come. But perhaps it's the surprise that makes you behave like this. Yet you ought to be used to surprises. The way you vanished! I shall never forget it. The best magic I've ever seen. How did you do it?"

"Oh, never mind about that now," said Robert. "You see you've gone and upset all those people, and I expect they'll fetch the police. And we don't want to see you collared and put in prison."

"You can't put queens in prison," she said loftily.

"Oh, can't you?" said Cyril. "We cut off a king's head here once."

"In this miserable room? How frightfully interesting."

"No, no, not in this room; in history."

"Oh, in *that*," said the Queen disparagingly. "I thought you'd done it with your own hands."

The girls shuddered.

"What a hideous city yours is," the Queen went on pleasantly, "and what horrid, ignorant people. Do you know they actually can't understand a single word I say."

"Can you understand them?" asked Jane.

"Of course not; they speak some vulgar, Northern dialect. I can understand *you* quite well."

I really am not going to explain *again* how it was that the children could understand other languages than their own so thoroughly, and talk them, too, so that it felt and sounded (to them) just as though they were talking English.

"Well," said Cyril bluntly, "now you've seen just how horrid it is, don't you think you might as well go home again?"

"Why, I've seen simply nothing yet," said the Queen, arranging her starry veil. "I wished to be at your door, and I was. Now I must go and see your King and Queen."

"Nobody's allowed to," said Anthea in haste; "but look here, we'll take you and show you anything you'd like to see—anything you *can* see," she added kindly, because she remembered how nice the Queen had been to them in Babylon, even if she had been a little deceitful in the matter of Jane and the Psammead.

"There's the Museum," said Cyril hopefully; "there are lots of things from your country there. If only we could disguise you a little."

"I know," said Anthea suddenly. "Mother's old theatre-cloak, and there are a lot of her old hats in the big box."

The blue-silk, lace-trimmed cloak did indeed hide some of the Queen's startling splendours, but the hat fitted very badly. It had pink roses in it; and there was something about the coat or the hat or the Queen, that made her look somehow not very respectable.

"Oh, never mind," said Anthea, when Cyril whispered this. "The thing is to get her out before Nurse has finished her forty winks. I should think she's about got to the thirty-ninth wink by now."

"Come on then," said Robert. "You know how dangerous it is. Let's make haste into the Museum. If any of those people you made guys of do fetch the police, they won't think of looking for you there."

The blue-silk cloak and the pink-rosed hat attracted almost as much attention as the royal costume had done; and the children were uncommonly glad to get out of the noisy streets into the gray quiet of the Museum.

"Parcels and umbrellas to be left here," said a man at the counter. The party had no umbrellas, and the only parcel was the bag containing the Psammead, which the Queen had insisted should be brought.

"*I'm* not going to be left," said the Psammead softly, "so don't you think it."

"I'll wait outside with you," said Anthea hastily, and went to sit on the seat near the drinking fountain.

"Don't sit so near that nasty fountain," said the creature crossly; "I might get splashed."

Anthea obediently moved to another seat and waited. Indeed she waited, and waited, and waited, and waited, and waited. The Psammead dropped into an uneasy slumber. Anthea had long ceased to watch the swing-door that always let out the wrong person, and was herself almost asleep, and still the others did not come back.

It was quite a start when Anthea suddenly realised that they had come back, and that they were not alone. Behind them was quite a crowd of men in uniform, and several gentlemen were there. Every one seemed very angry.

"Now go," said the nicest of the angry gentlemen. "Take the poor, demented thing home and tell your parents she ought to be properly looked after."

"If you can't get her to go we must send for the police," said the nastiest gentleman.

"But we don't wish to use harsh measures," added the nice one, who was really very nice indeed, and seemed to be over all the others.

"May I speak to my sister a moment first?" asked Robert.

The nicest gentleman nodded, and the officials stood round the Queen, and the others forming a sort of guard while Robert crossed over to Anthea.

"Everything you can think of," he replied to Anthea's glance of inquiry. "Kicked up the most frightful shine in there. Said those necklaces and earrings and things in the glass cases were all hers—would have them out of the cases. Tried to break the glass—she did break one bit! Everybody in the place has been at her. No good. I only got her out by telling her that was the place where they cut queens' heads off."

"Oh, Bobs, what a whacker!"

"You'd have told a whackinger one to get her out. Besides it wasn't. I meant *mummy* queens. How do you know they don't cut off mummies' heads to see how the embalming is done? What I want to say is, can't you get her to go with you quietly?"

"I'll try," said Anthea, and went up to the Queen.

"Do come home," she said; "the learned gentleman in our house has a much nicer necklace than anything they've got here. Come and see it."

The Queen nodded.

"You see," said the nastiest gentleman, "she does understand English."

"I was talking Babylonian, I think," said Anthea bashfully.

"My good child," said the nice gentleman, "what you're talking is not Babylonian, but nonsense. You just go home *at once*, and tell your parents exactly what has happened."

Anthea took the Queen's hand and gently pulled her away. The other children followed, and the black crowd of angry gentlemen stood on the steps watching them. It was when the little party of disgraced children, with the Queen who had disgraced them, had reached the middle of the courtyard that her eyes fell on the bag where the Psammead was. She stopped short.

"I wish," she said very loud and clear, "that all those Babylonian things would come out to me here—slowly, so that those dogs and slaves can see the working of the great Queen's magic."

"Oh, you *are* a tiresome woman," said the Psammead in its bag, but it puffed itself out.

Next moment there was a crash. The glass swing-doors and all their framework were smashed suddenly and completely. The crowd of angry gentlemen sprang aside when they saw what had done this. But the nastiest of them was not quick enough, and he was roughly pushed out of the way by an enormous stone bull that was floating steadily through the door. It came and stood beside the Queen in the middle of the courtyard.

It was followed by more stone images, by great slabs of carved stone, bricks, helmets, tools, weapons, fetters, wine-jars, bowls, bottles, vases, jugs, saucers, seals, and the round long things, something like rolling pins with marks on them like the print of little bird-feet, necklaces, collars, rings, arm-lets, earrings—heaps and heaps and heaps of things, far more than any one had time to count, or even to see distinctly.

All the angry gentlemen had abruptly sat down on the Museum steps except the nice one. He stood with his hands in his pockets just as though he was quite used to seeing great stone bulls and all sorts of small Babylonish objects float out into the Museum yard. But he sent a man to close the big iron gates.

A journalist, who was just leaving the musuem, spoke to Robert as he passed.

"Theosophy, I suppose?" he said. "Is she Mrs. Besant?"

"*Yes*," said Robert recklessly.

The journalist passed through the gates just before they were shut. He rushed off to Fleet Street, and his paper got out a new edition within half an hour.

"MRS. BESANT AND THEOSOPHY.

"Impertinent Miracle at the

British Museum."

People saw it in fat, black letters on the boards carried by the sellers of newspapers. Some few people who had nothing better to do went down to the Museum on the tops of omni-buses. But by the time they got there there was nothing to be seen. For the Babylonian Queen had suddenly seen the closed gates, had felt the threat of them, and had said—

"I wish we were in your house."

And, of course, instantly they were.

The Psammead was furious.

"Look here," it said, "they'll come after you, and they'll find *me*. There'll be a National Cage built for me at West-minster, and I shall have to work at politics. Why wouldn't you leave the things in their places?"

It was followed by more stone images

"What a temper you have, haven't you?" said the Queen serenely. "I wish all the things were back in their places. Will *that* do for you?"

The Psammead swelled and shrank and spoke very angrily.

"I can't refuse to give your wishes," it said, "but I can Bite. And I will if this goes on. Now then."

"Ah, don't," whispered Anthea close to its bristling ear; "it's dreadful for us too. Don't *you* desert us. Perhaps she'll wish herself at home again soon."

"Not she," said the Psammead a little less crossly.

"Take me to see your City," said the Queen.

The children looked at each other.

"If we had some money we could take her about in a cab. People wouldn't notice her so much then. But we haven't."

"Sell this," said the Queen, taking a ring from her finger.

"They'd only think we'd stolen it," said Cyril bitterly, "and put us in prison."

"All roads lead to prison with you, it seems," said the Queen.

"The learned gentleman!" said Anthea, and ran up to him with the ring in her hand.

"Look here," she said, "will you buy this for a pound?"

"Oh!" he said in tones of joy and amazement, and took the ring into his hand.

"It's my very own," said Anthea; "it was given to me to sell."

"I'll lend you a pound," said the learned gentleman, "with pleasure; and I'll take care of the ring for you. Who did you say gave it to you?"

"We call her," said Anthea carefully, "the Queen of Baby-lon."

"Is it a game?" he asked hopefully.

"It'll be a pretty game if I don't get the money to pay for cabs for her," said Anthea.

"I sometimes think," he said slowly, "that I am becoming insane, or that——"

"Or that I am; but I'm not, and you're not, and she's not."

"Does she *say* that she's the Queen of Babylon?" he uneasily asked.

"I'll lend you a pound," said the learned gentleman

"Yes," said Anthea recklessly.

"This thought-transference is more far-reaching than I imagined," he said. "I suppose I have unconsciously influenced *her*, too. I never thought my Babylonish studies would bear fruit like this. Horrible! There are more things in heaven and earth——"

"Yes," said Anthea, "heaps more. And the pound is the thing *I* want more than anything on earth."

He ran his fingers through his thin hair.

"This thought-transference!" he said. "It's undoubtedly a Babylonian ring—or it seems so to me. But perhaps I have hypnotised myself. I will see a doctor the moment I have corrected the last proofs of my book."

"Yes, do!" said Anthea, "and thank you so very much."

She took the sovereign and ran down to the others.

And now from the window of a four-wheeled cab the Queen of Babylon beheld the wonders of London. Buckingham Palace she thought uninteresting; Westminster Abbey and the Houses of Parliament little better. But she liked the Tower, and the River, and the ships filled her with wonder and delight.

"But how badly you keep your slaves. How wretched and poor and neglected they seem," she said, as the cab rattled along the Mile End Road.

"They aren't slaves; they're working-people," said Jane.

"Of course they're working. That's what slaves are. Don't you tell me. Do you suppose I don't know a slave's face when I see it? Why don't their masters see that they're better fed and better clothed? Tell me in three words."

No one answered. The wage-system of modern England is a little difficult to explain in three words even if you understand it—which the children didn't.

"You'll have a revolt of your slaves if you're not careful," said the Queen.

"Oh, no," said Cyril; "you see they have votes—that makes them safe not to revolt. It makes all the difference. Father told me so."

"What is this vote?" asked the Queen. "Is it a charm? What do they do with it?"

"I don't know," said the harassed Cyril; "it's just a vote, that's all! They don't do anything particular with it."

"I see," said the Queen; "a sort of plaything. Well, I wish that all these slaves may have in their hands this moment their full of their favourite meat and drink."

Instantly all the people in the Mile End Road, and in all the other streets where poor people live, found their hands full of things to eat and drink. From the cab window could be seen persons carrying every kind of food, and bottles and cans as well. Roast meat, fowls, red lobsters, great yellowy crabs, fried fish, boiled pork, beef-steak puddings, baked onions, mutton pies; most of the young people had oranges and sweets and cake. It made an enormous change in the look of the Mile End Road—brightened it up, so to speak, and brightened up, more than you can possibly imagine, the faces of the people.

"Makes a difference, doesn't it?" said the Queen.

"That's the best wish you've had yet," said Jane with cordial approval.

Just by the Bank the cabman stopped.

"I ain't agoin' to drive you no further," he said. "Out you gets."

They got out rather unwillingly.

"I wants my tea," he said; and they saw that on the box of the cab was a mound of cabbage, with pork chops and apple sauce, a duck, and a spotted currant pudding. Also a large can.

"You pay me my fare," he said threateningly, and looked down at the mound, muttering again about his tea.

"We'll take another cab," said Cyril with dignity. "Give me change for a sovereign, if you please."

But the cabman, as it turned out, was not at all a nice character. He took the sovereign, whipped up his horse, and disappeared in the stream of cabs and omnibuses and wagons, without giving them any change at all.

Already a little crowd was collecting round the party.

"Come on," said Robert, leading the wrong way.

The crowd round them thickened. They were in a narrow

All the people in that street found their hands full of things to eat and drink

street where many gentlemen in black coats and without hats were standing about on the pavement talking very loudly.

"How ugly their clothes are," said the Queen of Babylon. "They'd be rather fine men, some of them, if they were dressed decently, especially the ones with the beautiful long, curved noses. I wish they were dressed like the Babylonians of my court."

And, of course, it was so.

The moment the almost fainting Psammead had blown itself out every man in Throgmorton Street appeared abruptly in Babylonian full dress.

All were carefully powdered, their hair and beards were scented and curled, their garments richly embroidered. They wore rings and armlets, flat gold collars and swords, and impossible-looking head-dresses.

A stupefied silence fell on them.

"I say," a youth who had always been fair haired broke that silence, "it's only fancy of course—something wrong with my eyes—but you chaps do look so rum."

"Rum," said his friend. "Look at *you*. You in a sash! My hat! And your hair's gone black and you've got a beard. It's my belief we've been poisoned. You do look a jackape."

"Old Levinstein don't look so bad. But how was it *done*— that's what I want to know. How *was* it done? Is it conjuring, or what?"

"I think it is chust a ver' bad tream," said old Levinstein to his clerk; "all along Bishopsgate I haf seen the gommon people have their hants full of of food—*goot* food. Oh yes, without doubt a very bad tream!"

"Then I'm dreaming too, sir," said the clerk, looking down at his legs with an expression of loathing. "I see my feet in beastly sandals as plain as plain."

"All that goot food wasted," said old Mr. Levinstein. "A bad tream—a bad tream."

The Members of the Stock Exchange are said to be at all times a noisy lot. But the noise they made now to express their disgust at the costumes of ancient Babylon, was far louder than their ordinary row. One had to shout before one could here oneself speak.

"I only wish," said the clerk who thought it was conjuring— he was quite close to the children and they trembled, because they knew that whatever he wished would come true. "I only wish we knew who'd done it."

And, of course, instantly they did know, and they pressed round the Queen.

"Scandalous! Shameful! Ought to be put down by law. Give her in charge. Fetch the police," two or three hundred voices shouted at once.

The Queen recoiled.

"What is it?" she asked. "They sound like caged lions—lions by the thousand. What is it that they say?"

"They say 'Police!'" said Cyril briefly. "I knew they would sooner or later. And I don't blame them, mind you."

"I wish my guards were here!" cried the Queen. The exhausted Psammead was panting and trembling, but the Queen's guards in red and green garments, and brass and iron gear, choked Throgmorton Street, and bared weapons flashed round the Queen.

"I'm mad," said a Mr. Rosenbaum; "dat's what it is—mad!"

"It's a judgment on you, Rosy," said his partner. "I always said you were too hard in that matter of Flowerdew. It's a judgment, and I'm in it too."

The members of the Stock Exchange had edged carefully away from the gleaming blades, the mailed figures, the hard, cruel Eastern faces. But Throgmorton Street is narrow, and the crowd was too thick for them to get away as quickly as they wished.

"Kill them," cried the Queen. "Kill the dogs!"

The guards obeyed.

"It *is* all a dream," cried Mr. Levinstein, cowering in a doorway behind his clerk.

"It isn't," said the clerk. "It isn't. Oh, my good gracious! those foreign brutes are killing everybody. Henry Hirsh is down now, and Prentice is cut in two—oh, Lord! and Huth, and there goes Lionel Cohen with his head off, and Guy Nickalls has lost his head now. A dream? I wish to goodness it was all a dream."

And, of course, instantly it was! The entire Stock Exchange rubbed its eyes and went back to close, to over, and either side of seven-eighths, and Trunks, and Kaffirs, and Steel Common, and Contangoes, and Backwardations, Double Options, and all the interesting subjects concerning which they talk in the Street without ceasing.

No one said a word about it to any one else. I think I have explained before that business men do not like it to be known that they have been dreaming in business hours. Especially mad dreams including such dreadful things as hungry people getting dinners, and the destruction of the Stock Exchange.

The children were in the dining-room at 300, Fitzroy Street, pale and trembling. The Psammead crawled out of the embroidered bag, and lay flat on the table, its legs stretched out, looking more like a dead hare than anything else.

"Thank Goodness that's over," said Anthea, drawing a deep breath.

"She won't come back, will she?" asked Jane tremulously.

"No," said Cyril. "She's thousands of years ago. But we spent a whole precious pound on her. It'll take all our pocket-money for ages to pay that back."

"Not if it was *all* a dream," said Robert. "The wish said *all* a dream, you know, Panther; you cut up and ask if he lent you anything."

"I beg your pardon," said Anthea politely, following the sound of her knock into the presence of the learned gentleman, "I'm *so* sorry to trouble you, but *did* you lend me a pound to-day?"

"No," said he, looking kindly at her through his spectacles. "But it's extraordinary that you should ask me, for I dozed for a few moments this afternoon, a thing I very rarely do, and I dreamed quite distinctly that you brought me a ring that you said belonged to the Queen of Babylon, and that I lent you a sovereign, and that you left one of the Queen's rings here. The ring was a magnificent specimen." He sighed. "I wish it hadn't been a dream," he said smiling. He was really learning to smile quite nicely.

Anthea could not be too thankful that the Psammead was not there to grant his wish.

CHAPTER IX

ATLANTIS

YOU WILL understand that the adventure of the Babylonian Queen in London was the only one that had occupied any time at all. But the children's time was very fully taken up by talking over all the wonderful things seen and done in the Past, where, by the power of the Amulet, they seemed to spend hours and hours, only to find when they got back to London that the whole thing had been briefer than a lightning flash.

They talked of the Past at their meals, in their walks, in the dining-room, in the first-floor drawing-room, but most of all on the stairs. It was an old house; it had once been a fashionable one, and was a fine one still. The banister rails of the stairs were excellent for sliding down, and in the corners of the landings were big alcoves that had once held graceful statues, and now quite often held the graceful forms of Cyril, Robert, Anthea, and Jane.

One day Cyril and Robert in tight white underclothing had spent a pleasant hour in reproducing the attitudes of statues seen either in the British Museum, or in Father's big photograph book. But the show ended abruptly because Robert wanted to be the Venus of Milo, and for this purpose pulled at the sheet which served for drapery at the very moment when Cyril, looking really quite like the Discobolos—with a gold and white saucer for the disc—was standing on one foot, and under that one foot was the sheet.

Of course the Discobolos and his disc and the would-be Venus came down together, and everyone was a good deal hurt, especially the saucer, which would never be the same again, however neatly one might join its uneven bits with Seccotine or the white of an egg.

"I hope you're satisfied," said Cyril, holding his head where a large lump was rising.

"Quite, thanks," said Robert bitterly. His thumb had caught in the banisters and bent itself back almost to breaking point.

"I *am* so sorry, poor, dear Squirrel," said Anthea; "and you were looking so lovely. I'll get a wet rag. Bobs, go and hold your hand under the hot-water tap. It's what ballet girls do with their legs when they hurt them. I saw it in a book."

"What book?" said Robert disagreeably. But he went.

When he came back Cyril's head had been bandaged by his sisters, and he had been brought to the state of mind where he was able reluctantly to admit that he supposed Robert hadn't done it on purpose.

Robert replying with equal suavity, Anthea hastened to lead the talk away from the accident.

"I suppose you don't feel like going anywhere through the Amulet," she said.

"Egypt!" said Jane promptly. "I want to see the pussy cats."

"Not me—too hot," said Cyril. "It's about as much as I can stand here—let alone Egypt." It was indeed, hot, even on the second landing, which is the coolest place in the house. "Let's go to the North Pole."

"I don't suppose the Amulet was ever there—and we might get our fingers frost-bitten so that we could never hold it up to get home again. No thanks," said Robert.

"I say," said Jane, "let's get the Psammead and ask its advice. It will like us asking, even if we don't take it."

The Psammead was brought up in its green silk embroidered bag, but before it could be asked anything the door of the learned gentleman's room opened and the voice of the visitor who had been lunching with him was heard on the stairs. He seemed to be speaking with the door handle in his hand.

"You see a doctor, old boy," he said; "all that about thought-transference is just simply twaddle. You've been over-working. Take a holiday. Go to Dieppe."

"I'd rather go to Babylon," said the learned gentleman.

"I wish you'd go to Atlantis some time, while we're about it, so as to give me some tips for my *Nineteenth Century* article when you come home."

"I wish I could," said the voice of the learned gentleman.

"Good-bye. Take care of yourself."

The door was banged, and the visitor came smiling down the stairs—a stout, prosperous, big man. The children had to get up to let him pass.

"Hullo, Kiddies," he said, glancing at the bandages on the head of Cyril and the hand of Robert, "been in the wars?"

"It's all right," said Cyril. "I say, what was that Atlantic place you wanted him to go to? We couldn't help hearing you talk."

"You talk so very loud, you see," said Jane soothingly.

"Atlantis," said the visitor, "the lost Atlantis, garden of the Hesperides. Great continent—disappeared in the sea. You can read about it in Plato."

"Thank you," said Cyril doubtfully.

"Were there any Amulets there?" asked Anthea made anxious by a sudden thought.

"Hundreds, I should think. So *he's* been talking to you?"

"Yes, often. He's very kind to us. We like him awfully."

"Well, what he wants is a holiday; you persuade him to take one. What he wants is a change of scene. You see, his head is crusted so thickly inside with knowledge about Egypt and Assyria and things that you can't hammer anything into it unless you keep hard at it all day long for days and days. And I haven't time. But you live in the house. You can hammer almost incessantly. Just try your hands, will you? Right. So long!"

He went down the stairs three at a time, and Jane remarked that he was a nice man, and she thought he had little girls of his own.

"I should like to have them to play with," she added pensively.

The three elder ones exchanged glances. Cyril nodded.

"All right. *Let's* go to Atlantis," he said.

"Let's go to Atlantis and take the learned gentleman with us," said Anthea; "he'll think it's a dream, afterwards, but it'll certainly be a change of scene."

"Why not take him to nice Egypt?" asked Jane.

"Too hot," said Cyril shortly.

"Or Babylon, where he wants to go?"

"I've had enough of Babylon," said Robert, "at least for the present. And so have the others. I don't know why," he added, forestalling the question on Jane's lips, "but somehow we have. Squirrel, let's take off these beastly bandages and get into flannels. We can't go in our unders."

"He *wished* to go to Atlantis, so he's got to go some time; and he might as well go with us," said Anthea.

This was how it was that the learned gentleman, permitting himself a few moments of relaxation in his chair, after the fatigue of listening to opinions (about Atlantis and many other things) with which he did not at all agree, opened his eyes to find his four young friends standing in front of him in a row.

"Will you come," said Anthea, "to Atlantis with us?"

"To know that you are dreaming shows that the dream is nearly at an end," he told himself; "or perhaps it's only a game, like 'How many miles to Babylon?'"

So he said aloud: "Thank you very much, but I have only a quarter of an hour to spare."

"It doesn't take any time," said Cyril; "time is only a mode of thought, you know, and you've got to go some time, so why not with us?"

"Very well," said the learned gentleman, now quite certain that he was dreaming.

Anthea held out her soft, pink hand. He took it. She pulled him gently to his feet. Jane held up the Amulet.

"To just outside Atlantis," said Cyril, and Jane said the Name of Power.

"You owl!" said Robert, "it's an island. Outside an island's all water."

"I won't go. I *won't*," said the Psammead, kicking and struggling in its bag.

But already the Amulet had grown to a great arch. Cyril pushed the learned gentleman, as undoubtedly the first-born, through the arch—not into water, but on to a wooden floor, out of doors. The others followed. The amulet grew smaller again, and there they all were, standing on the deck of a ship whose sailors were busy making her fast with chains to rings on a white quay-side. The rings and the chains were of a metal that shone red-yellow like gold.

Everyone on the ship seemed too busy at first to notice the group of new-comers from Fitzroy Street. Those who seemed to be officers were shouting orders to the men.

They stood and looked across the wide quay to the town that rose beyond it. What they saw was the most beautiful sight any of them had ever seen—or ever dreamed of.

The blue sea sparkled in soft sunlight; little white-capped waves broke softly against the marble breakwaters that guarded the shipping of a great city from the wildness of winter winds and seas. The quay was of marble, white and sparkling with a veining bright as gold. The city was of marble, red and white. The greater buildings that seemed to be temples and places were roofed with what looked like gold and silver, but most of the roofs were of copper that glowed golden-red on the houses on the hills among which the city stood, and shaded into marvellous tints of green and blue and purple where they had been touched by the salt sea spray and the fumes of the dyeing and smelting works of the lower town.

Broad and magnificent flights of marble stairs led up from the quay to a sort of terrace that seemed to run along for miles, and beyond rose the town built on a hill.

The learned gentleman drew a long breath. "Wonderful!" he said, "wonderful!"

"I say, Mr.—what's your name," said Robert.

"He means," said Anthea, with gentle politeness, "that we never can remember your name. I know it's Mr. De Something."

"When I was your age I was called Jimmy," he said timidly. "Would you mind? I should feel more at home in a dream like this if I——Anything that made me seem more like one of you."

"Thank you—Jimmy," said Anthea with an effort. It seemed such cheek to be saying Jimmy to a grown-up man. "Jimmy, *dear*," she added, with no effort at all. Jimmy smiled and looked pleased.

But now the ship was made fast, and the Captain had time

to notice other things. He came towards them, and he was dressed in the best of all possible dresses for the seafaring life.

"What are you doing here?" he asked rather fiercely. "Do you come to bless or to curse?"

"To bless, of course," said Cyril. "I'm sorry if it annoys you, but we're here by magic. We come from the land of the sun-rising," he went on explanatorily.

"I see," said the Captain; no one had expected that he would. "I didn't notice at first, but of course I hope you're a good omen. It's needed. And this," he pointed to the learned gentleman, "your slave, I presume?"

"Not at all," said Anthea; "he's a very great man. A sage, don't they call it? And we want to see all your beautiful city, and your temples and things, and then we shall go back, and he will tell his friend, and his friend will write a book about it."

"What," asked the Captain, fingering a rope, "is a book?"

"A record—something written, or," she added hastily, remembering the Babylonian writing, "or engraved."

Some sudden impulse of confidence made Jane pluck the Amulet from the neck of her frock.

"Like this," she said.

The Captain looked at it curiously, but the other three were relieved to notice, without any of that overwhelming interest which the mere name of it had roused in Egypt and Babylon.

"The stone is of our country," he said; "and that which is engraved on it, it is like our writing, but I cannot read it. What is the name of your sage?"

"Ji—jimmy," said Anthea hesitatingly.

The Captain repeated "Ji—jimmy. Will you land?" he added. "And shall I lead you to the Kings?"

"Look here," said Robert, "does your King hate strangers?"

"Our Kings are ten," said the Captain, "and the Royal line, unbroken from Poseidon, the father of us all, has the noble tradition to do honour to strangers if they come in peace."

"Then lead on, please," said Robert, "though I *should* like to see all over your beautiful ship, and sail about in her."

"That shall be later," said the Captain; "just now we're afraid of a storm—do you notice that odd rumbling?"

"The stone is of our country," he said

"That's nothing, master," said an old sailor who stood near; "it's the pilchards coming in, that's all."

"Too loud," said the Captain.

There was a rather anxious pause; then the Captain stepped on to the quay, and the others followed him.

"Do talk to him—Jimmy," said Anthea as they went; "you can find out all sorts of things for your friend's book."

"Please excuse me," he said earnestly. "If I talk I shall wake up; and besides, I can't understand what he says."

No one else could think of anything to say, so that it was in complete silence that they followed the Captain up the marble steps and through the streets of the town. There were streets and shops and houses and markets.

"It's just like Babylon," whispered Jane, "only everything's perfectly different."

"It's a great comfort the ten Kings have been properly brought up—to be kind to strangers," Anthea whispered to Cyril.

"Yes," he said, "no deepest dungeons here."

There were no horses or chariots in the street, but there were handcarts and low trolleys running on thick log-wheels, and porters carrying packets on their heads, and a good many of the people were riding on what looked like elephants, only the great beasts were hairy, and they had not that mild expression we are accustomed to meet on the faces of the elephants at the Zoo.

"Mammoths!" murmured the learned gentleman, and stumbled over a loose stone.

The people in the streets kept crowding round them as they went along, but the Captain always dispersed the crowd before it grew uncomfortably thick by saying—

"Children of the Sun God and their High Priest—come to bless the City."

And then the people would draw back with a low murmur that sounded like a suppressed cheer.

Many of the buildings were covered with gold, but the gold on the bigger buildings was of a different colour, and they had sorts of steeples of burnished silver rising above them.

"Are all these houses real gold?" asked Jane.

"The temples are covered with gold, of course," answered the Captain, "but the houses are only oricalchum. It's not quite so expensive."

The learned gentleman, now very pale, stumbled along in a dazed way, repeating: —

"Oricalchum—oricalchum."

"Don't be frightened," said Anthea; "we can get home in a minute, just by holding up the charm. Would you rather go back now? We could easily come some other day without you."

"Oh, no, no," he pleaded fervently; "let the dream go on. Please, please do."

"The High Ji—jimmy is perhaps weary with his magic journey," said the Captain, noticing the blundering walk of the learned gentleman; "and we are yet very far from the Great Temple, where to-day the Kings make sacrifice."

He stopped at the gate of a great enclosure. It seemed to be a sort of park, for trees showed high above its brazen wall.

The party waited, and almost at once the Captain came back with one of the hairy elephants and begged them to mount.

This they did.

It was a glorious ride. The elephant at the Zoo—to ride on him is also glorious, but he goes such a very little way, and then he goes back again, which is always dull. But this great hairy beast went on and on and on along streets and through squares and gardens. It was a glorious city; almost everything was built of marble, red, or white, or black. Every now and then the party crossed a bridge.

It was not till they had climbed to the hill which is the centre of the town that they saw that the whole city was divided into twenty circles, alternately land and water, and over each of the water circles were the bridges by which they had come.

And now they were in a great square. A vast building filled up one side of it; it was overlaid with gold, and had a dome of silver. The rest of the buildings round the square were of oricalchum. And it looked more splendid than you can possibly imagine, standing up bold and shining in the sunlight.

It was a glorious ride

"You would like a bath," said the Captain, as the hairy elephant went clumsily down on his knees. "It's customary, you know, before entering the Presence. We have baths for men, women, horses, and cattle. The High Class Baths are here. Our Father Poseidon gave us a spring of hot water and one of cold."

The children had never before bathed in baths of gold.

"It feels very splendid," said Cyril, splashing.

"At least, of course, it's not gold; it's ori—what's its name," said Robert. "Hand over that towel."

The bathing hall had several great pools sunk below the level of the floor; one went down to them by steps.

"Jimmy," said Anthea timidly, when, very clean and boiled looking, they all met in the flowery courtyard of the Public Baths, "don't you think all this seems much more like *now* than Babylon or Egypt——? Oh, I forgot, you've never been there."

"I know a little of those nations, however," said he, "and I quite agree with you. A most discerning remark—my dear," he added awkwardly; "this city certainly seems to indicate a far higher level of civilisation than the Egyptian or Babylonish, and——"

"Follow me," said the Captain. "Now, boys, get out of the way." He pushed through a little crowd of boys who were playing with dried chestnuts fastened to a string.

"Ginger!" remarked Robert, "they're playing conkers, just like the kids in Kentish Town Road!"

They could see now that three walls surrounded the island on which they were. The outer-most wall was of brass, the Captain told them; the next, which looked liked silver, was covered with tin; and the innermost one was of oricalchum.

And right in the middle was a wall of gold, with golden towers and gates.

"Behold the Temples of Poseidon," said the Captain. "It is not lawful for me to enter. I will await your return here."

He told them what they ought to say, and the five people from Fitzroy Street took hands and went forward. The golden gates slowly opened.

"We are the children of the Sun," said Cyril, as he had been told, "and our High Priest, at least that's what the Captain calls him. We have a different name for him at home."

"What is his name?" asked a white-robed man who stood in the doorway with his arms extended.

"Ji—jimmy," replied Cyril, and he hesitated as Anthea had done. It really did seem to be taking a great liberty with so learned a gentleman. "And we have come to speak with your Kings in the Temple of Poseidon—does that word sound right?" he whispered anxiously.

"Quite," said the learned gentleman. "It's very odd I can understand what you say to them, but not what they say to you."

"The Queen of Babylon found that too," said Cyril; "it's part of the magic."

"Oh, what a dream!" said the learned gentleman.

The white-robed priest had been joined by others, and all were bowing low.

"Enter," he said, "enter, Children of the Sun, with your High Ji—jimmy."

In an inner courtyard stood the Temple—all of silver, with gold pinnacles and doors, and twenty enormous statues in bright gold of men and women. Also an immense pillar of the other precious yellow metal.

They went through the doors, and the priest led them up a stair into a gallery from which they could look down on to the glorious place.

"The ten Kings are even now choosing the bull. It is not lawful for me to behold," said the priest, and fell face downward on the floor outside the gallery. The children looked down.

The roof was of ivory adorned with the three precious metals, and the walls were lined with the favourite oricalchum.

At the far end of the Temple was a statue group, the like of which no one living has ever seen.

It was of gold, and the head of the chief figure reached to the roof. That figure was Poseidon, the Father of the City. He stood in a great chariot drawn by six enormous horses, and round about it were a hundred mermaids riding on dolphins.

Ten men, splendidly dressed and armed only with sticks and

"Behold the temple of Poseidon," said the Captain

ropes, were trying to capture one of some fifteen bulls who ran this way and that about the floor of the Temple. The children held their breath, for the bulls looked dangerous, and the great horned heads were swinging more and more wildly.

Anthea did not like looking at the bulls. She looked about the gallery, and noticed that another staircase led up from it to a still higher storey; also that a door led out into the open air, where there seemed to be a balcony.

So that when a shout went up and Robert whispered, "Got him," and she looked down and saw the herd of bulls being driven out of the Temple by whips, and the ten Kings following, one of them spurring with his stick a black bull that writhed and fought in the grip of a lasso, she answered the boy's agitated, "Now we shan't see anything more," with—

"Yes we can, there's an outside balcony."

So they crowded out.

But very soon the girls crept back.

"I don't like sacrifices," Jane said. So she and Anthea went and talked to the priest, who was no longer lying on his face, but sitting on the top step mopping his forehead with his robe, for it was a hot day.

"It's a special sacrifice," he said; "usually it's only done on the justice days every five years and six years alternately. And then they drink the cup of wine with some of the bull's blood in it, and swear to judge truly. And they wear the sacred blue robe, and put out all the Temple fires. But this to-day is because the City's so upset by the odd noises from the sea, and the god inside the big mountain speaking with his thunder-voice. But all that's happened so often before. If anything could make me uneasy it wouldn't be *that*."

"What would it be?" asked Jane kindly.

"It would be the Lemmings."

"Who are they—enemies?"

"They're a sort of rat; and every year they come swimming over from the country that no man knows, and stay here awhile, and then swim away. This year they haven't come. You know rats won't stay on a ship that's going to be wrecked. If anything horrible were going to happen to us, it's my belief those Lemmings would know; and that may be why they've fought shy of us."

"What do you call this country?" asked the Psammead, suddenly putting its head out of its bag.

"Atlantis," said the priest.

"Then I advise you to get on to the highest ground you can find. I remember hearing something about a flood here. Look here, you"—it turned to Anthea; "let's get home. The prospect's too wet for my whiskers."

The girls obediently went to find their brothers, who were leaning on the balcony railings.

"Where's the learned gentleman?" asked Anthea.

"There he is—below," said the priest, who had come with them. "Your High Ji—jimmy is with the Kings."

The ten Kings were no longer alone. The learned gentleman —no one had noticed how he got there—stood with them on the steps of an altar, on which lay the dead body of the black bull. All the rest of the courtyard was thick with people, seemingly of all classes, and all were shouting. "The sea—the sea!"

"Be calm," said the most kingly of the Kings, he who had lassoed the bull. "Our town is strong against the thunders of the sea and of the sky!"

"I want to go home," whined the Psammead.

"We can't go without *him*," said Anthea firmly.

"Jimmy," she called, "Jimmy!" and waved to him. He heard her, and began to come towards her through the crowd.

They could see from the balcony the sea-captain edging his way out from among the people. And his face was dead white, like paper.

"To the hills!" he cried in a loud and terrible voice. And above his voice came another voice, louder, more terrible— the voice of the sea.

The girls looked seaward.

Across the smooth distance of the sea something huge and black rolled towards the town. It was a wave, but a wave a hundred feet in height, a wave that looked like a mountain—a wave rising higher and higher till suddenly it seemed to break in two—one half of it rushed out to sea again; the other—

"Oh!" cried Anthea, "the town—the poor people!"

"It's all thousands of years ago, really," said Robert, but his voice trembled. They hid their eyes for a moment. They could not bear to look down, for the wave had broken on the face of the town, sweeping over the quays and docks, overwhelming the great storehouses and factories, tearing gigantic stones from forts and bridges, and using them as battering rams against the temples. Great ships were swept over the roofs of the houses and dashed down halfway up the hill among ruined gardens and broken buildings. The water ground brown fishing-boats to powder on the golden roofs of Palaces.

Then the wave swept back towards the sea.

"I want to go home," cried the Psammead fiercely.

"Oh, yes, yes!" said Jane, and the boys were ready—but the learned gentleman had not come.

Then suddenly they heard him dash up to the inner gallery, crying—

"I *must* see the end of the dream." He rushed up the higher flight. The others followed him. They found themselves in a sort of turret—roofed, but open to the air at the sides.

The learned gentleman was leaning on the parapet, and as they rejoined him the vast wave rushed back on the town. This time it rose higher—destroyed more.

"Come home," cried the Psammead; "*that's* the *last*, I know it is! That's the last—over there." It pointed with a claw that trembled.

"Oh, come!" cried Jane, holding up the Amulet.

"I *will see* the end of the dream," cried the learned gentleman.

"You'll never see anything else if you do," said Cyril.

"Oh, *Jimmy*!" appealed Anthea. "I'll *never* bring you out again!"

"You'll never have the chance if you don't go soon," said the Psammead.

"I *will* see the end of the dream," said the learned gentleman obstinately.

The hills around were black with people fleeing from the villages to the mountains. And even as they fled thin smoke

They all hid their eyes for a moment

broke from the great white peak, and then a faint flash of
flame. Then the volcano began to throw up its mysterious fiery
inside parts. The earth trembled; ashes and sulphur showered
down; a rain of fine pumice-stone fell like snow on all the dry
land. The elephants from the forests rushed up towards the
peaks; great lizards thirty yards long broke from the mountain
pools and rushed down towards the sea. The snows melted and
rushed down, first in avalanches, then in roaring torrents. Great
rocks cast up by the volcano fell splashing in the sea miles
away.

"Oh, this is horrible!" said Anthea. "Come home, come
home!"

"The end of the dream," gasped the learned gentleman.

"Hold up the Amulet," cried the Psammead suddenly. The
place where they stood was now crowded with men and
women, and the children were strained tight against the parapet. The turret rocked and swayed; the wave had reached the
golden wall.

Jane held up the Amulet.

"Now," cried the Psammead, "say the word!"

And as Jane said it the Psammead leaped from its bag and bit
the hand of the learned gentleman.

At the same moment the boys pushed him through the arch,
and all followed him.

He turned to look back, and through the arch he saw nothing
but a waste of waters, with above it the peak of the terrible
mountain with fire raging from it.

He staggered back to his chair.

"What a ghastly dream!" he gasped. "Oh, you're here, my—
er—dears. Can I do anything for you?"

"You've hurt your hand," said Anthea gently; "let me bind
it up."

The hand was indeed bleeding rather badly.

The Psammead had crept back to its bag. All the children
were very white.

"Never again," said the Psammead later on, "will I go into

the Past with a grown-up person! I will say for **you four, you** do do as you're told."

"We didn't even find the Amulet," said Anthea later still.

"Of course you didn't; it wasn't there. Only the stone it was made of was there. It fell on to a ship miles away that managed to escape and got to Egypt. I could have told you that."

"I wish you had," said Anthea, and her voice was still rather shaky. "Why didn't you?"

"You never asked me," said the Psammead very sulkily. "I'm not the sort of chap to go shoving my oar in where it's not wanted."

"Mr. Ji—jimmy's friend will have something worth having to put in his article now," said Cyril very much later indeed.

"Not he," said Robert sleepily. "The learned Ji—jimmy will think it's a dream, and it's ten to one he never tells the other chap a word about it at all."

Robert was quite right on both points. The learned gentleman did. And he never did.

CHAPTER X

THE LITTLE BLACK GIRL AND
JULIUS CÆSAR

A GREAT city swept away by the sea, a beautiful country
devastated by an active volcano—these are not the sort of
things you see every day of the week. And when you do see
them, no matter how many other wonders you may have seen
in your time, such sights are rather apt to take your breath
away. Atlantis had certainly this effect on the breaths of Cyril,
Robert, Anthea, and Jane.

They remained in a breathless state for some days. The
learned gentleman seemed as breathless as any one; he spent a
good deal of what little breath he had in telling Anthea about
a wonderful dream he had. "You would hardly believe," he
said, "that any one *could* have such a detailed vision."

But Anthea could believe it, she said, quite easily.

He had ceased to talk about thought-transference. He had
now seen too many wonders to believe that.

In consequence of their breathless condition none of the
children suggested any new excursions through the Amulet.
Robert voiced the mood of the others when he said that they
were "fed-up" with Amulet for a bit. They undoubtedly
were.

As for the Psammead, it went to sand and stayed there, worn
out by the terror of the flood and the violent exercise it had
had to take in obedience to the inconsiderate wishes of the
learned gentleman and the Babylonian queen.

The children let it sleep. The danger of taking it about
among strange people who might at any moment utter undesirable wishes was becoming more and more plain.

And there are pleasant things to be done in London without
any aid from Amulets or Psammeads. You can, for instance,
visit the Tower of London, the Houses of Parliament, the

158

National Gallery, the Zoological Gardens, the various Parks, the Musuems at South Kensington, Madame Tussaud's Exhibition of Waxworks, or the Botanical Gardens at Kew. You can go to Kew by a River steamer—and this is the way that the children would have gone if they had gone at all. Only they never did, because it was when they were discussing the arrangements for the journey, and what they should take with them to eat and how much of it, and what the whole thing would cost, that the adventure of the Little Black Girl began to happen.

The children were sitting on a seat in St. James's Park. They had been watching the pelican repulsing with careful dignity the advances of the seagulls who are always so anxious to play games with it. The pelican thinks, very properly, that it hasn't the figure for games, so it spends most of its time pretending that that is not the reason why it won't play.

The breathlessness caused by Atlantis was wearing off a little. Cyril, who always wanted to understand all about everything, was turning things over in his mind.

"I'm not; I'm only thinking," he answered when Robert asked him what he was so grumpy about. "I'll tell you when I've thought it all out."

"If it's about the Amulet I don't want to hear it," said Jane.

"Nobody asked you to," retorted Cyril mildly, "and I haven't finished my inside thinking about it yet. Let's go to Kew in the meantime."

"I'd rather go in a steamer," said Robert; and the girls laughed.

"That's right," said Cyril, "*be* funny. I would."

"Well, he was, rather," said Anthea.

"I wouldn't think, Squirrel, if it hurts you so," said Robert kindly.

"Oh, shut up," said Cyril, "or else talk about Kew."

"I want to see the palms there," said Anthea hastily, "to see if they're anything like the ones on the island where we united the Cook and the Burglar by the Reverend Half-Curate."

"All disagreeableness was swept away in a pleasant tide of

recollections, and "Do you remember . . . ?" they said. "Have you forgotten . . . ?"

"My hat!" remarked Cyril pensively, as the flood of reminiscence ebbed a little; "we have had some times."

"We have that," said Robert.

"Don't let's have any more," said Jane anxiously.

"That's what I was thinking about," Cyril replied; and just then they heard the Little Black Girl sniff. She was quite close to them.

She was not really a little black girl. She was shabby and not very clean, and she had been crying so much that you could hardly see, through the narrow chink between her swollen lids, how very blue her eyes were. It was her dress that was black, and it was too big and too long for her, and she wore a speckled black-ribboned sailor hat that would have fitted a much bigger head than her little flaxen one. And she stood looking at the children and sniffing.

"Oh, dear!" said Anthea, jumping up. "Whatever is the matter?"

She put her hand on the little girl's arm. It was rudely shaken off.

"You leave me be," said the little girl. "I ain't doing nothing to you."

"But what is it?" Anthea asked. "Has someone been hurting you?"

"What's that to you?" said the little girl fiercely. "*You're* all right."

"Come away," said Robert, pulling at Anthea's sleeve. "She's a nasty, rude little kid."

"Oh, no," said Anthea. "She's only dreadfully unhappy. What is it?" she asked again.

"Oh, *you're* all right," the child repeated; "*you* ain't agoin' to the Union."

"Can't we take you home?" said Anthea; and Jane added, "Where does your mother live?"

"She don't live nowheres—she's dead—so now!" said the little girl fiercely, in tones of miserable triumph. Then she opened her swollen eyes widely, stamped her foot in fury, and ran away. She ran no further than to the next bench, flung herself down there and began to cry without even trying not to.

Anthea, quite at once, went to the little girl and put her arms as tight as she could round the hunched-up black figure.

"Oh, don't cry so, dear, don't, don't!" she whispered under the brim of the large sailor hat, now very crooked indeed. "Tell Anthea all about it; Anthea'll help you. There, there, dear, don't cry."

The others stood at a distance. One or two passers-by stared curiously.

The child was now only crying part of the time; the rest of the time she seemed to be talking to Anthea.

Presently Anthea beckoned Cyril.

"It's horrible!" she said in a furious whisper, "her father was a carpenter and he was a steady man, and never touched a drop except on a Saturday, and he came up to London for work, and there wasn't any, and then he died; and her name is Imogen, and she's nine come next November. And now her mother's dead, and she's to stay to-night with Mrs. Shrobsall —that's a landlady that's been kind—and to-morrow the Believing Officer is coming for her, and she's going into the Union; that means the Workhouse. It's too terrible. What can we do?"

"Let's ask the learned gentleman," said Jane brightly.

And as no one else could think of anything better the whole party walked back to Fitzroy Street as fast as it could, the little girl holding tight to Anthea's hand and now not crying any more, only sniffing gently.

The learned gentleman looked up from his writing with the smile that had grown much easier to him than it used to be. They were quite at home in his room now; it really seemed to welcome them. Even the mummy case appeared to smile as if in its distant superior ancient Egyptian way it were rather pleased to see them than not.

Anthea sat on the stairs with Imogen, who was nine come next November, while the others went in and explained the difficulty.

The learned gentleman listened with grave attention.

"It really does seem rather rough luck," Cyril concluded, "because I've often heard about rich people who wanted children most awfully—though I know *I* never should—but they do. There must be somebody who'd be glad to have her."

"Gipsies are awfully fond of children," Robert hopefully said. "They're always stealing them. Perhaps they'd have her."

"She's quite a nice little girl really," Jane added; "she was only rude at first because we looked jolly and happy, and she wasn't. You understand that, don't you?"

"Yes," said he, absently fingering a little blue image from Egypt. "I understand that very well. As you say, there must be some home where she would be welcome." He scowled thoughtfully at the little blue image.

Anthea outside thought the explanation was taking a very long time. She was so busy trying to cheer and comfort the little black girl that she never noticed the Psammead who, roused from sleep by her voice, had shaken itself free of sand, and was coming crookedly up the stairs. It was close to her before she saw it. She picked it up and settled it in her lap.

"What is it?" asked the black child. "Is it a cat or a organ-monkey, or what?"

And then Anthea heard the learned gentleman say—

"Yes, I wish we could find a home where they would be glad to have her," and instantly she felt the Psammead begin to blow itself out as it sat on her lap.

She jumped up lifting the Psammead in her skirt, and holding Imogen by the hand, rushed into the learned gentleman's room.

"At least let's keep together," she cried. "All hold hands—quick!"

The circle was like that formed for the Mulberry Bush or Ring o' Roses. And Anthea was only able to take part in it by holding in her teeth the hem of her frock which, thus supported, formed a bag to hold the Psammead.

"Is it a game?" asked the learned gentleman feebly. No one **answered.**

There was a moment of suspense; then came that curious upside-down, inside-out sensation which one almost always feels when transported from one place to another by magic. Also there was that dizzy dimness of sight which comes on these occasions.

The mist cleared, the upside-down, inside-out sensation subsided, and there stood the six in a ring, as before, only their twelve feet, instead of standing on the carpet of the learned gentleman's room, stood on green grass. Above them, instead of the dusky ceiling of the Fitzroy Street top floor, was a pale blue sky. And where the walls had been and the painted mummy-case, were tall dark green trees, oaks and ashes, and in between the trees and under them tangled bushes and creeping ivy. There were beech-trees too, but there was nothing under them but their own dead red drifted leaves, and here and there a delicate green fern-frond.

And there they stood in a circle still holding hands, as though they were playing Ring o' Roses or the Mulberry Bush. Just six people hand in hand in a wood. That sounds simple, but then you must remember that they did not know *where* the wood was; and what's more they didn't know *when* the wood was. There was a curious sort of feeling that made the learned gentleman say—

"Another dream, dear me!" and made the children almost certain that they were in a time a very long while ago. As for little Imogen, she said, "Oh, my!" and kept her mouth very much open indeed.

"Where are we?" Cyril asked the Psammead.

"In Britain," said the Psammead.

"But when?" asked Anthea anxiously.

"About the year fifty-five before the year you reckon time from," said the Psammead crossly. "Is there anything else you want to know?" It added, sticking its head out of the bag formed by Anthea's blue linen frock, and turning it's snail's eyes to right and left. "I've been here before—it's very little changed."

"Yes, but why here?" asked Anthea.

"Your inconsiderate friend," the Psammead replied, "wished

to find some home where they would be glad to have that unattractive and immature female human being whom you have picked up—gracious knows how. In Megatherium days properly brought-up children didn't talk to shabby strangers in parks. Your thoughtless friend wanted a place where some one would be glad to have this undesirable stranger. And now here you are!"

"I see we are," said Anthea patiently, looking round on the tall gloom of the forest. "But why *here?* why *now?*"

"You don't suppose any one would want a child like that in *your* times—in *your* towns?" said the Psammead in irritated tones. "You've got your country into such a mess that there's no room for half your children—and no one to want them."

"That's not our doing, you know," said Anthea gently.

"And bringing me here without any waterproof or anything," said the Psammead still more crossly, "when every one knows how damp and foggy Ancient Britain was."

"Here, take my coat," said Robert, taking it off. Anthea spread the coat on the ground and, putting the Psammead on it, folded it round so that only the long eyes and furry ears showed.

"There," she said comfortingly. "Now if it does begin to look like rain, I can cover you up in a minute. Now what are we to do?"

The others who had stopped holding hands crowded round to hear the answer to this question. Imogen whispered in an awed tone—

"Can't the organ monkey talk neither! I thought it was only parrots!"

"Do?" replied the Psammead. "I don't care what you do!" And it drew head and ears into the tweed covering of Robert's coat.

The others looked at each other.

"It's only a dream," said the learned gentleman hopefully; "something is sure to happen if we can prevent ourselves from waking up."

And sure enough, something did.

Anthea spread the coat on the ground, and putting the Psammead on it, folded it round

The brooding silence of the dark forest was broken by the laughter of children and the sound of voices.

"Let's go and see," said Cyril.

"It's only a dream," said the learned gentleman to Jane, who hung back; "if you don't go with the tide of a dream—if you resist—you wake up, you know."

There was a sort of break in the undergrowth that was like a silly person's idea of a path. They went along this in Indian file, the learned gentleman leading.

Quite soon they came to a large clearing in the forest. There were a number of houses—huts perhaps you would have called them—with a sort of mud and wood fence.

"It's like the old Egyptian town," whispered Anthea.

And it was, rather.

Some children, with no clothes on at all, were playing what looked like Ring o' Roses or Mulberry Bush. That is to say, they were dancing round in a ring, holding hands. On a grassy bank several women, dressed in blue and white robes and tunics of beast-skins sat watching the playing children.

The children from Fitzroy Street stood on the fringe of the forest looking at the games. One woman with long, fair braided hair sat a little apart from the others, and there was a look in her eyes as she followed the play of the children that made Anthea feel sad and sorry.

"None of those little girls is her own little girl," thought Anthea.

The little black-clad London child pulled at Anthea's sleeve.

"Look," she said, "that one there—she's precious like mother; mother's 'air was somethink lovely, when she 'ad time to comb it out. Mother wouldn't never a-beat me if she'd lived 'ere—I don't suppose there's e'er a public nearer than Epping, do you, Miss?"

In her eagerness the child had stepped out of the shelter of the forest. The sad-eyed woman saw her. She stood up, her thin face lighted up with a radiance like sunrise, her long, lean arms stretched towards the London child.

"Imogen!" she cried—at least the word was more like that than any other word—"Imogen!"

There was a moment of great silence; the naked children paused in their play, the women on the bank stared anxiously.

"Oh, it *is* mother—it *is*!" cried Imogen-from-London, and rushed across the cleared space. She and her mother clung together—so closely, so strongly that they stood an instant like a statue carved in stone.

Then the women crowded round.

"It *is* my Imogen!" cried the woman. "Oh it is! And she wasn't eaten by wolves. She's come back to me. Tell me, my darling, how did you escape? Where have you been? Who has fed and clothed you?"

"I don't know nothink," said Imogen.

"Poor child!" whispered the women who crowded round, "the terror of the wolves has turned her brain."

"But you know *me*?" said the fair-haired woman.

And Imogen, clinging with black-clothed arms to the bare neck, answered—

"Oh, yes, mother, I know *you* right 'nough."

"What is it? What do they say?" the learned gentleman asked anxiously.

"You wished to come where someone wanted the child," said the Psammead. "The child says this is her mother."

"And the mother?"

"You can see," said the Psammead.

"But is she really? Her child, I mean?"

"Who knows?" said the Psammead; "but each one fills the empty place in the other's heart. It is enough."

"Oh," said the learned gentleman, "this is a good dream. I wish the child might stay in the dream."

The Psammead blew itself out and granted the wish. So Imogen's future was assured. She had found some one to want her.

"If only all the children that no one wants," began the learned gentleman—but the woman interrupted. She came towards them.

"Welcome, all!" she cried. "I am the Queen, and my child tells me that you have befriended her; and this I well believe, looking on your faces. Your garb is strange, but faces I can

"Oh, it is Mother—it is!" cried Imogen-from-London

read. The child is bewitched, I see that well, but in this she speaks truth. Is it not so?"

The children said it wasn't worth mentioning.

I wish you could have seen all the honours and kindnesses lavished on the children and the learned gentleman by those ancient Britons. You would have thought, to see them, that a child was something to make a fuss about, not a bit of rubbish to be hustled about the streets and hidden away in the work-house. It wasn't as grand as the entertainment at Babylon, but somehow it was more satisfying.

"I think you children have some wonderful influence on me," said the learned gentleman. "I never dreamed such dreams before I knew you."

It was when they were alone that night under the stars where the Britons had spread a heap of dried fern for them to sleep on, that Cyril spoke.

"Well," he said, "we've made it all right for Imogen, and had a jolly good time. I vote we get home again before the fighting begins."

"What fighting?" asked Jane sleepily.

"Why, Julius Cæsar, you little goat," replied her kind brother. "Don't you see that if this is the year fifty-five, Julius Cæsar may happen at any moment."

"I thought you liked Cæsar," said Robert.

"So I do—in the history. But that's different from being killed by his soldiers."

"If we saw Cæsar we might persuade him not to," said Anthea.

"*You* persuade *Cæsar*," Robert laughed.

The learned gentleman, before any one could stop him, said, "I only wish we could see Cæsar some time."

And, of course, in just the little time the Psammead took to blow itself out for wish-giving, the five, or six counting the Psammead, found themselves in Cæsar's camp, just outside Cæsar's tent. And they saw Cæsar. The Psammead must have taken advantage of the loose wording of the learned gentle-man's wish, for it was not the same time of day as that on which the wish had been uttered among the dried ferns. It was

Julius Cæsar sat on a chair outside his tent

sunset, and the great man sat on a chair outside his tent gazing over the sea towards Britain—every one knew without being told that it was towards Britain. Two golden eagles on the top of posts stood on each side of the tent, and on the flaps of the tent which was very gorgeous to look at were the letters S.P.Q.R.

The great man turned unchanged on the newcomers the august glance that he had turned on the violet waters of the Channel. Though they had suddenly appeared out of nothing, Cæsar never showed by the faintest movement of an eyelid, by the least tightening of that firm mouth, that they were not some long expected embassy. He waved a calm hand towards the sentinels, who sprang weapons in hand towards the newcomers.

"Back!" he said in a voice that thrilled like music. "Since when has Cæsar feared children and students?"

To the children he seemed to speak in the only language they knew; but the learned gentleman heard—in rather a strange accent, but quite intelligibly—the lips of Cæsar speaking in the Latin tongue, and in that tongue, a little stiffly he answered—

"It is a dream, O Cæsar."

"A dream?" repeated Cæsar. "What is a dream?"

"This," said the learned gentleman.

"Not it," said Cyril, "it's a sort of magic. We come out of another time and another place."

"And we want to ask you not to trouble about conquering Britain," said Anthea; "it's a poor little place, not worth bothering about."

"Are you from Britain?" the General asked. "Your clothes are uncouth, but well woven, and your hair is short as the hair of Roman citizens, not long like the hair of barbarians, yet such I deem you to be."

"We're not," said Jane with angry eagerness; "we're not barbarians at all. We come from the country where the sun never sets, and we've read about you in books; and our country's full of fine things—St. Paul's, and the Tower of London, and Madame Tussaud's Exhibition, and——"

Then the others stopped her.

"Don't talk nonsense," said Robert in a bitter undertone.

Cæsar looked at the children a moment in silence. Then he called a soldier and spoke with him apart. Then he said aloud—

"You three elder children may go where you will within the camp. Few children are privileged to see the camp of Cæsar. The student and the smaller girl-child will remain here with me."

Nobody liked this; but when Cæsar said a thing that thing was so, and there was an end of it. So the three went.

Left alone with Jane and the learned gentleman, the great Roman found it easy enough to turn them inside out. But it was not so easy, even for him, to make head or tail of the insides of their minds when he had got at them.

The learned gentleman insisted that the whole thing was a dream, and refused to talk much, on the ground that if he did he would wake up.

Jane, closely questioned, was full of information about railways, electric lights, balloons, men-of-war, cannons, and dynamite.

"And do they fight with swords?" asked the General.

"Yes, swords and guns and cannons."

Cæsar wanted to know what guns were.

"You fire them," said Jane, "and they go bang, and people fall down dead."

"But what are guns like?"

Jane found them hard to describe.

"But Robert has a toy one in his pocket," she said. So the others were recalled.

The boys explained the pistol to Cæsar very fully, and he looked at it with the greatest interest. It was a two-shilling pistol, the one that had done such good service in the old Egyptian village.

"I shall cause guns to be made," said Cæsar, "and you will be detained till I know whether you have spoken the truth. I had just decided that Britain was not worth the bother of invading. But what you tell me decides me that it is very much worth while."

They explained the gun to Cæsar very fully

"But it's all nonsense," said Anthea. "Britain is just a savage sort of island—all fogs and trees and big rivers. But the people are kind. We know a little girl there named Imogen. And it's no use your making guns because you can't fire them without gunpowder, and that won't be invented for hundreds of years, and we don't know how to make it, and we can't tell you. Do go straight home, dear Cæsar, and let poor little Britain alone."

"But this other girl-child says——" said Cæsar.

"All Jane's been telling you is what it's going to be," Anthea interrupted, "hundreds and hundreds of years from now."

"The little one is a prophetess, eh?" said Cæsar, with a whimsical look. "Rather young for the business, isn't she?"

"You can call her a prophetess if you like," said Cyril, "but what Anthea says is true."

"Anthea?" said Cæsar. "That's a Greek name."

"Very likely," said Cyril, worriedly. "I say, I do wish you'd give up this idea of conquering Britain. It's not worth while, really it isn't!"

"On the contrary," said Cæsar, "what you've told me has decided me to go, if it's only to find out what Britain is really like. Guards, detain these children."

"Quick," said Robert, "before the guards begin detaining. We had enough of that in Babylon."

Jane held up the Amulet away from the sunset, and said the word. The learned gentleman was pushed through and the others more quickly than ever before passed through the arch back into their own times and the quiet dusty sitting-room of the learned gentleman.

It is a curious fact that when Cæsar was encamped on the coast of Gaul—somewhere near Boulogne it was, I believe— he was sitting before his tent in the glow of the sunset, looking out over the violet waters of the English Channel. Suddenly he started, rubbed his eyes, and called his secretary. The young man came quickly from within the tent.

"Marcus," said Cæsar, "I have dreamed a very wonderful dream. Some of it I forget, but I remember enough to decide what was not before determined. To-morrow the ships that have been brought round from the Ligeris shall be provisioned. We shall sail for this three-cornered island. First, we will take out two legions. This, if what we have heard be true, should suffice. But if my dream be true, then a hundred legions will not suffice. For the dream I dreamed was the most wonderful that ever tormented the brain even of Cæsar. And Cæsar has dreamed some strange things in his time."

"And if you hadn't told Cæsar all that about how things are now, he'd never have invaded Britain," said Robert to Jane as they sat down to tea.

"Oh, nonsense," said Anthea, pouring out; "it was all settled hundreds of years ago."

"I don't know," said Cyril. "Jam, please. This about time being only a thingummy of thought is very confusing. If everything happens at the same time——"

"It *can't*!" said Anthea stoutly, "the present's the present and the past's the past."

"Not always," said Cyril.

"When we were in the Past the present was the future. Now then!" he added triumphantly.

And Anthea could not deny it.

"I should have liked to see more of the camp," said Robert.

"Yes, we didn't get much for our money—but Imogen is happy, that's one thing," said Anthea. "We left her happy in the Past. I've often seen about people being happy in the Past, in poetry books. I see what it means now."

"It's not a bad idea," said the Psammead sleepily, putting its head out of its bag and taking it in again suddenly, "being left in the Past."

Every one remembered this afterwards, when——

CHAPTER XI

BEFORE PHARAOH

I T W A S T H E day after the adventure of Julius Cæsar and the Little Black Girl that Cyril, bursting into the bathroom to wash his hands for dinner (you have no idea how dirty they were, for he had been playing shipwrecked mariners all the morning on the leads at the back of the house, where the water-cistern is), found Anthea leaning her elbows on the edge of the bath, and crying steadily into it.

"Hullo!" he said, with brotherly concern, "what's up now? Dinner'll be cold before you've got enough salt-water for a bath."

"Go away," said Anthea fiercely. "I hate you! I hate everybody!"

There was a stricken pause.

"*I* didn't know," said Cyril tamely.

"Nobody ever does know anything," sobbed Anthea.

"I didn't know you were waxy. I thought you'd just hurt your fingers with the tap again like you did last week," Cyril carefully explained.

"Oh—fingers!" sneered Anthea through her sniffs.

"Here, drop it, Panther," he said uncomfortably. "You haven't been having a row or anything?"

"No," she said. "Wash your horrid hands, for goodness' sake, if that's what you came for, or go."

Anthea was so seldom cross that when she was cross the others were always more surprised than angry.

Cyril edged along the side of the bath and stood beside her. He put his hand on her arm.

"Dry up, do," he said, rather tenderly for him. And, finding that though she did not at once take his advice she did not seem to resent it, he put his arm awkwardly across her shoulders and rubbed his head against her ear.

"There!" he said, in the tone of one administering a price-less cure for all possible sorrows. "Now, what's up?"

"Promise you won't laugh?"

"I don't feel laughish myself," said Cyril, dismally.

"Well, then," said Anthea, leaning her ear against his head, "it's Mother."

"What's the matter with Mother?" asked Cyril, with apparent want of sympathy. "She was all right in her letter this morning."

"Yes; but I want her so."

"You're not the only one," said Cyril briefly, and the brevity of his tone admitted a good deal.

"Oh, yes," said Anthea, "I know. We all want her all the time. But I want her now most dreadfully, awfully much. I never wanted anything so much. That Imogen child—the way the ancient British Queen cuddled her up! And Imogen wasn't me, and the Queen was Mother. And then her letter this morning! And about The Lamb liking the salt bathing! And she bathed him in this very bath the night before she went away —oh, oh, oh!"

Cyril thumped her on the back.

"Cheer up," he said. "You know my inside thinking that I was doing? Well, that was partly about Mother. We'll soon get her back. If you'll chuck it, like a sensible kid, and wash your face. I'll tell you about it. That's right. You let me get to the tap. Can't you stop crying? Shall I put the door-key down your back?"

"That's for noses," said Anthea, "and I'm not a kid any more than you are," but she laughed a little, and her mouth began to get back into its proper shape. You know what an odd shape your mouth gets into when you cry in earnest.

"Look here," said Cyril, working the soap round and round between his hands in a thick slime of gray soapsuds. "I've been thinking. We've only just *played* with the Amulet so far. We've got to *work* it now—work it for all it's worth. And it isn't only Mother either. There's Father out there all among the fighting. *I* don't howl about it, but I *think*—— Oh, bother the soap!" The gray-lined soap had squirted out under the pressure of his fingers, and had hit Anthea's chin with as much force as though it had been shot from a catapult.

"There now," she said regretfully, "now I shall have to wash my face."

"You'd have had to do that any way," said Cyril with conviction. "Now, my idea's this. You know missionaries?"

"Yes," said Anthea, who did not know a single one.

"Well, they always take the savages beads and brandy, and stays, and hats, and braces, and really useful things—things the savages haven't got, and never heard about. And the savages love them for their kind generousness, and give them pearls, and shells, and ivory, and cassowaries. And that's the way——"

"Wait a sec," said Anthea, splashing. "I can't hear what you're saying. Shells and——"

"Shells, and things like that. The great thing is to get people to love you by being generous. And that's what we've got to do. Next time we go into the Past we'll regularly fit out the expedition. You remember how the Babylonian Queen froze on to that pocket-book? Well, we'll take things like that. And offer them in exchange for a sight of the Amulet."

"A sight of it's not much good."

"No, silly. But, don't you see, when we've seen it we shall know where it is, and we can go and take it in the night when everybody is asleep."

"It wouldn't be stealing, would it?" said Anthea thoughtfully, "because it will be such an awfully long time ago when we do it. Oh, there's that bell again."

As soon as dinner was eaten (it was tinned salmon and lettuce, and a jam tart), and the cloth cleared away, the idea was explained to the others, and the Psammead was aroused from sand, and asked what it thought would be good merchandise with which to buy the affection of say, the Ancient Egyptians, and whether it thought the Amulet was likely to be found in the Court of Pharaoh.

But it shook its head, and shot out its snail's eyes hopelessly.

"I'm not allowed to play in this game," it said. "Of course I *could* find out in a minute where the thing was, only I mayn't.

But I may go so far as to own that your idea of taking things with you isn't a bad one. And I shouldn't show them all at once. Take small things and conceal them craftily about your persons."

This advice seemed good. Soon the table was littered over with things which the children thought likely to interest the Ancient Egyptians. Anthea brought dolls, puzzle blocks, a wooden tea-service, a green leather case with *Nécessaire* written on it in gold letters. Aunt Emma had once given it to Anthea, and it had then contained scissors, penknife, bodkin, stiletto, thimble, corkscrew, and glove-buttoner. The scissors, knife, and thimble, and penknife were, of course, lost, but the other things were there and as good as new. Cyril contributed lead soldiers, a cannon, a catapult, a tin-opener, a tie-clip, and a tennis-ball, and a padlock—no key. Robert collected a candle ("I don't suppose they ever saw a self-fitting paraffin one," he said), a penny Japanese pin-tray, a rubbery stamp with his father's name and address on it, and a piece of putty.

Jane added a key-ring, the brass handle of a poker, a pot that had held cold-cream, a smoked pearl button off her winter coat, and a key—no lock.

"We can't take all this rubbish," said Robert, with some scorn. "We must just each choose one thing."

The afternoon passed very agreeably in the attempt to choose from the table the four most suitable objects. But the four children could not agree what was suitable, and at last Cyril said—

"Look here, let's each be blindfolded and reach out, and the first thing you touch you stick to."

This was done.

Cyril touched the padlock.

Anthea got the *Nécessaire*.

Robert clutched the candle.

Jane picked up the tie-clip.

"It's not much," she said. "I don't believe Ancient Egyptians wore ties."

"Never mind," said Anthea. "I believe it's luckier not to really choose. In the stories it's always the thing the woodcutter's son picks up in the forest, and almost throws away because he thinks it's no good, that turns out to be the magic thing in the end; or else someone's lost it, and he is rewarded with the hand of the King's daughter in marriage."

"I don't want any hands in marriage, thank you," said Cyril firmly.

"Nor yet me," said Robert. "It's always the end of the adventures when it comes to the marriage hands."

"*Are* we ready?" said Anthea.

"It *is* Egypt we're going to, isn't it?—nice Egypt?" said Jane. "I won't go anywhere I don't know about—like that dreadful big-wavy burning-mountain city," she insisted.

Then the Psammead was coaxed into its bag.

"I say," said Cyril suddenly, "I'm rather sick of kings. And people notice you so in palaces. Besides the Amulet's sure to be in a Temple. Let's just go among the common people, and try to work ourselves up by degrees. We might get taken on as Temple assistants."

"Like beadles," said Anthea, "or vergers. They must have splendid chances of stealing the Temple treasures."

"Righto!" was the general rejoinder. The charm was held up. It grew big once again, and once again the warm golden Eastern light glowed softly beyond it.

As the children stepped through it loud and furious voices rang in their ears. They went suddenly from the quiet of Fitz-roy Street dining-room into a very angry Eastern crowd, a crowd much too angry to notice them. They edged through it to the wall of a house and stood there. The crowd was of men, women, and children. They were of all sorts of com-plexions, and pictures of them might have been coloured by any child with a shilling paint-box. The colours that child would have used for complexions would have been yellow ochre, red ochre, light red, sepia, and indian ink. But their faces were painted already—black eyebrows and lashes, and some red lips. The women wore a sort of pinafore with shoulder straps, and loose things wound round their heads and shoulders. The men wore very little clothing—for they were the working people—and the Egyptian boys and girls wore nothing at all, unless you count the little ornaments hung on chains round their necks and waists. The children saw all this before they could hear anything distinctly. Everyone was shouting so.

But a voice sounded above the other voices, and presently it was speaking in a silence.

"Comrades and fellow workers," it said, and it was the voice of a tall, coppery-coloured man who had climbed into a chariot that had been stopped by the crowd. Its owner had bolted, muttering something about calling the Guards, and now the man spoke from it. "Comrades and fellow workers, how long are we to endure the tyranny of our masters, who live in idleness and luxury on the fruit of our toil? They only give us a bare subsistence wage, and they live on the fat of the land. We labour all our lives to keep them in wanton luxury. Let us make an end of it!"

A roar of applause answered him.

"How are you going to do it?" cried a voice.

"You look out," cried another, "or you'll get yourself into trouble."

"I've heard almost every single word of that," whispered Robert, "in Hyde Park last Sunday!"

"Let us strike for more bread and onions and beer, and a longer mid-day rest," the speaker went on. "You are tired, you are hungry, you are thirsty. You are poor, your wives and children are pining for food. The barns of the rich are full to bursting with the corn we want, the corn our labour has grown. To the granaries!"

"To the granaries!" cried half the crowd; but another voice shouted clear above the tumult, "To Pharaoh! To the King! Let's present a petition to the King! He will listen to the voice of the oppressed!"

For a moment the crowd swayed one way and another—first towards the granaries and then towards the palace. Then, with a rush like that of an imprisoned torrent suddenly set free, it surged along the street towards the palace, and the children were carried with it. Anthea found it difficult to keep the Psammead from being squeezed very uncomfortably.

The crowd swept through the streets of dull-looking houses

"Let us strike for more bread and onions and beer"

with few windows, very high up, across the market where
people were not buying but exchanging goods. In a momentary
pause Robert saw a basket of onions exchanged for a hair comb
and five fish for a string of beads. The people in the market

seemed better off than those in the crowd; they had finer clothes, and more of them. They were the kind of people who, nowadays, would have lived at Brixton or Brockley.

"What's the trouble now?" a languid, large-eyed lady in a crimped, half-transparent linen dress, with her black hair very much braided and puffed out, asked of a date-seller.

"Oh, the working-men—discontented as usual," the man answered. "Listen to them. Any one would think it mattered whether they had a little more or less to eat. Dregs of society!" said the date-seller.

"Scum!" said the lady.

"And I've heard *that* before, too," said Robert.

At that moment the voice of the crowd changed, from anger to doubt, from doubt to fear. There were other voices shouting; they shouted defiance and menace, and they came nearer very quickly. There was the rattle of wheels and the pounding of hoofs. A voice shouted, "Guards!"

"The Guards! The Guards!" shouted another voice, and the crowd of workmen took up the cry. "The Guards! Pharaoh's Guards!" And swaying a little once more, the crowd hung for a moment as it were balanced. Then as the trampling hoofs came nearer the workmen fled dispersed, up alleys and into the courts of houses, and the Guards in their embossed leather chariots swept down the street at the gallop, their wheels clattering over the stones, and their dark-coloured, blue tunics blown open and back with the wind of their going.

"So *that* riot's over," said the crimped-linen-dressed lady; "that's a blessing! And did you notice the Captain of the Guard? What a very handsome man he was, to be sure!"

The four children had taken advantage of the moment's pause before the crowd turned to fly to edge themselves and drag each other into an arched doorway.

Now they each drew a long breath and looked at the others.

"We're well out of *that*," said Cyril.

"Yes," said Anthea, "but I do wish the poor men hadn't been driven back before they could get to the King. He might have done something for them."

"Not if he was the one in the Bible he wouldn't," said Jane. "He had a hard heart."

"Ah, that was the Moses one," Anthea explained. "The Joseph one was quite different. I should like to see Pharaoh's house. I wonder whether it's like the Egyptian Court in the Crystal Palace."

"I thought we decided to try to get taken on in a Temple," said Cyril in injured tones.

"Yes, but we've got to know someone first. Couldn't we make friends with a Temple doorkeeper—we might give him the padlock or something. I wonder which are temples and which are palaces," Robert added, glancing across the market-place to where an enormous gateway with huge side buildings towered towards the sky. To right and left of it were other buildings only a little less magnificent.

"Did you wish to seek out the Temple of Amen Rā?" asked a soft voice behind them, "or the Temple of Mut, or the Temple of Khonsu?"

They turned to find beside them a young man. He was shaved clean from head to foot, and on his feet were light papyrus sandals. He was clothed in a linen tunic of white, embroidered heavily in colours. He was gay with anklets, bracelets, and armlets of gold, richly inlaid. He wore a ring on his finger, and he had a short jacket of gold embroidery something like the Zouave soldiers wear, and on his neck was a gold collar with many amulets hanging from it. But among the amulets the children could see none like theirs.

"It doesn't matter which Temple," said Cyril frankly.

"Tell me your mission," said the young man. "I am a divine father of the Temple of Amen Rā and perhaps I can help you."

"Well," said Cyril, "we've come from the great Empire on which the sun never sets."

"I thought somehow that you'd come from some odd, out-of-the-way spot," said the priest with courtesy.

"And we've seen a good many palaces. We thought we should like to see a Temple, for a change," said Robert.

The Psammead stirred uneasily in its embroidered bag.

"Have you brought gifts to the Temple?" asked the priest cautiously.

"We *have* got some gifts," said Cyril with equal caution. "You see there's magic mixed up in it. So we can't tell you everything. But we don't want to give our gifts for nothing."

"Beware how you insult the god," said the priest sternly. "I also can do magic. I can make a waxen image of you, and I can say words which, as the wax image melts before the fire, will make you dwindle away and at last perish miserably."

"Pooh!" said Cyril stoutly, "that's nothing I can make *fire* itself!"

"I should jolly well like to see you do it," said the priest unbelievingly.

"Well, you shall," said Cyril, "nothing easier. Just stand close round me."

"Do you need no preparation—no fasting, no incantations?" The priest's tone was incredulous.

"The incantation's quite short," said Cyril, taking the hint; "and as for fasting, it's not needed in my sort of magic. Union Jack, Printing Press, Gunpowder, Rule Britannia! Come, Fire, at the end of this little stick!"

He had pulled a match from his pocket, and as he ended the incantation which contained no words that it seemed likely the Egyptian had ever heard he stooped in the little crowd of his relations and the priest and struck the match on his boot. He stood up, shielding the flame with one hand.

"See?" he said, with modest pride. "Here, take it into your hand."

"No, thank you," said the priest, swiftly backing. "Can you do that again?"

"Yes."

"Then come with me to the great double house of Pharaoh. He loves good magic, and he will raise you to honour and glory. There's no need of secrets between initiates," he went on confidentially. "The fact is, I am out of favour at present owing to a little matter of failure of prophecy. I told him a beautiful princess would be sent to him from Syria, and, lo! a woman thirty years old arrived. But she *was* a beautiful woman not so long ago. Time is only a mode of thought, you know."

The children thrilled to the familiar words.

"So you know that too, do you?" said Cyril.

"It is part of the mystery of all magic, is it not?" said the priest. "Now if I bring you to Pharaoh the little unpleasantness I spoke of will be forgotten. And I will ask Pharaoh, the Great House, Son of the Sun, and Lord of the South and North, to decree that you shall lodge in the Temple. Then you can have a good look round, and teach me your magic. And I will teach you mine."

This idea seemed good—at least it was better than any other which at that moment occurred to anybody, so they followed the priest through the city.

The streets were very narrow and dirty. The best houses, the priest explained, were built within walls twenty to twenty-five feet high, and such windows as showed in the walls were very high up. The tops of palm-trees showed above the walls. The poor people's houses were little square huts with a door and two windows, and smoke coming out of a hole in the back.

"The poor Egyptians haven't improved so very much in their building since the first time we came to Egypt" whispered Cyril to Anthea.

The huts were roofed with palm branches, and everywhere there were chickens, and goats, and little naked children kicking about in the yellow dust. On one roof was a goat, who had climbed up and was eating the dry palm-leaves with snorts and head-tossings of delight. Over every house door was some sort of figure or shape.

"Amulets," the priest explained, "to keep off the evil eye."

"I don't think much of your 'nice Egypt,'" Robert whispered to Jane; "it's simply not a patch on Babylon."

"Ah, you wait till you see the palace," Jane whispered back.

The palace was indeed much more magnificent than anything they had yet seen that day, though it would have made but a poor show beside that of the Babylonian King. They came to it through a great square pillared doorway of sandstone that stood in a high brick wall. The shut doors were of massive cedar, with bronze hinges, and were studded with bronze nails.

at the side was a little door and a wicket gate, and through this the priest led the children. He seemed to know a word that made the sentries make way for him.

Inside was a garden, planted with hundreds of different kinds of trees and flowering shrubs, a lake full of fish, with blue lotus flowers at the margin, and ducks swimming about cheerfully, and looking, as Jane said, quite modern.

"The guard-chamber, the store-houses, the Queen's house," said the priest, pointing them out.

They passed through open courtyards, paved with flat stones, and the priest whispered to a guard at a great inner gate.

"We are fortunate," he said to the children, "Pharaoh is even now in the Court of Honour. Now, don't forget to be overcome with respect and admiration. It won't do any harm if you fall flat on your faces. And whatever you do don't speak until you're spoken to."

"There used to be that rule in our country," said Robert, "when my father was a little boy."

At the outer end of the great hall a crowd of people were arguing with and even shoving the Guards, who seemed to make it a rule not to let anyone through unless they were bribed to do it. The children heard several promises of the utmost richness, and wondered whether they would ever be kept.

All round the hall were pillars of painted wood. The roof was of cedar, gorgeously inlaid. About half-way up the hall was a wide, shallow step that went right across the hall; then a little farther on another; and then a steep flight of narrower steps, leading right up to the throne on which Pharaoh sat. He sat there very splendid, his red and white double crown on his head, and his sceptre in his hand. The throne had a canopy of wood and wooden pillars painted in bright colours. On a low, broad bench that ran all round the hall sat the friends, relatives, and courtiers of the King, leaning on richly-covered cushions.

The priest led the children up the steps till they all stood before the throne; and then, suddenly, he fell on his face with hands outstretched. The others did the same, Anthea falling very carefully because of the Psammead.

"Raise them," said the voice of Pharaoh, "that they may speak to me."

The officers of the King's household raised them.

"Who are these strangers?" Pharaoh asked, and added very crossly, "And what do you mean, Rekh-marā, by daring to come into my presence while your innocence is not established?"

"Oh, great King," said the young priest, "you are the very image of Rā, and the likeness of his son Horus in every respect. You know the thoughts of the hearts of the gods and of men, and you have divined that these strangers are the children of the children of the vile and conquered Kings of the Empire where the sun never sets. They know a magic not known to the Egyptians. And they come with gifts in their hands as tribute to Pharaoh, in whose heart is the wisdom of the gods, and on his lips their truth."

"That is all very well," said Pharaoh, "but where are the gifts?"

The children, bowing as well as they could in their embarrassment at finding themselves the centre of interest in a circle more grand, more golden and more highly coloured than they could have imagined possible, pulled out the padlock, the *Nécessaire,* and the tie-clip. "But it's not tribute all the same," Cyril muttered. "England doesn't pay tribute!"

Pharaoh examined all the things with great interest when the chief of the household had taken them up to him. "Deliver them to the Keeper of the Treasury," he said to one near him. And to the children he said—

"A small tribute, truly, but strange, and not without worth. And the magic, O Rekh-marā?"

"These unworthy sons of a conquered nation . . ." began Rekh-marā.

"Nothing of the kind!" Cyril whispered angrily.

". . . of a vile and conquered nation, can make fire to spring from dry wood—in the sight of all."

"I should jolly well like to see them do it," said Pharaoh, just as the priest had done.

So Cyril, without more ado, did it.

Pharaoh examined all the things with great interest

"Do more magic," said the King, with simple appreciation.

"He cannot do any more magic," said Anthea suddenly, and all eyes were turned on her, "because of the voice of the free people who are shouting for bread and onions and beer and a long mid-day rest. If the people had what they wanted, he could do more."

"A rude-spoken girl," said Pharaoh. "But give the dogs what they want," he said, without turning his head. "Let them have their rest and their extra rations. There are plenty of slaves to work."

A richly-dressed official hurried out.

"You will be the idol of the people," Rekh-marā whispered joyously; "the Temple of Amen will not contain their offerings."

Cyril struck another match, and all the court was overwhelmed with delight and wonder. And when Cyril took the candle from his pocket and lighted it with the match, and then held the burning candle up before the King the enthusiasm knew no bounds.

"Oh, greatest of all, before whom sun and moon and stars bow down," said Rekh-marā insinuatingly, "am I pardoned? Is my innocence made plain?"

"As plain as it ever will be, I daresay," said Pharaoh shortly. "Get along with you. You are pardoned. Go in peace." The priest went with lightning swiftness.

"And what," said the King suddenly, "is it that moves in that sack? Show me, oh strangers."

There was nothing for it but to show the Psammead.

"Seize it," said Pharaoh carelessly. "A very curious monkey. It will be a nice little novelty for my wild beast collection."

And instantly, the entreaties of the children availing as little as the bites of the Psammead, though both bites and entreaties were fervent, it was carried away from before their eyes.

"Oh, do be careful!" cried Anthea. "At least keep it dry! Keep it in its sacred house!"

She held up the embroidered bag.

"It's a magic creature," cried Robert; "it's simply priceless!"

"You've no right to take it away," cried Jane incautiously. "It's a shame, a barefaced robbery, that's what it is!"

There was an awful silence. Then Pharaoh spoke.

"Take the sacred house of the beast from them," he said, "and imprison all. To-night after supper it may be our pleasure to see more magic. Guard them well, and do not torture them—yet!"

"Oh, dear!" sobbed Jane, as they were led away. "I knew exactly what it would be! Oh, I wish you hadn't!"

"Shut up, silly," said Cyril. "You know you *would* come to Egypt. It was your own idea entirely. Shut up. It'll be all right."

"I thought we should play ball with queens," sobbed Jane, "and have no end of larks! And now everything's going to be perfectly horrid!"

The room they were shut up in *was* a room, and not a dungeon, as the elder ones had feared. That, as Anthea said, was one comfort. There were paintings on the wall that at any other time would have been most interesting. And a sort of low couch, and chairs.

When they were alone Jane breathed a sigh of relief.

"Now we can get home all right," she said.

"And leave the Psammead?" said Anthea reproachfully.

"Wait a sec. I've got an idea," said Cyril. He pondered for a few moments. Then he began hammering on the heavy cedar door. It opened, and a guard put in his head.

"Stop that row," he said sternly, "or——"

"Look here," Cyril interrupted, "it's very dull for you isn't it? Just doing nothing but guard us. Wouldn't you like to see some magic? We're not too proud to do it for you. Wouldn't you like to see it?"

"I don't mind if I do," said the guard.

"Well then, you get us that monkey of ours that was taken away, and we'll show you."

"How do I know you're not making game of me?" asked the soldier. "Shouldn't wonder if you only wanted to get the creature so as to set it on me. I daresay its teeth and claws are poisonous."

"Well, look here," said Robert. "You see we've got nothing with us? You just shut the door, and open it again in five minutes, and we'll have got a magic—oh, I don't know—a magic flower in a pot for you."

"If you can do that you can do anything," said the soldier, and he went out and barred the door.

Then, of course, they held up the Amulet. They found the East by holding it up, and turning slowly till the Amulet began to grow big, walked home through it, and came back with a geranium in full scarlet flower from the staircase window of the Fitzroy Street house.

"Well!" said the soldier when he came in, "I really am——!"

"We can do much more wonderful things than that—oh, ever so much," said Anthea persuasively, "if we only have our monkey. And here's twopence for yourself."

The soldier looked at the twopence.

"What's this?" he said.

Robert explained how much simpler it was to pay money for things than to exchange them as the people were doing in the market. Later on the soldier gave the coins to his captain, who, later still, showed them to Pharaoh, who of course kept them and was much struck with the idea. That was really how coins first came to be used in Egypt. You will not believe this, I daresay, but really, if you believe the rest of the story, I don't see why you shouldn't believe this as well.

"I say," said Anthea, struck by a sudden thought, "I suppose it'll be all right about those workmen? The King won't go back on what he said about them just because he's angry with us?"

"Oh, no," said the soldier, "you see, he's rather afraid of magic. He'll keep to his word right enough."

"Then *that's* all right," said Robert; and Anthea said softly and coaxingly—

"Ah, do get us the monkey, and then you'll see some lovely magic. Do—there's a nice, kind soldier."

"I don't know where they've put your precious monkey, but if I can get another chap to take on my duty here I'll see what I can do," he said grudgingly, and went out.

"Well!" said the soldier when he came in, "I really am—"

"Do you mean," said Robert, "that we're going off without even *trying* for the other half of the Amulet?"

"I really think we'd better," said Anthea tremulously.

"Of course the other half of the Amulet's here somewhere, or our half wouldn't have brought us here. I do wish we could find it. It is a pity we don't know any *real* magic. Then we could find out. I do wonder where it is—exactly."

If they had only known it, something very like the other half of the Amulet was very near them. It hung round the neck of someone, and that someone was watching them through a chink, high up in the wall, specially devised for watching people who were imprisoned. But they did not know.

There was nearly an hour of anxious waiting. They tried to take an interest in the picture on the wall, a picture of harpers playing very odd harps and women dancing at a feast. They examined the painted plaster floor, and the chairs were of white painted wood with coloured stripes at intervals.

But the time went slowly, and every one had time to think of how Pharaoh had said, "Don't torture them—*yet*."

"If the worst comes to the worst," said Cyril, "we must just bunk, and leave the Psammead. I believe it can take care of itself well enough. They won't kill it or hurt it when they find it can speak and give wishes. They'll build it a temple, I shouldn't wonder."

"I couldn't bear to go without it," said Anthea, "and Pharaoh said 'After supper', that won't be just yet. And the soldier was curious. I'm sure we're all right for the present."

All the same, the sound of the door being unbarred seemed one of the prettiest sounds possible.

"Suppose he hasn't got the Psammead?" whispered Jane.

But that doubt was set at rest by the Psammead itself; for almost before the door was open it sprang through the chink of it into Anthea's arms, shivering and hunching up its fur.

"Here's its fancy overcoat," said the soldier, holding out the bag, into which the Psammead immediately crept.

"Now," said Cyril, "what would you like us to do? Anything you'd like us to get for you?"

"Any little trick you like," said the soldier. "If you can get a strange flower blooming in an earthenware vase you can get anything, I suppose," he said. "I just wish I'd got two men's loads of jewels from the King's treasury. That's what I've always wished for."

At the word "*wish*" the children knew that the Psammead

The soldier fell flat on his face among the jewels

would attend to that bit of magic. It did, and the floor was littered with a spreading heap of gold and precious stones.

"Any other little trick?" asked Cyril loftily. "Shall we become invisible? Vanish?"

"Yes, if you like," said the soldier; "but not through the door, you don't."

He closed it carefully and set his broad Egyptian back against it.

"No! no!" cried a voice high up among the tops of the tall wooden pillars that stood against the wall. There was a sound of someone moving above.

The soldier was as much surprised as anybody.

"That's magic, if you like," he said.

And then Jane held up the Amulet, uttering the word of Power. At the sound of it and at the sight of the Amulet growing into the great arch the soldier fell flat on his face among the jewels with a cry of awe and terror.

The children went through the arch with a quickness born of long practice. But Jane stayed in the middle of the arch and looked back.

The others, standing on the dining-room carpet in Fitzroy Street, turned and saw her still in the arch. "Some one's holding her," cried Cyril. "We must go back."

But they pulled at Jane's hands just to see if she would come, and, of course, she did come.

Then, as usual, the arch was little again and there they all were.

"Oh, I do wish you hadn't!" Jane said crossly. "It *was* so interesting. The priest had come in and he was kicking the soldier, and telling him he'd done it now, and they must take the jewels and flee for their lives."

"And did they?"

"I don't know. You interfered," said Jane ungratefully. "I *should* have liked to see the last of it."

As a matter of fact, none of them had seen the last of it—if by "it" Jane meant the adventure of the Priest and the Soldier.

CHAPTER XII

THE SORRY-PRESENT AND THE
EXPELLED LITTLE BOY

"Look here," said Cyril, sitting on the dining-table and swinging his legs; "I really have got it."

"Got what?" was the not unnatural rejoinder of the others.

Cyril was making a boat with a penknife and a piece of wood, and the girls were making warm frocks for their dolls, for the weather was growing chilly.

"Why, don't you see? It's really not any good our going into the Past looking for that Amulet. The Past's as full of different times as—as—as the sea is of sand. We're simply bound to hit upon the wrong time. We might spend our lives looking for the Amulet and never see a sight of it. Why, it's the end of September already. It's like looking for a needle in——"

"A bottle of hay—I know," interrupted Robert; "but if we don't go on doing that, what are we to do?"

"That's just it," said Cyril in mysterious accents. "Oh, *bother*!"

Old Nurse had come in with the tray of knives, forks, and glasses, and was getting the tablecloth and table-napkins out of the chiffonier drawer.

"It's always meal-times just when you come to anything interesting."

"And a nice interesting handful *you'd* be, Master Cyril," said old Nurse, "if I wasn't to bring your meals up to time. Don't you begin grumbling now, fear you get something to grumble *at*."

"I wasn't grumbling," said Cyril quite untruly; "but it does always happen like that."

"You deserve to *have* something happen," said old Nurse. "Slave, slave, slave for you day and night, and never a word of thanks. . . ."

"Why, you do everything beautifully," said Anthea.

"It's the first time any of you's troubled to say so, anyhow," said Nurse shortly.

"What's the use of *saying*?" inquired Robert. "We *eat* our meals fast enough, and almost always two helps. *That* ought to show you!"

"Ah!" said old Nurse, going round the table and putting the knives and forks in their places; "you're a man all over, Master Robert. There was my poor Green, all the years he lived with me I never could get more out of him than 'It's all right!' when I asked him if he'd fancied his dinner. And yet, when he lay a-dying, his last words to me was, 'Maria, you was always a good cook!'" She ended with a trembling voice.

"And so you are," cried Anthea, and she and Jane instantly hugged her.

When she had gone out of the room Anthea said—

"I know exactly how she feels. Now, look here! Let's do a penance to show we're sorry we didn't think about telling her before what nice cooking she does, and what a dear she is."

"Penances are silly," said Robert.

"Not if the penance is something to please someone else. I didn't mean old peas and hair shirts and sleeping on the stones, I mean we'll make her a sorry-present," explained Anthea. "Look here! I vote Cyril doesn't tell us his idea until we've done something for old Nurse. It's worse for us than him," she added hastily, "because he knows what it is and we don't. Do you all agree?"

The others would have been ashamed not to agree, so they did. It was not till quite near the end of dinner—mutton fritters and blackberry and apple pie—that out of the earnest talk of the four came an idea that pleased everybody and would, they hoped, please Nurse.

Cyril and Robert went out with the taste of apple still in their mouths and the purple of blackberries on their lips—and, in the case of Robert, on the wristband as well—and bought a big sheet of cardboard at the stationer's. Then at the plumber's shop, that has tubes and pipes and taps and gas-fittings in the window, they bought a pane of glass the same size as the cardboard. The man cut it with a very interesting tool that had a bit of diamond at the end, and he gave them, out of his own free generousness, a large piece of putty and a small piece of glue.

While they were out the girls had floated four photographs of the four children off their cards in hot water. These were now stuck in a row along the top of the cardboard. Cyril put the glue to melt in a jampot, and put the jampot in a saucepan and the saucepan on the fire, while Robert painted a wreath of poppies round the photographs. He painted rather well and very quickly, and poppies are easy to do if you've once been shown how. Then Anthea drew some printed letters and Jane coloured them. The words were:

> "With all our loves to shew
> We like the thigs to eat."

And when the painting was dry they all signed their names at the bottom and put the glass on, and glued brown paper round the edge and over the back, and put two loops of tape to hang it up by.

Of course every one saw when too late that there were not enough letters in "things," so the missing "n" was put in. It was impossible, of course, to do the whole thing over again for just one letter.

"There!" said Anthea, placing it carefully, face up, under the sofa. "It'll be hours before the glue's dry. Now, Squirrel, fire ahead!"

"Well, then," said Cyril in a great hurry, rubbing at his gluey hands with his pocket handkerchief. "What I mean to say is this."

There was a long pause.

"Well," said Robert at last, "*what* is it that you mean to say?"

"It's like this," said Cyril, and again stopped short.

"Like *what*?" asked Jane.

"How can I tell you if you will all keep on interrupting?" said Cyril sharply.

So no one said any more, and with wrinkled frowns he arranged his ideas.

"Look here," he said, "what I really mean is—we can remember now what we did when we went to look for the Amulet. And if we'd found it we should remember that too."

"Rather!" said Robert. "Only, you see we haven't."

"But in the future we shall have."

"Shall we, though?" said Jane.

"Yes—unless we've been made fools of by the Psammead. So then, where we want to go to is where we shall remember about where we did find it."

"I see," said Robert, but he didn't.

"*I* don't," said Anthea, who did, very nearly. "Say it again, Squirrel, and very slowly."

"If," said Cyril, very slowly indeed, "we go into the future —after we've found the Amulet——"

"But we've got to find it first," said Jane.

"Hush!" said Anthea.

"There will be a future," said Cyril, driven to greater clearness by the blank faces of the other three, "there will be a time *after* we've found it. Let's go into *that* time—and then we shall remember *how* we found it. And then we can go back and do the finding really."

"I see," said Robert, and this time he did, and I hope *you* do.

"Yes," said Anthea. "Oh, Squirrel, how clever of you!"

"But will the Amulet work both ways?" inquired Robert.

"It ought to," said Cyril, "if time's only a thingummy of whatsitsname. Anyway we might try."

"Let's put on our best things, then," urged Jane. "You know what people say about progress and the world growing better and brighter. I expect people will be awfully smart in the future."

"All right," said Anthea, "we should have to wash anyway, I'm all thick with glue."

When everyone was clean and dressed, the charm was held up.

"We want to go into the future and see the Amulet after

Right in front of them, under a glass case, was the amulet

we've found it," said Cyril, and Jane said the word of Power.
They walked through the big arch of the charm straight into
the British Museum. They knew it at once, and there, right
in front of them, under a glass case, was the Amulet—their
own half of it, as well as the other half they had never been
able to find—and the two were joined by a pin of red stone
that formed a hinge.

"Oh, glorious!" cried Robert. "Here it is!"

"Yes," said Cyril, very gloomily, "here it is. But we can't
get it out."

"No," said Robert, remembering how impossible the Queen
of Babylon had found it to get anything out of the glass cases
in the Museum—except by Psammead magic, and then she-
hadn't been able to take anything away with her; "no—but we
remember where we got it, and we can——"

"Oh, *do* we?" interrupted Cyril bitterly, "do *you* remember
where we got it?"

"No," said Robert, "I don't, exactly, now I come to think of
it."

Nor did any of the others!

"But *why* can't we?" said Jane.

"Oh, *I* don't know," Cyril's tone was impatient, "some silly
old enchanted rule I suppose. I wish people would teach you
magic at school like they do sums—or instead of. It would be
some use having an Amulet then."

"I wonder how far we are in the future," said Anthea, "the
Museum looks just the same, only lighter and brighter, somehow."

"Let's go back and try the Past again," said Robert.

"Perhaps the Museum people could tell us how we got it,"
said Anthea with sudden hope. There was no one in the room,
but in the next gallery, where the Assyrian things are and still
were, they found a kind, stout man in a loose, blue gown, and
stockinged legs.

"Oh, they've got a new uniform, how pretty!" said Jane.

When they asked him their question he showed them a label
on the case. It said, "From the collection of——." A name
followed, and it was the name of the learned gentleman who,

among themselves, and to his face when he had been with them at the other side of the Amulet, they had called Jimmy.

"*That's* not much good," said Cyril, "thank you."

"How is it you're not at school?" asked the kind man in blue. "Not expelled for long I hope?"

"We're not expelled at all," said Cyril rather warmly.

"Well, I shouldn't do it again, if I were you," said the man, and they could see he did not believe them. There is no company so little pleasing as that of people who do not believe you.

"Thank you for showing us the label," said Cyril. And they came away.

As they came through the doors of the Museum they blinked at the sudden glory of sunlight and blue sky. The houses opposite the Museum were gone. Instead there was a big garden, with trees and flowers and smooth green lawns, and not a single notice to tell you not to walk on the grass and not to destroy the trees and shrubs and not to pick the flowers. There were comfortable seats all about, and arbours covered with roses, and long, trellised walks, also rose-covered. Whispering, plashing fountains fell into full white marble basins, white statues gleamed among the leaves, and the pigeons that swept about among the branches or pecked on the smooth, soft gravel were not black and tumbled like the Museum pigeons are now, but bright and clean and sleek as birds of new silver. A good many people were sitting on the seats, and on the grass babies were rolling and kicking and playing—with very little on indeed. Men, as well as women, seemed to be in charge of the babies and were playing with them.

"It's like a lovely picture," said Anthea, and it was. For the people's clothes were of bright, soft colours and all beautifully and very simply made. No one seemed to have any hats or bonnets, but there were a great many Japanese-looking sunshades. And among the trees were hung lamps of coloured glass.

"I expect they light those in the evening," said Jane. "I *do* wish we lived in the future!"

They walked down the path, and as they went the people

on the benches looked at the four children very curiously, but not rudely or unkindly. The children, in their turn, looked— I hope they did not stare—at the faces of these people in the beautiful soft clothes. Those faces were worth looking at. Not that they were all handsome, though even in the matter of handsomeness they had the advantage of any set of people the children had ever seen. But it was the expression of their faces that made them worth looking at. The children could not tell at first what it was.

"I know," said Anthea suddenly. "They're not worried; that's what it is."

And it was. Everybody looked calm, no one seemed to be in a hurry, no one seemed to be anxious, or fretted, and though some did seem to be sad, not a single one look worried.

But though the people looked kind everyone looked so interested in the children that they began to feel a little shy and turned out of the big main path into a narrow little one that wound among trees and shrubs and mossy, dripping springs.

It was here, in a deep, shadowed cleft between tall cypresses, that they found the expelled little boy. He was lying face downward on the mossy turf, and the peculiar shaking of his shoulders was a thing they had seen, more than once, in each other. So Anthea knelt down by him and said—

"What's the matter?"

"I'm expelled from school," said the boy between his sobs.

This was serious. People are not expelled for light offences.

"Do you mind telling us what you'd done?"

"I—I tore up a sheet of paper and threw it about in the playground," said the child, in the tone of one confessing an unutterable baseness. "You won't talk to me any more now you know that," he added without looking up.

"Was that all?" asked Anthea.

"It's about enough," said the child; "and I'm expelled for the whole day!"

"I don't quite understand," said Anthea, gently. The boy lifted his face, rolled over, and sat up.

There was a big garden with trees and flowers and smooth green lawns

"Why, whoever on earth are you?" he said.

"We're strangers from a far country," said Anthea. "In our country it's not a crime to leave a bit of paper about."

"It is here," said the child. "If grown-ups do it they're fined. When we do it we're expelled for the whole day."

"Well, but," said Robert, "that just means a day's holiday."

"You *must* come from a long way off," said the little boy. "A holiday's when you all have play and treats and jolliness, all of you together. On your expelled days no one'll speak to you. Everyone sees you're an Expelleder or you'd be in school."

"Suppose you were ill?"

"Nobody is—hardly. If they are, of course they wear the badge, and everyone is kind to you. I know a boy that stole his sister's illness badge and wore it when he was expelled for a day. *He* got expelled for a week for that. It must be awful not to go to school for a week."

"Do you *like* school, then?" asked Robert incredulously.

"Of course I do. It's the loveliest place there is. I chose railways for my special subject this year, there are such splendid models and things, and now I shall be all behind because of that torn-up paper."

"You choose your own subject?" asked Cyril.

"Yes, of course. Where *did* you come from? Don't you know *anything*?"

"No," said Jane definitely; "so you'd better tell us."

"Well, on Midsummer Day school breaks up and everything's decorated with flowers, and you choose your special subject for next year. Of course you have to stick to it for a year at least. Then there are all your other subjects, of course, reading, and painting, and the rules of Citizenship."

"Good gracious!" said Anthea.

"Look here," said the child, jumping up, "it's nearly four. The expelledness only lasts till then. Come home with me. Mother will tell you all about everything."

"Will your mother like you taking home strange children?" asked Anthea.

"I don't understand," said the child, settling his leather belt

A lady in soft green clothes came out

over his honey-coloured smock and stepping out with hard little bare feet. "Come on."

So they went.

The streets were wide and hard and very clean. There were no horses, but a sort of motor carriage that made no noise. The Thames flowed between green banks, and there were trees at the edge, and people sat under them, fishing, for the stream was clear as crystal. Everywhere there were green trees and there was no smoke. The houses were set in what seemed like one green garden.

The little boy brought them to a house, and at the window was a good, bright mother-face. The little boy rushed in, and through the window they could see him hugging his mother then his eager lips moving and his quick hands pointing.

A lady in soft green clothes came out, spoke kindly to them, and took them into the oddest house they had ever seen. It was very bare, there were no ornaments, and yet every single thing was beautiful, from the dresser with its rows of bright china, to the thick squares of Eastern-looking carpet on the floors. I can't describe that house; I haven't the time. And I haven't heart either, when I think how different it was from our houses. The lady took them all over it. The oddest thing of all was the big room in the middle. It had padded walls and a soft, thick carpet, and all the chairs and tables were padded. There wasn't a single thing in it that any one could hurt itself with.

"Whatever's this for?—lunatics?" asked Cyril.

The lady looked very shocked.

"No! It's for the children, of course," she said. "Don't tell me that in your country there are no children's rooms."

"There are nurseries," said Anthea doubtfully, "but the furniture's all cornery and hard, like other rooms."

"How shocking!" said the lady; "you must be *very* much behind the times in your country! Why, the children are more than half of the people; it's not much to have one room where they can have a good time and not hurt themselves."

"But there's no fireplace," said Anthea.

"Hot-air pipes, of course," said the lady. "Why, how could you have a fire in a nursery? A child might get burned."

"In our country," said Robert suddenly, "more than three thousand children are burned to death every year. Father told me," he added, as if apologising for this piece of information, "once when I'd been playing with fire."

The lady turned quite pale.

"What a frightful place you must live in!" she said.

"What's all the furniture padded for?" Anthea asked, hastily turning the subject.

"Why, you couldn't have little tots of two or three running about in rooms where the things were hard and sharp! They might hurt themselves."

Robert fingered the scar on his forehead where he had hit it against the nursery fender when he was little.

"But does everyone have rooms like this, poor people and all?" asked Anthea.

"There's a room like this wherever there's a child, of course," said the lady. "How refreshingly ignorant you are!—no, I don't mean ignorant, my dear. Of course, you're awfully well up in Ancient History. But I see you haven't done your Duties of Citizenship Course yet."

"But beggars, and people like that?" persisted Anthea; "and tramps and people who haven't any homes?"

"People who haven't any homes?" repeated the lady. "I really *don't* understand what you're talking about."

"It's all different in our country," said Cyril carefully; "and I have read that it used to be different in London. Usedn't people to have no homes and beg because they were hungry? and wasn't London very black and dirty once upon a time? and the Thames all muddy and filthy? and narrow streets, and——"

"You must have been reading very old-fashioned books," said the lady. "Why, all that was in the dark ages! My husband can tell you more about it than I can. He took Ancient History as one of his special subjects."

"I haven't seen any working people," said Anthea.

"Why, we're all working people," said the lady; "at least my husband's a carpenter."

"Good gracious!" said Anthea; "but you're a lady!"

"Ah," said the lady, "that quaint old world! Well, my husband *will* enjoy a talk with you. In the dark ages every one was allowed to have a smoky chimney, and those nasty horses all over the streets, and all sorts of rubbish thrown into the Thames. And, of course, the sufferings of the people will hardly bear thinking of. It's very learned of you to know it all. Did *you* make Ancient History your special subject?"

"Not exactly," said Cyril, rather uneasily. "What is the Duties of Citizenship Course about?"

"Don't you *really* know? Aren't you pretending—just for fun? Really not? Well, that course teaches you how to be a good citizen, what you must do and what you mayn't do, so as to do your full share of the work of making your town a beautiful and happy place for people to live in. There's a quite simple little thing they teach the tiny children. How does it go . . . ?"

> " 'I must not steal and I must learn,
>   Nothing is mine that I do not earn.
>   I must try in work and play
>   To make things beautiful every day.
>   I must be kind to every one,
>   And never let cruel things be done.
>   I must be brave, and I must try
>   When I am hurt never to cry,
>   And always laugh as much as I can,
>   And be glad that I'm going to be a man
>   To work for my living and help the rest,
>   And never do less than my very best.' "

"That's very easy," said Jane. "*I* could remember that."

"That's only the very beginning, of course," said the lady; "there are heaps more rhymes. There's the one beginning—

> " 'I must not litter the beautiful street
>   With bits of paper or things to eat;
>   I must not pick the public flowers,
>   They are not *mine*, but they are *ours*.' "

"Oh, look at their faces, their horrible faces!" she cried

"And 'things to eat' reminds me—are you hungry? Wells, run and get a tray of nice things."

"Why do you call him 'Wells'?" asked Robert as the boy ran off.

"It's after the great reformer—surely you've heard of *him*? He lived in the dark ages, and he saw that what you ought to do is to find out what you want and then try to get it. Up to then people had always tried to tinker up what they'd got. We've got a great many of the things he thought of. Then 'Wells' means springs of clear water. It's a nice name, don't you think?"

Here Wells returned with strawberries and cakes and lemonade on a tray, and everybody ate and enjoyed.

"Now, Wells," said the lady, "run off or you'll be late and not meet your Daddy."

Wells kissed her, waved to the others, and went.

"Look here," said Anthea suddenly, "would you like to come to *our* country, and see what it's like? It wouldn't take you a minute."

The lady laughed. But Jane held up the charm and said the word.

"What a splendid conjuring trick!" cried the lady, enchanted with the beautiful, growing arch.

"Go through," said Anthea.

The lady went, laughing. But she did not laugh when she found herself, suddenly, in the dining-room at Fitzroy Street.

"Oh, what a *horrible* trick!" she cried. "What a hateful, dark, ugly place!"

She ran to the window and looked out. The sky was gray, the street was foggy, a dismal organ-grinder was standing opposite the door, a beggar and a man who sold matches were quarrelling at the edge of the pavement on whose greasy black surface people hurried along, hastening to get to the shelter of their houses.

"Oh, look at their faces, their horrible faces!" she cried. "What's the matter with them all?"

"They're poor people, that's all," said Robert.

"But it's *not* all! They're ill, they're unhappy, they're

wicked! Oh, do stop it, there's dear children. It's very, very clever. Some sort of magic-lantern trick, I suppose, like I've read of. But *do* stop it. Oh! their poo·, tired, miserable, wicked faces!"

The tears were in her eyes. Anthea signed to Jane. The arch grew, they spoke the words, and pushed the lady through it into her own time and place, where London is clean and beautiful, and the Thames runs clear and bright, and the green trees grow, and no one is afraid, or anxious, or in a hurry.

There was a silence. Then—

"I'm glad we went," said Anthea, with a deep breath.

"I'll never throw paper about again as long as I live," said Robert.

"Mother always told us not to," said Jane.

"I would like to take up the Duties of Citizenship for a special subject," said Cyril. "I wonder if Father could put me through it. I shall ask him when he comes home."

"If we'd found the Amulet, Father could be home *now*," said Anthea, "and Mother and The Lamb."

"Let's go into the future *again*," suggested Jane brightly. "Perhaps we could remember if it wasn't such an awful way off."

So they did. This time they said, "The future, where the Amulet is, not so far away."

And they went through the familiar arch into a large, light room with three windows. Facing them was the familiar mummy case. And at a table by the window sat the learned gentleman. They knew him at once, though his hair was white. His was one of the faces that do not change with age. In his hand was the Amulet—complete and perfect.

He rubbed his other hand across his forehead in the way they were so used to.

"Dreams, dreams!" he said; "old age is full of them!"

"You've been in dreams with us before now," said Robert, "don't you remember?"

"I do, indeed," said he. The room had many more books than the Fitzroy Street room, and far more curious and wonderful Assyrian and Egyptian objects. "The most wonderful dreams I ever had, had you in them."

"Where," asked Cyril, "did you get that thing in your hand?"

"If you weren't just a dream," he answered, smiling, "you'd remember that you gave it to me."

"But where did we get it?" Cyril asked eagerly.

"Ah, you never would tell me that," he said, "you always had your little mysteries. You dear children! What a difference you made to that old Bloomsbury house! I wish I could dream you oftener. Now you're grown up you're not like you used to be."

"Grown up?" said Anthea.

The learned gentleman pointed to a frame with four photographs in it.

"There you are," he said.

The children saw four grown-up people's portraits—two ladies, two gentlemen—and looked on them with loathing.

"Shall we grow up like *that*?" whispered Jane. "How perfectly horrid!"

"If we're ever like that, we sha'n't know it's horrid, I expect," Anthea with some insight whispered back. "You see, you get used to yourself while you're changing. It's—it's being so sudden makes it seem so frightful now."

The learned gentleman was looking at them with wistful kindness. "Don't let me undream you just yet," he said. There was a pause.

"Do you remember *when* we gave you that Amulet?" Cyril asked suddenly.

"You know, or you would if you weren't a dream, that it was on the 3rd December, 1905. I shall never forget *that* day."

"Thank you," said Cyril, earnestly; "oh, thank you very much."

"You've got a new room," said Anthea, looking out of the window, "and what a lovely garden!"

"Yes," said he, "I'm too old now to care even about being near the Museum. This is a beautiful place. Do you know—I can hardly believe you're just a dream, you do look so exactly real. Do you know..." his voice dropped, "I can say it to *you*, though, of course, if I said it to anyone that wasn't a

At a table by the window sat the learned gentleman

dream they'd call me mad; there was something about that Amulet you gave me—something very mysterious."

"There was that," said Robert.

"Ah, I don't mean your pretty little childish mysteries about where you got it. But about the thing itself. First, the wonderful dreams I used to have, after you'd shown me the first half of it! Why, my book on Atlantis, that I did, was the beginning of my fame and my fortune, too. And I got it all out of a dream! And then, 'Britain at the Time of the Roman Invasion' —that was only a pamphlet, but it explained a lot of things people hadn't understood."

"Yes," said Anthea, "it would."

"That was the beginning. But after you'd given me the whole of the Amulet—ah, it was generous of you!—then, somehow, I didn't need to theorise, I seemed to *know* about the old Egyptian civilisation. And they can't upset my theories"— he rubbed his thin hands and laughed triumphantly—"they can't, though they've tried. Theories, they call them, but they're more like—I don't know—more like memories. I *know* I'm right about the secret rites of the Temple of Amen."

"I'm so glad you're rich," said Anthea. "You weren't, you know, at Fitzroy Street."

"Indeed I wasn't," said he, "but I am now. This beautiful house and this lovely garden—I dig in it sometimes; you remember, you used to tell me to take more exercise? Well, I feel I owe it all to you—and the Amulet."

"I'm so glad," said Anthea, and kissed him. He started.

"*That* didn't feel like a dream," he said, and his voice trembled.

"It isn't exactly a dream," said Anthea softly, "it's all part of the Amulet—it's a sort of extra special, real dream, dear Jimmy."

"Ah," said he, "when you call me that, I know I'm dreaming. My little sister—I dream of her sometimes. But it's not real like this. Do you remember the day I dreamed you brought me the Babylonish ring?"

"We remember it all," said Robert. "Did you leave Fitzroy Street because you were too rich for it?"

"Oh, no!" he said reproachfully. "You know I should never have done such a thing as that. Of course, I left when your old Nurse died and—what's the matter!"

"Old Nurse *dead*?" said Anthea. "Oh, no!"

"Yes, yes, it's the common lot. It's a long time ago now."

Jane held up the Amulet in a hand that twittered.

"Come!" she cried, "oh, come home! She may be dead before we get there, and then we can't give it to her. Oh, come!"

"Ah, don't let the dream end now!" pleaded the learned gentleman.

"It must," said Anthea firmly, and kissed him again.

"When it comes to people dying," said Robert, "goodbye! I'm so glad you're rich and famous and happy."

"*Do* come!" cried Jane, stamping in her agony of impatience.

And they went. Old Nurse brought in tea almost as soon as they were back in Fitzroy Street. As she came in with the tray, the girls rushed at her and nearly upset her and it.

"Don't die!" cried Jane, "oh, don't!" and Anthea cried, "Dear, ducky, darling old Nurse, don't die!"

"Lord, love you!" said Nurse, "I'm not agoin' to die yet a while, please Heaven! Whatever on earth's the matter with the chicks?"

"Nothing. Only don't!"

She put the tray down and hugged the girls in turn. The boys thumped her on the back with heartfelt affection.

"I'm as well as ever I was in my life," she said. "What nonsense about dying! You've been a sitting too long in the dusk, that's what it is. Regular blind man's holiday. Leave go of me, while I light the gas.

The yellow light illuminated four pale faces.

"We do love you so," Anthea went on, "and we've made you a picture to show you how we love you. Get it out, Squirrel."

The glazed testimonial was dragged out from under the sofa and displayed.

"The glue's not dry yet," said Cyril, "look out!"

"What a beauty!" cried old Nurse. "Well, I never! And

your pictures and the beautiful writing and all. Well, I always did say your hearts was in the right place, if a bit careless at times. Well! I never did! I don't know as I was ever pleased better in my life."

She hugged them all, one after the other. And the boys did not mind it, somehow, that day.

"How is it we can remember all about the future, *now*?" Anthea woke the Psammead with laborious gentleness to put the question. "How is it we can remember what we saw in the future, and yet, when we *were* in the future, we could not remember the bit of the future that was past then, the time of finding the Amulet?"

"Why, what a silly question!" said the Psammead, "of course you cannot remember what hasn't happened yet."

"But the *future* hasn't happened yet," Anthea persisted, "and we remember that all right."

"Oh, that isn't what's happened, my good child," said the Psammead, rather crossly, "that's prophetic vision. And you remember dreams, don't you? So why not visions? You never do seem to understand the simplest thing."

It went to sand again at once.

Anthea crept down in her nightgown to give one last kiss to old Nurse, and one last look at the beautiful testimonial hanging, by its tapes, its glue now firmly set, in glazed glory on the wall of the kitchen.

"Good-night, bless your loving heart," said old Nurse, "if only you don't catch your deather-cold!"

CHAPTER XIII

THE SHIPWRECK ON THE
TIN ISLANDS

"Blue and red," said Jane softly, "make purple."

"Not always they don't," said Cyril, "it has to be crimson lake and Prussian blue. If you mix Vermilion and Indigo you get the most loathsome slate colour.'

"Sepia's the nastiest colour in the box, I think," said Jane, sucking her brush.

They were all painting. Nurse in the flush of grateful emotion, excited by Robert's border of poppies, had presented each of the four with a shilling paint-box, and had supplemented the gift with a pile of old copies of the *Illustrated London News*.

"Sepia," said Cyril instructively, "is made out of beastly cuttle-fish."

"Purple's made out of a fish, as well as out of red and blue," said Robert. "Tyrian purple was, I know."

"Out of lobsters?" said Jane dreamily. "They're red when they're boiled, and blue when they aren't. If you mixed live and dead lobsters you'd get Tyrian purple."

"*I* shouldn't like to mix anything with a live lobster" said Anthea, shuddering.

"Well, there aren't any other red and blue fish," said Jane; "you'd have to."

"I'd rather not have the purple," said Anthea.

"The Tyrian purple wasn't that colour when it came out of the fish, nor yet afterwards, it wasn't," said Robert; "it was scarlet really, and Roman Emperors wore it. And it wasn't any nice colour while the fish had it. It was a yellowish-white liquid of a creamy consistency."

"How do you know?" asked Cyril.

"I read it," said Robert with the meek pride of superior knowledge.

"Where?" asked Cyril.

"In print," said Robert, still more proudly meek.

"You think everything's true if it's printed," said Cyril, naturally annoyed, "but it isn't. Father said so. Quite a lot of lies get printed, especially in newspapers."

"You see, as it happens," said Robert, in what was really a rather annoying tone, "it wasn't a newspaper, it was in a book."

"How sweet Chinese white is!" said Jane, dreamily sucking her brush again.

"I don't believe it," said Cyril to Robert.

"Have a suck yourself," suggested Robert.

"I don't mean about the Chinese white. I mean about the cream fish turning purple and——"

"Oh!" cried Anthea, jumping up very quickly, "I'm tired of painting. Let's go somewhere by Amulet. I say—let's let *it* choose."

Cyril and Robert agreed that this was an idea. Jane consented to stop painting because, as she said, Chinese white, though certainly sweet, gives you a queer feeling in the back of the throat if you paint with it too long.

The Amulet was held up.

"Take us somewhere," said Jane, "anywhere you like in the Past—but somewhere where you are." Then she said the word.

Next moment everyone felt a queer rocking and swaying—something like what you feel when you go out in a fishing boat. And that was not wonderful, when you come to think of it, for it was in a boat that they found themselves. A queer boat, with high bulwarks pierced with holes for oars to go through. There was a high seat for the steersman, and the prow was shaped like the head of some great animal with big, staring eyes. The boat rode at anchor in a bay, and the bay was very smooth. The crew were dark, wiry fellows with black beards and hair. They had no clothes except a tunic from waist to knee, and round caps with knobs on the top. They were very busy, and what they were doing was so interesting to the children that at first they did not even wonder where the Amulet had brought them.

And the crew seemed too busy to notice the children. They

They were fastening rush baskets to a long rope

were fastening rush baskets to a long rope with a great piece of cork at the end, and in each basket they put mussels or little frogs. Then they cast out the ropes, the baskets sank, but the cork floated. And all about on the blue water were other boats and all the crews of all the boats were busy with ropes and baskets and frogs and mussels.

"Whatever are you doing?" Jane suddenly asked a man who had rather more clothes than the others, and seemed to be a sort of captain or overseer. He started and stared at her, but he had seen too many strange lands to be very much surprised at these queerly-dressed stowaways.

"Setting lines for the dye shell-fish," he said shortly. "How did you get here?"

"A sort of magic," said Robert carelessly. The Captain fingered an Amulet that hung round his neck.

"What is this place?" asked Cyril.

"Tyre, of course," said the man. Then he drew back and spoke in a low voice to one of the sailors.

"Now we shall know about your precious cream-jug fish," said Cyril.

"But we never *said* come to Tyre," said Jane.

"The Amulet heard us talking, I expect. I think it's *most* obliging of it," said Anthea.

"And the Amulet's here too," said Robert. "We ought to be able to find it in a little ship like this. I wonder which of them's got it."

"Oh—look, look!" cried Anthea suddenly. On the bare breast of one of the sailors gleamed something red. It was the exact counterpart of their precious half-Amulet.

A silence, full of emotion, was broken by Jane.

"Then we've found it!" she said. "Oh do let's take it and go home!"

"Easy to say 'take it,'" said Cyril; "he looks very strong."

He did—yet not so strong as the other sailors.

"It's odd," said Anthea musingly, "I do believe I've seen that man somewhere before."

"He's rather like our learned gentleman," said Robert, "but I'll tell you who he's much more like——"

At this moment that sailor looked up. His eyes met Robert's —and Robert and the others had no longer any doubt as to where they had seen him before. It was Rekh-marā, the priest who had led them to the palace of Pharaoh—and whom Jane had looked back at through the arch, when he was counselling Pharaoh's guard to take the jewels and fly for his life.

Nobody was quite pleased, and nobody quite knew why.

Jane voiced the feelings of all when she said, fingering *their* Amulet through the folds of her frock, "We can go back in a minute if anything nasty happens."

For the moment nothing worse happened than an offer of food—figs and cucumbers it was, and very pleasant.

"I see," said the Captain, "that you are from a far country. Since you have honoured my boat by appearing on it, you must stay here till morning. Then I will lead you to one of our great ones. He loves strangers from far lands."

"Let's go home," Jane whispered, "all the frogs are drowning *now*. I think the people here are cruel."

But the boys wanted to stay and see the lines taken up in the morning.

"It's just like eel-pots and lobster-pots," said Cyril, "the baskets only open from outside—I vote we stay."

So they stayed.

"That's Tyre over there," said the Captain, who was evidently trying to be civil. He pointed to a great island rock, that rose steeply from the sea, crowned with huge walls and towers. There was another city on the mainland.

"That's part of Tyre, too," said the Captain; "it's where the great merchants have their pleasure-houses and gardens and farms."

"Look, look!" Cyril cried suddenly; "what a lovely little ship!"

A ship in full sail was passing swiftly through the fishing fleet. The Captain's face changed. He frowned, and his eyes blazed with fury.

"Insolent young barbarian!" he cried. "Do you call the ships of Tyre *little*? None greater sail the seas. That ship has been on a three years' voyage. She is known in all the great trading ports from here to the Tin Islands. She comes back rich and glorious. Her very anchor is of silver."

"I'm sure we beg your pardon," said Anthea hastily. "In our country we say 'little' for a pet name. Your wife might call you her dear little husband, you know."

"I should like to catch her at it," growled the Captain, but he stopped scowling.

"It's a rich trade," he went on. "For cloth *once* dipped, second-best glass, and the rough images our young artists carve for practice, the barbarian King in Tessos lets us work the silver mines. We get so much silver there that we leave them our iron anchors and come back with silver ones."

"How splendid!" said Robert. "Do go on. What's cloth once dipped?"

"You *must* be barbarians from the outer darkness," said the Captain scornfully. "All wealthy nations know that our finest stuffs are twice dyed—dibaptha. They're only for the robes of kings and priests and princes."

"What do the rich merchants wear," asked Jane, with interest, "in the pleasure-houses?"

"They wear the dibaptha. *Our* merchants *are* princes," scowled the skipper.

"Oh, don't be cross, we do so like hearing about things. We want to know *all* about the dyeing," said Anthea cordially.

"Oh, you do, do you?" growled the man. "So that's what you're here for? Well, you won't get the secrets of the dye trade out of *me*."

He went away, and everyone felt snubbed and uncomfortable. And all the time the long, narrow eyes of the Egyptian were watching, watching. They felt as though he was watching them through the darkness, when they lay down to sleep on a pile of cloaks.

Next morning the baskets were drawn up full of what looked like whelk shells.

The children were rather in the way, but they made themselves as small as they could. While the skipper was at the other end of the boat they did ask one question of a sailor, whose face was a little less unkind than the others.

"That's jolly good," said Robert, as the naked brown body cleft the water

"Yes," he answered, "this is the dye-fish. It's a sort of murex —and there's another kind that they catch at Sidon—and then, of course, there's the kind that's used for the dibaptha. But that's quite different. It's——"

"Hold your tongue!" shouted the skipper. And the man held it.

The laden boat was rowed slowly round the end of the island, and was made fast in one of the two great harbours that lay inside a long breakwater. The harbour was full of all sorts of ships, so that Cyril and Robert enjoyed themselves much more than their sisters. The breakwater and the quays were heaped with bales and baskets, and crowded with slaves and sailors. Farther along some men were practising diving.

"That's jolly good," said Robert, as a naked brown body cleft the water.

"I should think so," said the skipper. "The pearl-divers of Persia are not more skilful. Why, we've got a fresh-water spring that comes out at the bottom of the sea. Our divers dive down and bring up the fresh water in skin bottles! Can your barbarian divers do as much?"

"I suppose not," said Robert, and put away a wild desire to explain to the Captain the English system of waterworks, pipes, taps, and the intricacies of the plumbers' trade.

As they neared the quay the skipper made a hasty toilet. He did his hair, combed his beard, put on a garment like a jersey with short sleeves, an embroidered belt, a necklace of beads, and a big signet ring.

"Now," said he, "I'm fit to be seen. Come along?"

"Where to?" said Jane cautiously.

"To Pheles, the great sea-captain," said the skipper. "The man I told you of, who loves barbarians."

Then Rekh-marā came forward, and, for the first time, spoke.

"I have known these children in another land," he said. "You know my powers of magic. It was my magic that brought these barbarians to your boat. And you know how they will profit you. I read your thoughts. Let me come with you and see the end of them, and then I will work the spell I promised you in return for the little experience you have so kindly given me on your boat."

The skipper looked at the Egyptian with some disfavour.

"So it was *your* doing," he said. "I might have guessed it. Well, come on."

So he came, and the girls wished he hadn't. But Robert whispered—

"Nonsense—as long as he's with us we've got *some* chance of the Amulet. We can always fly if anything goes wrong."

The morning was so fresh and bright; their breakfast had been so good and so unusual; they had actually seen the Amulet round the Egyptian's neck. One or two, or all these things, suddenly raised the children's spirits. They went off quite cheerfully through the city gate—it was not arched, but roofed over with a great flat stone—and so through the streets, which smelt horribly of fish and garlic and a thousand other things even less agreeable. But far worse than the street scents was the scent of the factory, where the skipper called in to sell his night's catch. I wish I could tell you all about that factory, but I haven't time, and perhaps after all you aren't interested in dyeing works. I will only mention that Robert was triumphantly proved to be right. The dye *was* a yellowish-white liquid of a creamy consistency, and it smelt more strongly of garlic than garlic itself does.

While the skipper was bargaining with the master of the dye works the Egyptian came close to the children, and said, suddenly and softly—

"Trust me."

"I wish we could," said Anthea.

"You feel," said the Egyptian, "that I want your Amulet. That makes you distrust me."

"Yes," said Cyril bluntly.

"But you also, you want my Amulet, and I am trusting you."

"There's something in that," said Robert.

"We have the two halves of the Amulet," said the Priest, "but not yet the pin that joined them. Our only chance of getting that is to remain together. Once part these two halves and they may never again be found in the same time and place. Be wise. Our interests are the same."

Before anyone could say more the skipper came back, and with him the dye-master. His hair and beard were curled like the men's in Babylon, and he was dressed like the skipper, but with added grandeur of gold and embroidery. He had necklaces of beads and silver, and a glass amulet with a man's face, very like his own, set between two bulls' heads, as well as gold and silver bracelets and armlets. He looked keenly at the children. Then he said—

"My brother Pheles has just come back from Tarshish. He's at his garden house—unless he's hunting wild boar in the marshes. He gets frightfully bored on shore."

"Ah," said the skipper, "he's a true-born Phœnician. 'Tyre, Tyre for ever! Oh, Tyre rules the waves!' as the old song says. I'll go at once, and show him my young barbarians."

"I should," said the dye-master. "They are very rum, aren't they? What frightful clothes, and what a lot of them! Observe the covering of their feet. Hideous indeed."

Robert could not help thinking how easy, and at the same time pleasant it would be to catch hold of the dye-master's feet and tip him backward into the great sunken vat just near him. But if he had, flight would have had to be the next move, so he restrained his impulse.

There was something about this Tyrian adventure that was different from all the others. It was, somehow, calmer. And there was the undoubted fact that the charm was there on the neck of the Egyptian.

So they enjoyed everything to the full, the row from the Island City to the shore, the ride on the donkeys that the skipper hired at the gate of the mainland city, and the pleasant country—palms and figs and cedars all about. It was like a garden—clematis, honeysuckle, and jasmine clung about the olive and mulberry trees, and there were tulips and gladiolus, and clumps of mandrake, which has bell-flowers that look as though they were cut out of dark blue jewels. In the distance were the mountains of Lebanon.

The house they came to at last was rather like a bungalow—

long and low, with pillars all along the front. Cedars and sycamores grew near it and sheltered it pleasantly.

Everyone dismounted, and the donkeys were led away.

"Why is this like Rosherville?" whispered Robert, and instantly supplied the answer.

"Because it's the place to spend a happy day."

"It's jolly decent of the skipper to have brought us to such a ripping place," said Cyril.

"Do you know," said Anthea, "this feels more real than anything else we've seen? It's like a holiday in the country at home."

The children were left alone in a large hall. The floor was mosaic, done with wonderful pictures of ships and sea-beasts and fishes. Through an open doorway they could see a pleasant courtyard with flowers.

"I should like to spend a week here," said Jane, "and donkey ride every day."

Everyone was feeling very jolly. Even the Egyptian looked pleasanter than usual. And then, quite suddenly, the skipper came back with a joyous smile. With him came the master of the house. He looked steadily at the children and nodded twice.

"Yes," he said, "my steward will pay you the price. But I shall not pay at that high rate for the Egyptian dog."

The two passed on.

"This," said the Egyptian, "is a pretty kettle of fish."

"What is?" asked all the children at once.

"Our present position," said Rekh-marā. "Our seafaring friend," he added, "has sold us all for slaves!"

A hasty council succeeded the shock of this announcement. The Priest was allowed to take part in it. His advice was "stay", because they were in no danger, and the Amulet in its completeness must be somewhere near, or, of course, they could not have come to that place at all. And after some discussion they agreed to this.

The children were treated more as guests than as slaves, but the Egyptian was sent to the kitchen and made to work.

Pheles, the master of the house, went off that very evening, by the King's orders, to start on another voyage. And when he was gone his wife found the children amusing company, and kept them talking and singing and dancing till quite late, "To distract my mind from my sorrows," she said.

"I do like being a slave," remarked Jane cheerfully, as they curled up on the big, soft cushions that were to be their beds.

It was black night when they were awakened, each by a hand passed softly over its face, and a low voice that whispered—

"Be quiet, or all is lost."

So they were quiet.

"It's me, Rekh-marā, the Priest of Amen," said the whisperer. "The man who brought us has gone to sea again, and he has taken my Amulet from me by force, and I know no magic to get it back. Is there magic for that in the Amulet you bear?"

Everyone was instantly awake by now.

"We can go after him," said Cyril, leaping up; "but he might take *ours* as well; or he might be angry with us for following him."

"I'll see to *that*," said the Egyptian in the dark. "Hide your Amulet well."

There in the deep blackness of that room in the Tyrian country house the Amulet was once more held up and the word spoken.

All passed through on to a ship that tossed and tumbled on a wind-blown sea. They crouched together there till morning, and Jane and Cyril were not at all well. When the dawn showed, dove-coloured, across the steely waves, they stood up as well as they could for the tumbling of the ship. Pheles, that hardy sailor and adventurer, turned quite pale when he turned round suddenly and saw them.

"Well!" he said, "well, I never did!"

"Master," said the Egyptian, bowing low, and that was even more difficult than standing up, "we are here by the magic of the sacred Amulet that hangs round your neck."

"I never did!" repeated Pheles. "Well, well!"

"What port is the ship bound for?" asked Robert, with a nautical air.

But Pheles said, "Are you a navigator?" Robert had to own that he was not.

"Then," said Pheles, "I don't mind telling you that we're bound for the Tin Isles. Tyre alone knows where the Tin Isles are. It is the splendid secret we keep from all the world. It is as great a thing to us as your magic to you."

He spoke in quite a new voice, and seemed to respect both the children and the Amulet a good deal more than he had done before.

"The King sent you, didn't he?" said Jane.

"Yes," answered Pheles, "he bade me set sail with half a score brave gentlemen and this crew. You shall go with us, and see many wonders." He bowed and left them.

"What are we going to do now?" said Robert, when Pheles had caused them to be left alone with a breakfast of dried fruits and a sort of hard biscuit.

"Wait till he lands in the Tin Isles," said Rekh-marā, "then we can get the barbarians to help us. We will attack him by night and tear the sacred Amulet from his accursed heathen neck," he added, grinding his teeth.

"When shall we get to the Tin Isles?" asked Jane.

"Oh—six months, perhaps, or a year," said the Egyptian cheerfully.

"A *year* of this?" cried Jane, and Cyril, who was still feeling far too unwell to care about breakfast, hugged himself miserably and shuddered.

It was Robert who said—

"Look here, we can shorten that year. Jane, out with the Amulet! Wish that we were where the Amulet will be when the ship is twenty miles from the Tin Islands. That'll give us time to mature our plans."

It was done—the work of a moment—and there they were on the same ship, between gray northern sky and gray northern sea. The sun was setting in a pale yellow line. It was the same ship, but it was changed, and so were the crew. Weather-worn and dirty were the sailors, and their clothes

*Pheles, crouched beside a dim lantern, steered by the
shilling compass*

torn and ragged. And the children saw that, of course, though
they had skipped the nine months, the ship had had to live
through them. Pheles looked thinner, and his face was rugged
and anxious.

"Ha!" he cried, "the charm has brought you back! I have
prayed to it daily these nine months—and now you are here?
Have you no magic that can help?"

"What is your need?" asked the Egyptian quietly.

"I need a great wave that shall whelm away the foreign ship that follows us. A month ago it lay in wait for us, by the pillars of the gods, and it follows, follows, to find out the secret of Tyre—the place of the Tin Islands. If I could steer by night I could escape them yet, but to-night there will be no stars."

"My magic will not serve you here," said the Egyptian.

But Robert said, "My magic will not bring up great waves, but I can show you how to steer without stars."

He took out the shilling compass, still, fortunately, in working order, that he had bought off another boy at school for fivepence, a piece of indiarubber, a strip of whalebone, and half a stick of red sealing-wax.

And he showed Pheles how it worked. And Pheles wondered at the compass's magic truth.

"I will give it to you," Robert said, "in return for that charm about your neck."

Pheles made no answer. He first laughed, snatched the compass from Robert's hand, and turned away still laughing.

"Be comforted," the Priest whispered, "our time will come."

The dusk deepened, and Pheles, crouched beside a dim lantern, steered by the shilling compass from the Crystal Palace.

No one ever knew how the other ship sailed, but suddenly, in the deep night, the look-out man at the stern cried out in a terrible voice—

"She is close upon us!"

"And we," said Pheles, "are close to the harbour." He was silent a moment, then suddenly he altered the ship's course, and then he stood up and spoke.

"Good friends and gentlemen," he said, "who are bound with me in this brave venture by our King's command, the false, foreign ship is close on our heels. If we land, they land, and only the gods know whether they might not beat us in fight, and themselves survive to carry back the tale of Tyre's secret island to enrich their own miserable land. Shall this be?"

"Never!" cried the half-dozen men near him. The slaves were rowing hard below and could not hear his words.

The Egyptian leaped upon him; suddenly, fiercely, as a wild beast leaps. "Give me back my Amulet," he cried, and caught at the charm. The chain that held it snapped, and it lay in the Priest's hand.

Pheles laughed, standing balanced to the leap of the ship that answered the oarstroke.

"This is no time for charms and mummeries," he said. "We've lived like men, and we'll die like gentlemen for the honour and glory of Tyre, our splendid city. 'Tyre, Tyre for ever! It's Tyre that rules the waves.' I steer her straight for the Dragon rocks, and we go down for our city, as brave men should. The creeping cowards who follow shall go down as slaves—and slaves they shall be to us—when we live again. Tyre, Tyre for ever!"

A great shout went up, and the slaves below joined in it.

"Quick, the Amulet," cried Anthea, and held it up. Rekh-marā held up the one he had snatched from Pheles. The word was spoken, and the two great arches grew on the plunging ship in the shrieking of wind under the dark sky. From each Amulet a great and beautiful green light streamed and shone far out over the waves. It illuminated, too, the black faces and jagged teeth of the great rocks that lay not two ships' lengths from the boat's peaked nose.

"Tyre, Tyre for ever! It's Tyre that rules the waves!" the voices of the doomed rose in a triumphant shout. The children scrambled through the arch, and stood trembling and blinking in the Fitzroy Street parlour, and in their ears still sounded the whistle of the wind, the rattle of the oars, the crash of the ship's bow on the rocks, and the last shout of the brave gentle-men-adventures who went to their death singing, for the sake of the city they loved.

* * * *

"And so we've lost the other half of the Amulet again," said Anthea, when they had told the Psammead all about it.

"Nonsense, pooh!" said the Psammead. "That wasn't the other half. It was the same half that you've got—the one that wasn't crushed and lost."

The word was spoken, and the two great arches grew

"But how could it be the same?" said Anthea gently.

"Well, not exactly, of course. The one you've got is a good many years older, but at any rate it's not the other one."

"What did you say when you wished?"

"I forget," said Jane.

"I don't," said the Psammead. "You said, 'Take us where *you* are'—and it did, so you see it was the same half."

"I see," said Anthea.

"But you mark my words," the Psammead went on, "you'll have trouble with that Priest yet."

"Why, he was quite friendly," said Anthea.

"All the same you'd better beware of the Reverend Rekh-marā."

"Oh, I'm sick of the Amulet," said Cyril, "we shall never get it."

"Oh yes we shall," said Robert. "Don't you remember December 3rd?"

"Jinks!" said Cyril, "I'd forgotten that."

"I don't believe it," said Jane, "and I don't feel at all well."

"If I were you," said the Psammead, "I should not go out into the Past again till that date. You'll find it safer not to go where you're likely to meet that Egyptian any more just at present."

"Of course we'll do as you say," said Anthea soothingly, "though there's something about his face that I really do like."

"Still, you don't want to run after him, I suppose," snapped the Psammead. "You wait till the 3rd, and then see what happens."

Cyril and Jane were feeling far from well, Anthea was always obliging, so Robert was overruled. And they promised. And none of them, not even the Psammead, at all foresaw, as you no doubt do quite plainly, exactly what it was that *would* happen on that memorable date.

CHAPTER XIV

THE HEART'S DESIRE

I F I O N L Y had time I could tell you lots of things. For instance, how, in spite of the advice of the Psammead, the four children did, one very wet day, go through their Amulet Arch into the golden desert, and there find the great Temple of Baalbec and meet with the Phœnix whom they never thought to see again. And how the Phœnix did not remember them at all until it went into a sort of prophetic trance—if that can be called remembering. But, alas! I *haven't* time, so I must leave all that out though it was a wonderfully thrilling adventure. I must leave out, too, all about the visit of the children to the Hippo-drome with the Psammead in its travelling bag, and about how the wishes of the people round about them were granted so suddenly and surprisingly that at last the Psammead had to be taken hurriedly home by Anthea, who consequently missed half the performance. Then there was the time when, Nurse hav-ing gone to tea with a friend out Ivalunk way, they were play-ing "devil in the dark"—and in the midst of that most creepy pastime the postman's knock frightened Jane nearly out of her life. She took in the letters, however, and put them in the back of the hat-stand drawer, so that they should be safe. And safe they were, for she never thought of them again for weeks and weeks.

One really good thing happened when they took the Psam-mead to a magic-lantern show and lecture at the boys' school at Camden Town. The lecture was all about our soldiers in South Africa. And the lecturer ended up by saying, "And I hope every boy in this room has in his heart the seeds of courage and heroism and self-sacrifice, and I wish that every one of you may grow up to be noble and brave and unselfish, worthy citizens of this great Empire for whom our soldiers have freely given their lives."

237

And, of course, this came true—which was a distinct score for Camden Town.

As Anthea said, it was unlucky that the lecturer said boys, because now she and Jane would have to be noble and unselfish, if at all, without any outside help. But Jane said, "I daresay we are already because of our beautiful natures. It's only boys that have to be made brave by magic"—which nearly led to a first-class row.

And I daresay you would like to know all about the affair of the fishing rod, and the fish-hooks, and the cook next door—which was amusing from some points of view, though not perhaps the cook's—but there really is no time even for that.

The only thing that there's time to tell about is the Adventure of Maskelyne and Cooke's, and the Unexpected Apparition—which is also the beginning of the end.

It was Nurse who broke into the gloomy music of the autumn rain on the window panes by suggesting a visit to the Egyptian Hall, Engand's Home of Mystery. Though they had good, but private reasons to know that their own particular personal mystery was of a very different brand, the four all brightened at the idea. All children, as well as a good many grown-ups, love conjuring.

"It's in Piccadilly," said old Nurse, carefully counting out the proper number of shillings into Cyril's hand, "not so very far down on the left from the Circus. There's big pillars outside, something like Carter's seed place in Holborn, as used to be Day and Martin's blacking when I was a gell. And something like Euston Station, only not so big."

"Yes, I know," said everybody.

So they started.

But though they walked along the left-hand side of Piccadilly they saw no pillared building that was at all like Carter's seed warehouse or Euston Station or England's Home of Mystery as they remembered it.

At last they stopped a hurried lady, and asked her the way to Maskelyne and Cooke's.

"I don't know, I'm sure," she said, pushing past them. "I

always shop at the Stores." Which just shows, as Jane said, how ignorant grown-up people are.

It was a policeman who at last explained to them that England's Mysteries are now appropriately enough enacted at St. George's Hall. So they tramped to Langham Place, and missed the first two items in the programme. But they were in time for the most wonderful magic appearances and disappearances, which they could hardly believe—even with all their knowledge of a larger magic—was not really magic after all.

"If only the Babylonians could have seen *this* conjuring," whispered Cyril. "It takes the shine out of their old conjurers, doesn't it?"

"Hush!" said Anthea and several other members of the audience.

Now there was a vacant seat next to Robert. And it was when all eyes were fixed on the stage where Mr. Devant was pouring out glasses of all sorts of different things to drink, out of one kettle with one spout, and the audience were delightedly tasting them, that Robert felt someone in that vacant seat. He did not feel someone sit down in it. It was just that one moment there was no one sitting there, and the next moment, suddenly, there was someone.

Robert turned. The someone who had suddenly filled that empty place was Rekh-marā, the Priest of Amen!

Though the eyes of the audience were fixed on Mr. David Devant, Mr. David Devant's eyes were fixed on the audience. And it happened that his eyes were more particularly fixed on that empty chair. So that he saw quite plainly the sudden appearance, from nowhere, of the Egyptian Priest.

"A jolly good trick," he said to himself, "and worked under my own eyes, in my own hall. I'll find out how that's done." He had never seen a trick that he could not do himself if he tried.

By this time a good many eyes in the audience had turned on the clean-shaven, curiously-dressed figure of the Egyptian Priest.

"Ladies and gentlemen," said Mr. Devant, rising to the

occasion, "this is a trick I have never before performed. The empty seat, third from the end, second row, gallery—you will now find occupied by an Ancient Egyptian, warranted genuine."

He little knew how true his words were.

And now all eyes were turned on the Priest and the children, and the whole audience, after a moment's breathless surprise, shouted applause. Only the lady on the other side of Rekh-mará drew back a little. She *knew* no one had passed her, and, as she said later, over tea and cold tongue, "it was that sudden it made her flesh creep."

Rekh-mará seemed very much annoyed at the notice he was exciting.

"Come out of this crowd," he whispered to Robert. "I must talk with you apart."

"Oh, no," Jane whispered. "I did so want to see the Mascot Moth, and the Ventriloquist."

"How did you get here?" was Robert's return whisper.

"How did you get to Egypt and to Tyre?" retorted Rekh-mará. "Come, let us leave this crowd."

"There's no help for it, I suppose," Robert shrugged angrily. But they all got up.

"Confederates!" said a man in the row behind. "Now they go round to the back and take part in the next scene."

"I wish we did," said Robert.

"Confederate yourself!" said Cyril. And so they got away, the audience applauding to the last.

In the vestibule of St. George's Hall they disguised Rekh-mará as well as they could, but even with Robert's hat and Cyril's Inverness cape he was too striking a figure for foot-exercise in the London streets. It had to be a cab, and it took the last, least money of all of them. They stopped the cab a few doors from home, and then the girls went in and engaged old Nurse's attention by an account of the conjuring and a fervent entreaty for dripping-toast with their tea, leaving the front door open so that while Nurse was talking to them the boys could creep quietly in with Rekh-mará and smuggle him, unseen, up the stairs into their bedroom.

When the girls came up they found the Egyptian Priest sitting on the side of Cyril's bed, his hands on his knees, looking like a statue of a king.

"Come on," said Cyril impatiently. "He won't begin till we're all here. And shut the door, can't you?"

When the door was shut the Egyptian said—

The priest was jerked back by a rope thrown over his head

"My interests and yours are one."

"Very interesting," said Cyril, "and it'll be a jolly sight more interesting if you keep following us about in a decent country with no more clothes on than *that*!"

"Peace," said the Priest. "What is this country? and what is this *time*?"

"The country's England," said Anthea, "and the time's about six thousand years later than *your* time."

"The Amulet, then," said the Priest, deeply thoughtful, "gives the power to move to and fro in time as well as in space?"

"That's about it," said Cyril gruffly. "Look here, it'll be tea-time directly. What are we to do with you?"

"You have one-half of the Amulet, I the other," said Rekh-marā. "All that is now needed is the pin to join them."

"Don't you think it," said Robert. "The half you've got is the same half as the one we've got."

"But the same thing cannot be in the same place and the same time, and yet be not one, but twain," said the Priest. "See, here is my half." He laid it on the Marcella counterpane. "Where is yours?"

Jane watching the eyes of the others, unfastened the string of the Amulet and laid it on the bed, but too far off for the Priest to seize it, even if he had been so dishonourable. Cyril and Robert stood beside him, ready to spring on him if one of his hands had moved but ever so little towards the magic treasure that was theirs. But his hands did not move, only his eyes opened very wide, and so did everyone else's, for the Amulet the Priest had now quivered and shook; and then, as steel is drawn to the magnet, it was drawn across the white counterpane, nearer and nearer to the Amulet, warm from the neck of Jane. And then, as one drop of water mingles with another on a rain-wrinkled window-pane, as one bead of quick-silver is drawn into another bead, Rekh-marā's Amulet slipped into the other one, and, behold! there was no more but the one Amulet!

"Black magic!" cried Rekh-marā, and sprang forward to snatch the Amulet that had swallowed his. But Anthea caught it up, and at the same moment the Priest was jerked back by a rope thrown over his head. It drew, tightened with the pull of his forward leap, and bound his elbows to his sides. Before he had time to use his strength to free himself, Robert had knotted the cord behind him and tied it to the bedpost. Then the four children, overcoming the priest's wrigglings and kickings, tied his legs with more rope.

"I thought," said Robert, breathing hard, and drawing the last knot tight, "he'd have a try for *Ours*, so I got the ropes out of the box-room, so as to be ready."

The girls, with rather white faces, applauded his foresight.

"Loosen these bonds!" cried Rekh-marā in fury, "before I blast you with the seven secret curses of Amen-Rā!"

"We shouldn't be likely to loose them *after*," Robert retorted.

"Oh, don't quarrel!" said Anthea desperately. "Look here, he *has* just as much right to the thing as we have. This," she took up the Amulet that had swallowed the other one, "this has got his in it as well as being ours. Let's go shares."

"Let me go!" cried the Priest, writhing.

"Now, look here," said Robert, "if you make a row we can just open that window and call the police—the guards, you know—and tell them you've been trying to rob us. *Now* will you shut up and listen to reason?"

"I suppose so," said Rekh-marā sulkily.

But reason could not be spoken to him till a whispered counsel had been held in the far corner by the wash-hand-stand and the towel-horse, a counsel rather long and very earnest.

At last Anthea detached herself from the group, and went back to the Priest.

"Look here," she said in her kind little voice, "we want to be friends. We want to help you. Let's make a treaty. Let's join together to *get* the Amulet—the whole one, I mean. And then it shall belong to you as much as to us, and we shall all get our hearts' desire."

"Fair words," said the Priest, "grow no onions."

"*We* say, 'Butter no parsnips,'" Jane put in. "But don't you see we *want* to be fair? Only we want to bind you in the chains of honour and upright dealing."

"Will you deal fairly by us?" said Robert.

"I will," said the Priest. "By the sacred, secret name that is written under the Altar of Amen-Rā, I will deal fairly by you. Will you, too, take the oath of honourable partnership?"

"No," said Anthea, on the instant, and added rather rashly, "We don't swear in England, except in police-courts, where the guards are, you know, and you don't want to go there. But when we *say* we'll do a thing—it's the same as an oath to us—we do it. You trust us, and we'll trust you." She began to unbind his legs, and the boys hastened to untie his arms.

When he was free he stood up, stretched his arms, and laughed.

"Now," he said, "I am stronger than you and my oath is void. I have sworn by nothing, and my oath is nothing likewise. For there *is* no secret, sacred name under the altar of Amen-Rā."

"Oh, yes there is!" said a voice from under the bed. Everyone started—Rekh-marā most of all.

Cyril stooped and pulled out the bath of sand where the Psammead slept.

"You don't know everything, though you *are* a Divine Father of the Temple of Amen," said the Psammead shaking itself till the sand fell tinkling on the bath edge. "There *is* a secret, sacred name beneath the altar of Amen-Rā. Shall I call on that name?"

"No, no!" cried the Priest in terror. "No," said Jane, too. "Don't let's have any calling names."

"Besides," said Rekh-marā, who had turned very white indeed under his natural brownness, "I was only going to say that though there isn't any name under——"

"There *is*," said the Psammead threateningly.

"Well, even if there *wasn't*, I will be bound by the wordless oath of your strangely upright land, and having said that I will be your friend—I will be it."

"Then that's all right," said the Psammead; "and there's the tea-bell. What are young going to do with your distinguished partner? He can't go down to tea like that, you know."

"You see we can't do anything till the 3rd of December," said Anthea, "that's when we are to find the whole charm. What can we do with Rekh-marā till then?"

"Box-room," said Cyril briefly, "and smuggle up his meals. It will be rather fun."

"Like a fleeing Cavalier concealed from exasperated Round-heads," said Robert. "Yes."

So Rekh-mará was taken up to the box-room and made as comfortable as possible in a snug nook between an old nursery fender and the wreck of a big four-poster. They gave him a big rag-bag to sit on, and an old, moth-eaten fur coat off the nail on the door to keep him warm. And when they had had their own tea they took him some. He did not like the tea at all, but he liked the bread and butter, and cake that went with it. They took it in turns to sit with him during the evening, and left him fairly happy and quite settled for the night.

But when they went up in the morning with a kipper, a quarter of which each of them had gone without at breakfast, Rekh-mará was gone! There was the cosy corner with the rag-bag, and the moth-eaten fur coat—but the cosy corner was empty.

"Good riddance!" was naturally the first delightful thought in each mind. The second was less pleasing, because everyone at once remembered that since his Amulet had been swallowed up by theirs—which hung once more round the neck of Jane —he could have no possible means of returning to his Egyptian past. Therefore he must be still in England, and prob-ably somewhere quite near them, plotting mischief.

The attic was searched, to prevent mistakes, but quite vainly.

"The best thing we can do," said Cyril, "is to go through the half Amulet straight away, get the whole Amulet, and come back."

"I don't know," Anthea hesitated. "Would that be quite fair? Perhaps he isn't really a base deceiver. Perhaps some-thing's happened to him."

"Happened?" said Cyril, "not it! Besides, what *could* happen?"

"I don't know," said Anthea. "Perhaps burglars came in the night, and accidentally killed him, and took away the—all that was mortal of him, you know—to avoid discovery."

"Or perhaps," said Cyril, "they hid the—all that was mortal, in one of those big trunks in the box-room. *Shall we go back and look?*" he added grimly.

"No, no!" Jane shuddered. "Let's go and tell the Psammead and see what it says."

"No," said Anthea, "let's ask the learned gentleman. If anything *has* happened to Rekh-mará a gentleman's advice would be more useful than a Psammead's. And the learned gentleman'll only think it's a dream, like he always does."

They tapped at the door, and on the "Come in" entered. The learned gentleman was sitting in front of his untasted breakfast. Opposite him, in the easy chair, sat Rekh-mará!

"Hush!" said the learned gentleman very earnestly, "please, hush! or the dream will go. I am learning. . . . Oh, what have I not not learned in the last hour!"

"In the gray dawn," said the Priest, "I left my hiding-place, and finding myself among these treasures from my own country, I remained. I feel more at home here somehow."

"Of course I know it's a dream," said the learned gentleman feverishly, "but, oh, ye gods! what a dream! By jove! . . ."

"Call not upon the gods," said the Priest, "lest ye raise greater ones than ye can control. Already," he explained to the children, "he and I are as brothers, and his welfare is dear to me as my own."

"He has told me," the learned gentleman began, but Robert interrupted. This was no moment for manners.

"Have you told him," he asked the Priest, "all about the Amulet?"

"No," said Rekh-mará.

"Then tell him now. He is very learned. Perhaps he can tell us what to do."

Rekh-mará hesitated, then told—and, oddly enough, none of the children ever could remember afterwards what it was that he did tell. Perhaps he used some magic to prevent their remembering.

When he had done the learned gentleman was silent, leaning his elbow on the table and his head on his hand.

"Dear Jimmy," said Anthea gently, "don't worry about it. We are sure to find it to-day, somehow."

"Yes," said Rekh-marā, "and perhaps, with it, Death."

"It's to bring us our hearts' desire," said Robert.

"Who knows," said the Priest, "what things undreamed-of and infinitely desirable lie beyond the dark gates?"

"Oh, don't," said Jane, almost whimpering.

The learned gentleman raised his head suddenly.

"Why not," he suggested, "go back into the Past? At a moment when the Amulet is unwatched. Wish to be with it, and that it shall be under your hand."

It was the simplest thing in the world! And yet none of them had ever thought of it.

"Come," cried Rekh-marā, leaping up. "Come *now*!"

"May—may I come?" the learned gentleman timidly asked. "It's only a dream, you know."

"Come, and welcome, oh brother," Rekh-marā was beginning, but Cyril and Robert with one voice cried, "*No.*"

"You weren't with us in Atlantis," Robert added, "or you'd know better than to let him come."

"Dear Jimmy," said Anthea, "please don't ask to come. We'll go and be back again before you have time to know that we're gone."

"And he, too?"

"We must keep together," said Rekh-marā, "since there is but one perfect Amulet to which I and these children have equal claims."

Jane held up the Amulet—Rekh-marā went first—and they all passed through the great arch into which the Amulet grew at the Name of Power.

The learned gentleman saw through the arch a darkness lighted by smoky gleams. He rubbed his eyes. And he only rubbed them for ten seconds.

The children and the Priest were in a small, dark chamber. A square doorway of massive stone let in gleams of shifting light, and the sound of many voices chanting a slow, strange hymn. They stood listening. Now and then the chant quickened and the light grew brighter, as though fuel had been thrown on a fire.

"Where are we?" whispered Anthea.

"And when?" whispered Robert.

"This is some shrine near the beginnings of belief," said the Egyptian shivering. "Take the Amulet and come away. It is cold here in the morning of the world."

And then Jane felt that her hand was on a slab or table of stone, and, under her hand, something that felt like the charm that had so long hung round her neck, only it was thicker. Twice as thick.

"It's *here*!" she said, "I've got it!" And she hardly knew the sound of her own voice.

"Come away," repeated Rekh-marā.

"I wish we could see more of this Temple," said Robert resistingly.

"Come away," the Priest urged, "there is death all about, and strong magic. Listen."

The chanting voices seemed to have grown louder and fiercer, the light stronger.

"They are coming!" cried Rekh-marā. "Quick, quick, the Amulet!"

Jane held it up.

"What a long time you've been rubbing your eyes!" said Anthea; "don't you see we've got back?" The learned gentleman merely stared at her.

"Miss Anthea—Miss Jane!" It was Nurse's voice, very much higher and squeaky and more exalted than usual.

"Oh, bother!" said everyone. Cyril adding, "You just go on with the dream for a sec. Mr. Jimmy, we'll be back directly. Nurse'll come up if we don't. *She* wouldn't think Rekh-marā was a dream."

Then they went down. Nurse was in the hall, an orange envelope in one hand, and a pink paper in the other.

"Your Pa and Ma's come home. 'Reach London 11.15. Prepare rooms as directed in letter,' and signed in their two names."

"Oh, hooray! hooray! hooray!" shouted the boys and Jane. But Anthea could not shout, she was nearer crying.

"They are coming!" cried Rekh-marā

"Oh," she said almost in a whisper, "then it *was* true. And we *have* got our hearts' desire."

"But I don't understand about the letter," Nurse was saying. "I haven't *had* no letter."

"*Oh!*" said Jane in a queer voice, "I wonder whether it was one of those . . . they came that night—you know, when we were playing 'devil in the dark'—and I put them in the hat-stand drawer, behind the clothes-brushes and"—she pulled out the drawer as she spoke—"and here they are!"

There was a letter for Nurse and one for the children. The letters told how Father had done being a war-correspondent and was coming home; and how Mother and The Lamb were going to meet him in Italy and all come home together; and how The Lamb and Mother were quite well; and how a telegram would be sent to tell the day and the hour of their homecoming.

"Mercy me!" said old Nurse. "I declare if it's not too bad of you, Miss Jane. I shall have a nice to-do getting things straight for your Pa and Ma."

"Oh, never mind, Nurse," said Jane, hugging her; "isn't it just too lovely for anything!"

"We'll come and help you," said Cyril. "There's just something upstairs we've got to settle up, and then we'll all come and help you."

"Get along with you," said old Nurse, but she laughed jollily. "Nice help *you'd* be. I know you. And it's ten o'clock now."

* * * *

There was, in fact, something upstairs that they had to settle. Quite a considerable something, too. And it took much longer than they expected.

A hasty rush into the boys' room secured the Psammead, very sandy and very cross.

"It doesn't matter how cross and sandy it is though," said Anthea, "it ought to be there at the final council."

"It'll give the learned gentleman fits, I expect," said Robert, "when he sees it."

But it didn't.

"The dream is growing more and more wonderful," he exclaimed, when the Psammead had been explained to him by Rekh-marā. "I have dreamed this beast before."

"Now," said Robert, "Jane has got the half Amulet and I've got the whole. Show up, Jane."

Jane untied the string and laid her half Amulet on the table, littered with dusty papers, and the clay cylinders marked all over with little marks like the little prints of birds' little feet.

Robert laid down the whole Amulet, and Anthea gently restrained the eager hand of the learned gentleman as it reached out yearningly towards the "perfect specimen".

And then, just as before on the Marcella quilt, so now on the dusty litter of papers and curiosities, the half Amulet quivered and shook, and then, as steel is drawn to a magnet, it was drawn across the dusty manuscripts, nearer and nearer to the perfect Amulet, warm from the pocket of Robert. And then, as one drop of water mingles with another when the panes of the window are wrinkled with rain, as one bead of mercury is drawn into another bead, the half Amulet, that was the children's and was also Rekh-marā's, slipped into the whole Amulet, and, behold! there was only one—the perfect and ultimate Charm.

"And *that's* all right," said the Psammead, breaking a breathless silence.

"Yes," said Anthea, "and we've got our hearts' desire. Father and Mother and The Lamb are coming home to-day."

"But what about me?" said Rekh-marā.

"What *is* your heart's desire?" Anthea asked.

"Great and deep learning," said the Priest, without a moment's hesitation. "A learning greater and deeper than that of any man of my land and my time. But learning too great is useless. If I go back to my own land and my own age, who will believe my tales of what I have seen in the future? Let me stay here, be the great knower of all that has been, in that our time, so living to me, so old to you, about which your learned men speculate unceasingly, and often, *he* tells me, vainly."

"If I were you," said the Psammead, "I should ask the Amulet about that. It's a dangerous thing, trying to live in a time that's not your own. You can't breathe an air that's thousands of centuries ahead of your lungs without feeling the effects of it, sooner or later. Prepare the mystic circle and consult the Amulet."

"Oh, *what* a dream!" cried the learned gentleman. "Dear children, if you love me—and I think you do, in dreams and out of them—prepare the mystic circle and consult the Amulet!"

They did. As once before, when the sun had shone in August splendour, they crouched in a circle on the floor. Now the air outside was thick and yellow with the fog that by some strange decree always attends the Cattle Show week. And in the street costers were shouting. "Ur Hekau Setcheh," Jane said the Name of Power. And instantly the light went out, and all the sounds went out too, so that there was a silence and a darkness, both deeper than any darkness or silence that you have ever even dreamed of imagining. It was like being deaf or blind, only darker and quieter even than that.

Then out of that vast darkness and silence came a light and a voice. The light was too faint to see anything by, and the voice was too small for you to hear what it said. But the light and the voice grew. And the light was the light that no man may look on and live, and the voice was the sweetest and most terrible voice in the world. The children cast down their eyes. And so did everyone.

"I speak," said the voice. "What is it that you would hear?"

There was a pause. Everyone was afraid to speak.

"What are we to do about Rekh-marā?" said Robert suddenly and abruptly. "Shall he go back through the Amulet to his own time, or——"

"No one can pass through the Amulet now," said the beautiful, terrible voice, "to any land or any time. Only when it was imperfect could such things be. But men may pass through the perfect charm to the perfect union, which is not of time or space."

"Would you be so very kind," said Anthea tremulously, "as

The children cast down their eyes. And so did every one

to speak so that we can understand you? The Psammead said
something about Rekh-marā not being able to live here, and
if he can't get back——" She stopped, her heart was beating
desperately in her throat, as it seemed.

"Nobody can continue to live in a land and in a time not
appointed," said the voice of glorious sweetness. "But a soul

may live, if in that other time and land there be found a soul so akin to it as to offer it refuge, in the body of that land and time, that thus they two may be one soul in one body."

The children exchanged discouraged glances. But the eyes of Rekh-marā and the learned gentleman met, and were kind to each other, and promised each other many things, secret and sacred and very beautiful.

Anthea saw the look.

"Oh, but," she said, without at all meaning to say it, "dear Jimmy's soul isn't at all like Rekh-marā's. I'm certain it isn't. I don't want to be rude, but it *isn't*, you know. Dear Jimmy's soul is as good as gold, and——"

"Nothing that is not good can pass beneath the double arch of my perfect Amulet," said the voice. "If both are willing, say the word of Power, and let the two souls become one for ever and ever more."

"Shall I?" asked Jane.

"Yes."

"Yes."

The voices were those of the Egyptian Priest and the learned gentleman, and the voices were eager, alive, thrilled with hope and the desire of great things.

So Jane took the Amulet from Robert and held it up between the two men, and said, for the last time, the word of Power.

"Ur Hekau Setcheh."

The perfect Amulet grew into a double arch; the two arches leaned to each other ∧ making a great A.

"A. stands for Amen," whispered Jane; "what he was a priest of."

"Hush!" breathed Anthea.

The great double arch glowed in and through the green light that had been there since the Name of Power had first been spoken—it glowed with a light more bright yet more soft than the other light—a glory and splendour and sweetness unspeakable.

"Come!" cried Rekh-marā, holding out his hands.

"Come!" cried the learned gentleman, and he also held out his hands.

Each moved forward under the glowing, glorious arch of the perfect Amulet.

Then Rekh-marā quavered and shook, and as steel is drawn to a magnet he was drawn, under the arch of magic, nearer and nearer to the learned gentleman. And, as one drop of water mingles with another, when the window-glass is rain-wrinkled, as one quick-silver bead is drawn to another quick-silver bead, Rekh-marā, Divine Father of the Temple of Amen-Rā, was drawn into, slipped into, disappeared into, and was one with Jimmy, the good, the beloved, the learned gentleman.

And suddenly it was good daylight and the December sun shone. The fog has passed away like a dream.

The Amulet was there—little and complete in Jane's hand, and there were the other children and the Psammead, and the learned gentleman. But Rekh-marā—or the body of Rekh-marā—was not there any more. As for his soul. . . .

"Oh, the horrid thing!" cried Robert, and put his foot on a centipede as long as your finger, that crawled and wriggled and squirmed at the learned gentleman's feet.

"*That*," said the Psammead, "*was* the evil in the soul of Rekh-marā."

There was a deep silence.

"Then Rekh-marā's him now?" said Jane at last.

"All that was good in Rekh-marā," said the Psammead.

"He ought to have his heart's desire, too," said Anthea, in a sort of stubborn gentleness.

"*His* heart's desire," said the Psammead, "is the perfect Amulet you hold in your hand. Yes—and has been ever since he first saw the broken half of it."

"We've got ours," said Anthea softly.

"Yes," said the Psammead—its voice was crosser than they had ever heard it—"your parents are coming home. And what's to become of *me*? I shall be found out, and made a show of, and degraded in every possible way. I *know* they'll make me go into Parliament—hateful place—all mud and no sand. That beautiful Baalbec temple in the desert! Plenty of good sand there, and no politics! I wish I were there, safe in the Past—that I do."

"I wish you were," said the learned gentleman absently, yet polite as ever.

The Psammead swelled itself up, turned its long snail's eyes in one last lingering look at Anthea—a loving look, she always said, and thought—and—vanished.

"Well," said Anthea, after a silence, "I suppose it's happy. The only thing it ever did really care for was *sand*."

"My dear children," said the learned gentleman, "I must have fallen asleep. I've had the most extraordinary dream."

"I hope it was a nice one," said Cyril with courtesy.

"Yes. . . . I feel a new man after it. Absolutely a new man."

There was a ring at the front-door bell. The opening of a door. Voices.

"It's *them*!" cried Robert, and a thrill ran through four hearts.

"Here!" cried Anthea, snatching the Amulet from Jane and pressing it into the hand of the learned gentleman. "Here—it's *yours*—your very own—a present from us, because you're Rekh-marā as well as . . . I mean, because you're such a dear."

She hugged him briefly but fervently, and the four swept down the stairs to the hall, where a cabman was bringing in boxes, and where, heavily disguised in travelling cloaks and wraps, was their hearts' desire—three-fold—Mother, Father, and The Lamb.

"Bless me!" said the learned gentleman, left alone, "bless me! What a treasure! The dear children! It must be their affection that has given me these luminous *aperçus*. I seem to see so many things now—things I never saw before! The dear children! The dear, dear children!"

THE END

Printed in Great Britain by
Clarke, Doble & Brendon, Limited, Plymouth